remind me

THE MADISON RIDGE SERIES: HOMECOMING

ELIZA PEAKE

CAFFEINATED WORDS PUBLISHING, LLC

REMIND ME

By Eliza Peake

Copyright © 2020 Caffeinated Words Publishing, LLC

All Rights Reserved

ISBN #: 978-0-9912976-4-1

Cover design by Julianne Fangmann at Heart to Cover

Editing by: Happily Editing Anns

www.elizapeake.com

❀ Created with Vellum

about this book

He wasn't over her. Nowhere near it.

As the sexy star of the hit home renovation show Property Ace, Del Reynolds lived life in the fast lane. After ten years away, unexpected news brings him home and face to face with smart, strong-willed Addison Davenport—the woman he left behind to pursue his career, but never stopped loving.

Forced to work side by side, it becomes clear that the love between them hasn't diminished despite the years apart. Her touch still sets him on fire. Her kisses still leave him weak in the knees. Her sharp mind still turns him inside out.

Day after day she reminds him of everything he missed.

But a devastating secret could ruin their new foundation and he soon realizes a second chance for their love might not be written in any script. Still, Del knows how to see potential when it seems all is lost and he wants nothing more than to make Addison his again.

Forever.

REMIND ME is a steamy, emotional interconnected stand-alone small town romance. It has an HEA, no cheating, and sizzling chemistry. Remind Me is the second book in the Madison Ridge: Homecoming series set in the fictional Georgia town, Madison Ridge.

CHAPTER ONE

welcome home, ace

DELANEY REYNOLDS NEEDED a coffee the size of his head. Better yet, mainlining the rich brew his sister's cafe served up would suit him just fine, which is why he was beating feet to her place at the moment.

He'd had a rough night, a common occurrence for him over the last six months. But today he needed to get his shit together. He wasn't looking forward to the meeting that awaited him at the end of the next half hour. The summons from Lee Mitchum, his family's attorney, was cryptic and bad timing. He had enough on his plate with the end of his show and trying to fulfill a contract before he was in legal hot water.

Ten seasons was a long time in the home renovation television show world. At thirty-six years old, he was ready for a new adventure. But the fact he was forced to change course pissed him off. He liked making his own terms, but it appeared life had other plans for him.

Too bad life hadn't let him in on what those plans were, though.

Truth be told, he was glad to be back in Madison Ridge. He'd missed his family and the town his ancestors founded two hundred years ago. His gaze took in the sights around him. There were some new shops here and there like The Sweet Spot, his sister Amelia's cafe and bakery she'd opened a year or so ago. But the old mainstays like the general store, the pizza shop, and Maggie's diner—this time of morning the place was hopping—still stood strong.

The mountain air was clear—unlike the air he'd never quite gotten used to in Southern California—and all was quiet in the late spring weekday morning, but Del knew the weekends would be crowded with tourists. That's what happened when southern hospitality meets a glowing write-up in a mainstream magazine. Del's lips quirked thinking some of the stalwarts of the town were probably sitting in Maggie's grumbling about people and yet making money hand over fist.

Even though he'd missed it, Del had his reasons for staying away. Unfortunately, some of those reasons he couldn't outrun no matter how many corners of the globe he'd seen.

He pushed open the door to The Sweet Spot and a bell rung above his head causing the dark haired woman behind the counter to turn and look his way. "Well, if it isn't my big brother, Mr. Property Ace!" His sister Amelia rounded the corner of the counter and bounded over to him. Del barely caught her when she launched herself into his arms.

"Hey, Ames," he said on a laugh before lifting her off the floor in a bear hug.

"When did you get back?"

Del set her back down on her feet and smiled at the adorable picture his little sister made in her apron, jeans, and messy knot on top of her head. "Yesterday." He glanced around the blessedly empty dining area. "The place looks great. You added seating."

Amelia put her hands on her hips and looked around with a proud look on her face. "Yeah, I've done some upgrades since you were here last." She focused on him, her denim-blue eyes serious and scanning his face. "You look tired."

Del grinned. "Good to see you haven't changed a bit, brat." She folded her arms over her chest and leveled him with a stare. Damn, but she looked like their mother, scolding them without saying a word. "Okay, yeah. I'm tired. But right now, I'm late. I'm headed to Mitchum's office and I need the biggest coffee you got."

"You got it." Amelia swung back behind the counter and started to fill a tall cardboard cup with coffee from a carafe. "So what's your meeting with Mitchum about?"

Del shrugged. "Don't know. He didn't give me any details." He picked up the cup she slid across the counter and sipped. A whole lotta *hell yeah* screamed through his blood when the caffeinated magic hit his tongue. "Ahhh, damn, that's good."

Amelia smirked. "Yeah, I know." The smirk dropped to a frown as her gaze shifted behind him. "You still get mobbed when you go places?"

Dread set up camp in Del's gut. "Usually. Why?"

Amelia lifted her chin to the door. "If you're in a hurry, you better head out. There's a group of young women headed this way that have tourist written all over them." She hitched a thumb over her shoulder. "Go, quick. Out the back."

Del kicked his expensive but battered work boots into gear and headed toward the back of the store. The bell of the front door and Amelia's bright greeting reached his ears as he opened the back door. "Good morning, ladies. What can I get you?"

The door led out into a small alleyway between two historical buildings. It was open on either end, but he took a left that would dump him out onto the sidewalk that ran along the storefronts on Main Street. He jogged across the crosswalk, weaved around the back side of the historic courthouse in the center of the square, and made his way to a two-story red brick building on the corner.

There were four sets of double doors across the front of the building, with gold stenciling scrolled across the last set, announcing Mitchum and Associates was on the second floor. Comfort settled into Del's bones, noting some things never changed.

But when he opened the door to the attorney's office, the main reason he stayed away from his hometown sat on the loveseat in the waiting room, typing away on her phone.

Addison Davenport.

He'd know that strawberry-blonde hair anywhere. In all of his travels around the world, there was only one woman whose hair was that special mix of red and blonde.

Del's stomach met his feet, which decided they no longer knew how to move. This girl—scratch that, she was all woman now—had monopolized his thoughts since he had first learned how to shave. But they hadn't spoken in nearly ten years, even though he'd caught glimpses of her here and there when he'd been home.

Hell yeah, he'd avoided her. She had a temper as fiery as her hair when the mood struck and he had no desire to be on the receiving end again. Even though he deserved her temper in spades.

He'd fucked up royally.

Before he could say anything, she glanced up briefly from her phone. As though it sank in who she just saw, her head popped back up, those forest-green eyes of hers wide.

He closed the door behind him, effectively closing them in the room together. "Hey, Addie." Shoving his hands into the pockets of his jeans, he grinned, as though the breath hadn't backed up in his lungs.

For the next few beats, all they did was stare at each other. Much to Del's dismay, Addison Davenport had grown into a stunning woman in the last ten years. She'd always been beautiful but to get a look at her this close...even *stunning* didn't do her justice.

Addison let the phone drop to her lap, and as quick as a blink, her surprise blanked away. Her green eyes were cold and steady on him. "Del. What are you doing here?"

Her voice was smooth and yet held a smoky tone he hadn't remembered her having before. And damned if it didn't go straight to his cock. He strode over to sign in, then walked over to a chair opposite her and sat down. Kicking his legs out in front of him, he crossed them at the ankles with a grin, in spite of the thumping behind his sternum. "Nice to see you, too, Addie," he drawled.

She narrowed her eyes. "Nice to see you haven't lost your accent," she retorted. She tilted her head. "I heard you were back in town, but I didn't believe it. And yet, here you are. The elusive Delaney Reynolds, Property Ace." The way she said his name made it sound like she'd tasted something sour.

Her sharp tongue had been honed to slicing perfection over the years. While he knew the temper that lay beneath the surface of her porcelain skin, her eyes were cold like bits of a green glass bottle.

He continued to smile at her, an action that belied the bundle of nerves that sat like a rock in his belly. He lifted his hands off the armrest in a casual gesture. "Here I am."

She shifted, crossing her legs, causing the fabric of her skirt to rustle against the leather of the small sofa. A ping from her phone drew her attention away from him, giving him a chance to take in the whole of her without her noticing. His eyes drifted down to the long legs on display and fucking hell if they weren't even more shapely than they had been when she was younger.

Longing burned in his gut. It seemed there wasn't a day in his life Del hadn't wanted the woman sitting across from him.

"You look good, Addie."

Her thumbs hitched a moment before continuing for a couple of clicks. She set the phone aside and pushed a strand of hair behind her ear, keeping her eyes averted from his. "Thanks."

He pulled in his legs and leaned closer toward her, his voice low. "I'm sorry about your parents."

Addison's eyes met his and the shadows that clouded the green depths nearly made his knees buckle. They were no longer the eyes of the carefree girl he'd grown up and fallen in love with in high school. No, these were the eyes of a woman that had seen things and experienced things, not all of them good. His heart twisted at the loss.

She swallowed hard but straightened her shoulders before speaking. "I figured Jackson had called you when I saw you at the funeral."

He nodded. "I flew out and stayed with him for a few days." His gaze held hers. He'd wanted to contact her but the last few times they'd talked, it hadn't ended well. Del wanted to save her any extra stress so he stayed away from her, including at the funeral.

Addison blinked. "I...I didn't know that. He never said anything."

"Well, you know how tight-lipped Jackson can be sometimes."

"Yes, I do."

The door leading back to the offices opened. "Ms. Davenport, Mr. Reynolds. Mr. Mitchum will see you now."

What the fuck? The thought bounced around Del's head when Addison's gaze snapped to his and her jaw dropped.

Del gave the receptionist his best smile when he stood. "Are you sure he's meeting with us at the same time?"

The older woman nodded and stood aside. "Yes, Mr. Reynolds," she responded without cracking a smile.

He looked over at Addison, who bit her lip and lifted a brow before standing. "You're losing your touch, Ace," she murmured as she walked by him. Her trademark scent of vanilla and lavender drifted to him as she passed, and it was a feat to keep his knees from locking up.

They were taken to a small conference room, where they were asked to sit side by side at a small table. Tense silence stretched between them until Del wanted to climb the walls. He swiveled his chair in her direction and studied her profile. He shouldn't push, should just leave well enough alone. But now that she was here—and who knows when he'd see her again—there were things to say.

"I know it's been a while since we spoke…" She scoffed at his words and looked away. While a flare of anger lit in his chest, it was quickly extinguished knowing she had every right to be wary of anything he told her.

She turned her chair to face him, and this time her gaze held no shadows. "A while, Del? Try nearly ten years. You've managed to avoid me the few times you came back."

Damn it all to hell. After all of this time that fire in her eyes still made his blood burn hot. He looked away, forcing himself to focus on the small town outside the large picture window in the room to bring his brain back online from the gutter. When he thought he could look at her without wanting to drag her to him and kiss the hell out of her, Del shifted his stare back to hers and held up his hands in a surrender gesture. "Okay, fine. I deserved that. But I was going to say if you want to talk, call me."

Addison froze, then leaned forward, the chair creaking under her. "Call you? Did you say call you?" She leaned back, her lip curled. "I don't think so. I have friends, Delaney. Friends that don't leave me high and dry when I need them. Besides," she crossed her legs and turned her chair so she faced away from him, "the last time I tried to call you, the number you had was disconnected."

Shit, this wasn't awkward, was it? In a span of less than two minutes, all of the old hurts reared their ugly heads. Del sighed and ran a hand over his short hair. "Fine. I get your point. But I am sorry,

Addie. I'm sorry you lost your parents so suddenly. They were some of the best people I knew. And I understand the heartbreak of losing a parent."

The starch in Addison's spine let go and she shoved a lock of hair behind her ear. "I know," she said on a sigh and turned her head to meet his stare. "Your family has been great to me." Her eyes filled with tears, which she quickly blinked away and set her shoulders. "I'm sorry. What happened between us is water under the bridge. And I'm still a bit raw about…a lot of things apparently," she muttered the last part, her eyes darting away from his.

When she looked back over at him, her eyes were sad and resigned. A million memories flooded his mind and caused a bone-deep ache. Addison may have been sitting mere inches from him, but she was a thousand miles away now.

And he had no one but himself to blame.

She licked her lips before she spoke. "Our families are close, but maybe you could do me a favor and just stay elusive. The thing is, I put you and all those years we were together in a box," she made a box shape with her fingers, "and buried it in the back of my closet. And that's where I'd like it to stay. It's how I got over you." She paused. "The town has grown in your absence. After this meeting, there should be no reason we need to see each other again."

If she'd stabbed him in the gut, it would have hurt less. His first instinct over the years when it came to Addie had been dead-on. *Out of sight, out of mind* had been his motto when it came to her. Being around each other only served to hurt each other more. Wasn't time supposed to heal all wounds? In his case, time had worked some magic, but obviously not as much as he'd thought. He thought back to the custom, white gold solitaire ring sitting in a black velvet box that he never left home without.

All the years, the women, the traveling hadn't done a fucking thing when he came face to face with her. The fact was he wasn't over her at all.

Nowhere near it.

life amended

WHY THE HELL was Delaney Reynolds back in Madison Ridge?

The last thing she needed right now was to have her past show up with a "hi, how are ya?". Seeing him again in the flesh had thrown her completely out of whack. Thankfully, the first time they'd come face to face in years, she managed to look put together. At least on the outside. On the inside, she was an utter hot mess.

Of course, Del was devastatingly gorgeous as usual. Time had been kind and he'd grown into his rugged good looks. His sky-blue eyes still reminded her of a clear summer day. The dark blond hair was cut short, crew cut style, as opposed to the headful of waves he'd worn in the past, but that only served to accentuate the strong jaw covered by a five o'clock shadow. Although the timbre of his voice had been deeper than she remembered, that sexy, southern drawl hadn't waned a bit and added to the sex appeal he exuded so well.

And damn, her skin was hot like she'd been branded when his gaze traveled down her body.

Del rubbed the back of his neck and sighed. But before he could respond to her "keeping him in a box" speech, Lee walked into the room. He closed the door firmly behind him, as though putting the final punctuation on the conversation. He smiled and looked between them. "Addison, Delaney. Good to see you both." He shook hands with both before settling down and opening the thick folder in front of him.

"Let's get started. I'm sure you're wondering what's going on. As you know, your fathers were working on a project together before Paul died." Regret punched her in the gut. Regardless of all that transpired between them, she and Del were now part of the same dead dads' club no one wanted to join.

Lee cleared his throat and continued. "Addison, there's an amendment to your father's will we didn't go over at the reading of the will."

"Okay," she drew out the word until it sounded like a question. "What's in the amendment?"

Lee shuffled some papers. "When Paul died, the estate they had joint ownership of reverted to Stephen Davenport. In the event of his death, he bequeathed the ownership to you."

What. The. Hell. A flutter started deep in her belly and she leaned forward. "What? Why would he do that?"

Lee raised a brow. "I can't say for sure what his motives were, but Jackson always made it known he wanted no part of that business."

Addison nodded, thinking back to all the times her father and brother butted heads over that subject. "That's true. But my dad never…"

Addison drew in a deep breath and closed her eyes. She'd loved her dad with all her heart, but they hadn't always seen eye to eye. When Jackson decided he didn't want to follow in Dad's footsteps and instead went to law school, Addison had hoped she'd be able to step up and learn the family business. She'd even obtained her real estate license to help with the land deals. But while their father was supportive of her real estate acumen and even created a real estate firm for her to run, he'd left her out of the land development side of the business.

So why this project? One so near and dear to his heart?

"Addison?"

She opened her eyes and turned her head toward the rich baritone voice of the man sitting next to her. "Yeah?"

"You okay?" Del's blue eyes held a concern she didn't want to acknowledge.

He held her gaze for a moment until she turned her head away. Addison ignored the pain in her chest and focused on Lee. "Okay, so I own the estate now." She blew out a breath.

Lee cleared his throat. "Yes, but there are stipulations."

Addison frowned. "What kind of stipulations?"

Del shifted in his seat. "Lee, I hate to be a pain in the ass, but if the house has been left to Addison, what does this have to do with me?"

Lee glanced over at Del briefly. "I'm getting to that." He returned his attention back to Addison. "It means the estate your father left you is to be renovated into a museum based on the history of Madison Ridge. And be completed in time for the bicentennial celebration."

Her jaw dropped. "What? But that's just a couple of months away."

"I'm aware."

Addison liked Lee, but she wanted to tighten the tie around his neck a little tighter. "Are you freaking kidding me? These old houses take a long time to restore. And how the hell am I supposed to fund this?"

Lee slipped on a pair of reading glasses and shifted some paper. "He has an account set up for this particular project." He passed the bank statement across the large pine desk to her.

Addison's brow lifted at the amount that sat in a local bank account. "Holy hell."

Lee cleared his throat. "There's more." He shuffled some more papers around. "Your father was very detailed about what he wanted done with the property in the event of his death. The instructions are very specific." He ran a hand over his gray hair and straightened his tie. He peered at them over his glasses. "Ready for it?"

Del nodded silently. She rubbed her temples. "Yeah, I'm ready."

"Okay. If he should pass before the bicentennial celebration, his daughter, Addison Davenport, is bequeathed the estate, and if time permits, is to complete the project one week before the anniversary date, to the specifications on the blueprints housed in the family safe at the Madison Ridge residence. Reynolds Construction and Renovation is the contractor of choice and in the event they are not in business or otherwise unavailable, the contractor should be one recommended by Delaney Reynolds."

Addison's heart stopped. *Breathe, girl. Just breathe.*

Del coughed before leaning forward, his elbows on his thighs. "It specifically spells my name out?"

Lee nodded.

"But why me? Why not Noah? He's run the company for over ten years now."

"Look," Lee laid the paper on the table and folded his hands over it. "I know this is a shock for both of you. The amendment was made after Paul died. It had to be changed to reflect the new beneficiary. It was at that point he added Del as the manager of the project."

Addison hazarded a glance over to Del. Their eyes met and a million memories flashed between them. When Paul died, Del was the one to take over the company, not to mention she and Del were already in a serious relationship at the time.

Of all the places her dad dropped the ball, it had to be with a project involving her ex-fiancé. She rubbed her forehead and tried to harness the thoughts running in her head.

How can I get out of renovating the house?

"Lee, what would happen if I decided to sell the house instead of renovating it for the museum?"

Lee raised a brow. "I wasn't kidding when I said your father was detailed. He made a contract with the town of Madison Ridge. The agreement stated it would be renovated and ownership passed over to the town within ninety days of the anniversary date. This agreement extends to the current owner as well. So if you sell it, you will be in breach of contract."

Son of a bitch. "So what you're telling me is, I'm on the hook to renovate this thing no matter what?" she asked.

"Yes." Lee said.

"And I'm on the hook for helping her renovate it?" Del asked, his tone laced with something akin to annoyance mixed with resignation.

Another nod from the legal bearer of bad news.

All at once, Addison was tired. She leaned back in the chair with a sigh. "Is there anything else?" she asked when Lee continued to stay silent. She just wanted to get the hell out of this room that seemed to be getting smaller by the second.

He nodded. "Just a few more things." His eyes scanned down the page. "Your father worked with the historical society, donating quite a bit of money over the years. They had an agreement that he could use several artifacts to go into the museum. There's a contract for that as well. I'll give you a copy of all of this." He laid a hand on the bank statement. "We went over the funds. I think that's it."

Addison's mind whirled with all the information that was just dumped in her lap. Her dad had been meticulous in details, yes, but he'd also made things harder by not bringing her in on things. Life had thrown her the shittiest of curveballs over the last few months and wasn't done with her just yet.

Lee's throat clearing brought her focus back to him. "Luckily, your father had already started some work on the project. All of the paperwork for the permits was completed. You'll just need to update them."

As he continued to talk, Del glanced at his watch and frowned. Addison narrowed her eyes. *Keeping you from something, hot shot?*

"That's it for now," Lee said, straightening the stack of papers. "Write down your emails before you leave, and I'll email you both a copy of the paperwork."

After she wrote down her information, Addison gathered her purse and stood. "Thank you, Lee. I appreciate all your help." They shook hands and she turned on her heel.

She made it down the stairs and to the front door of the building before Del caught up with her. "Addison, wait." As much as she wanted to keep walking, she had to face the music.

Addison pushed open the door before stopping and facing her past. "What?"

"Listen, I know this isn't ideal for either of us. But we can make this work. We can get this done."

Addison scoffed and folded her arms over her chest, doing her best not to gaze into his bright blue eyes. "We? There's no 'we', Del. This is my issue to handle."

He mimicked her stance, his forearms—damn, he'd really honed those muscles over the years—covering his broad chest and one side of his full lips tilted into a half smirk. "Well, according to the will, your issue involves me. Why don't we make it easy on each other and just work together on the estate?"

Addison turned her head away and counted to ten under her breath. "Look, I know what the will said. It also said the contractor of choice is Reynolds Construction. I'll get Noah to help me." Relief warmed her blood and she straightened her shoulders. Yes, that's what she would do. Whew. Delaney Reynolds wouldn't be in her world for long.

Del just continued to half smirk at her. Holding her stare, he pulled out his phone and hit a button. A ringing phone came through the speaker. "What's up, man?" Noah's deep voice answered.

"Hey, bro. I'm standing here with Addison—"

"Oh shit." Her lips twitched at Noah's tone of incredulity and humor and Del's frown.

"Is there any way we can meet with you?"

"I can't—" Addison started. Del just held up a hand in a stop sign motion. Anger whipped its way through her body, and she wanted to smack at his hand. But that would only make her look childish.

Deep breaths. In, out. In, out.

"Yeah, I'm here a while longer before I head over to the inn."

"Great, see you in a minute." Del ended the call and slipped the phone into his back pocket. "You ready?"

"Why do you have to be there?"

"Addie," Del stepped forward and closed the distance between them. "You're going to have to come to the realization we are in this together, one way or another."

She tilted her head back to look up into his dark blue eyes. Even after ten years and the fact she wanted to scoop his heart out with a spoon, the one-two combination punch of his eyes and voice still made her want to melt into a puddle at his feet.

He moved in closer still until the heat of his body came to her in waves. The faint scent of sandalwood drifted around her, making her want to lean in closer to him.

Don't forget how he left you. Remember how devastated you were?

Right. She needed to remember *that.* Not how good he smelled or that sexy little smirk or the way he always left her the last chocolate donut. Nope, nope, nope.

She narrowed her eyes at him. Keeping her voice low, she put all of the venom she could muster into it. "I don't know why you're back in Madison Ridge, Delaney. And frankly, I don't care. I'll go with you to see Noah. But we aren't in this project together. It's mine now. After this meeting with him, I want you to stay as far away as possible." She stepped back from him and walked away.

After a few steps, she stopped and glanced over her shoulder. "After almost ten years of silence that shouldn't be too hard for you to do."

karma was a real bitch

ADDISON SAT with her back ramrod straight and her jaw set. It appeared she hadn't lost that stubborn streak, and the passing years hadn't mellowed her any.

Del turned his head away to hide a small smile. In a sick, twisted way, it was one of the things he loved about her and he was glad to see she hadn't changed much. Not that it was going to make working with her any easier.

There was little more than stony silence between them as they sat in the waiting room of Noah's office. The clicking on the assistant's keyboard and the occasional ringing phone were the only sounds around them.

Frustration at the inability to get along with Addie built in Del's chest. *This is ridiculous.*

He turned in his chair, ready to go head-to-head with the little minx, when Noah opened his door and walked out. His gaze went from Del to Addison and back, before raising a brow. "Hey, y'all come on in."

Addison popped up from the chair as though she sat on a bed of nails and walked ahead of Del. Noah smiled at her as she breezed into his office and then looked back at Del. He clapped his hand on Del's shoulder. "How are you?" His voice was low enough only Del could hear him.

Del nodded. "Today is a good day. Well, at least on that front anyway." He cut his gaze to the woman sitting in the office. "Otherwise? I've had better."

Noah nodded and shut the door behind them. "Sorry you had to wait. I couldn't get Commissioner Daniels off the phone," he said as he rounded his desk and sat down.

Del sat and tilted his head. "Daniels? As in Tommy Daniels?"

Noah nodded. "One and the same."

The class clown of Madison Ridge High School was a commissioner? He *had* been away a long time.

Noah leaned back in the well-worn leather office chair, rocking it slightly. "So..." He drew out the last syllable as his gaze darted back and forth between Del and Addison. "It's been a while since I've seen you two in the same room. At least when you're not trying to avoid each other."

Addison cleared her throat and sat up straighter. Del frowned at his older brother. He leaned forward with his forearms on his thighs. "Well, it seems Addison is now the proud owner of the estate dad and Stephen were working on years ago."

Addison sighed and Noah stopped the rocking of his chair, the creaking ceasing along with it. "There hasn't been any work done on it in a while." He rubbed his chin, the scruff rasping under his hand. "Stephen did mention about six months ago that he had all the new permits in place and wanted to get started on the house again. He even dropped off some plans. Something about a town anniversary thing." He shrugged. "But then he never followed up with it." He frowned. "And then...well..."

"He died." Addison's voice was cold and blunt, causing Del to lift a brow. There was something there, but a snowball had a better chance in hell than he did of finding out any info from her.

Addison leaned forward. "Apparently, he and the town had a deal to turn the house into a museum. Make it a historic town thing." She waved her hand and leaned back hard. "I don't know. All I do know is that I'm responsible for fixing it up before the anniversary celebration in a couple months."

Noah's brow furrowed. "What are you guys not telling me? There's a reason you're both here."

"I'm getting to that." Addison huffed out a breath. "According to my dad's will, should the estate be left to me and I become responsible for renovating it, Reynolds Construction is the contractor of choice and if they are unable to do it…" she trailed off and looked sideways at Del as though he were akin to a venomous snake. "Then Del is responsible for choosing the contractor." She paused. "Please tell me you're available, Noah."

Noah bit his bottom lip and looked down at his desk. Del narrowed his eyes. Big brother was enjoying this just a bit too much.

He's going to pay for this later.

Noah cleared his throat and leaned forward on his elbows. "I'm sorry, Addie. I'm slammed from now until the end of the year. I've had to hire some extra hands and may have to hire more." He glanced over to Del before focusing back on Addison. "I'm going to have to defer to Del on this one."

Her eyes widened. "Are you sure?" She scooted to the edge of her chair and leaned in close to Noah. "You have to help me, Noah. We go way back, right? I was almost your sis—" She leaned back quickly. "Never mind. But we've known each other for a long time. Can't you fit me in somewhere?"

Del scoffed and rolled his eyes. "For God's sake, Addie. I'm not going to hire some hack to do this for you. You have to trust my judgment." Even as he said it, the thought pinged in his chest that her trust was something he lost a long time ago.

She turned her head toward him, her green eyes all ice. "Trust you? You really think I'm going to trust you of all people?"

All Del could do was stare back at her. Nope. Her trust was not an option.

"Addie," Noah said in a coaxing tone and waited for her to drag her stare away from Del. Relief bloomed in his chest to ease some of the ache there. He didn't know how much longer he'd be able to look into her eyes and not remember the past, both good and bad, when all she remembered was the bad.

Not that he could blame her.

"What?" she asked. Her shoulders started to slump as though she smelled defeat coming her way.

"Do you trust me?"

She nodded. "Sure. He's the only Reynolds man I don't trust," she said, hitching her chin toward Del.

Del groaned and rubbed his eyes with his thumb and forefinger. He understood her hesitation, but for the love of all that is holy, he was getting tired of the barbs she kept lobbing his way.

Noah cleared his throat again. "Okay, then you're going to have to trust me when I tell you that Del is going to make a sound decision in whoever does the reno." He tilted his head. "Okay?"

Addison closed her eyes and dropped her chin to her chest. A moment later, she stood and lifted her handbag over her shoulder. Noah and Del followed suit. "I appreciate your time, Noah." She faced Del. "Let me know when you've figured out who you've chosen. I'm late for an appointment."

Before either man could reply, Addison was out the door as fast as her stilettos would take her.

"Shit," Del muttered, and for the second time that day, he found himself chasing after her. When he caught up with her on the sidewalk outside of Noah's office, he walked ahead of her and turned to face her, causing her to stop in her tracks.

She gritted her teeth and tried to move past him. He moved in sync with her, blocking her getaway. "Knock it off, Delaney. I'm not in the mood for games." She tried to move again, but once again he blocked her. Addison closed her eyes and sighed.

"Addison," he said, since they were at the point of using full names now, "listen to me. This is going to be hard enough as it is. But worse if you don't give a little." She opened her eyes and the depth of her pain in them nearly knocked him to his knees. He seriously underestimated how much she was hurting. While he was part of it, he wasn't all of it.

"I don't want to give a little with you. I just don't."

"Starshine, wait a—" The old nickname he'd given her slipped out of his mouth.

She pointed a finger into his chest. "Don't call me that. You lost the privilege years ago."

He held up his hands in an "I surrender" gesture. "Fine. *Addison*. Look, I'm not going to screw you over."

Addison crossed her arms over her chest. "Again. You're not going to screw me over, again."

Del jammed his hands on his hips and looked at the ground. Son of a bitch, the woman was going to kill him. When he thought he could speak without wanting to scream, he looked up. "Right. I'm not going to screw you over, *again*. You have my word I'll pick the best contractor for the job. This was my father's legacy too, Addison."

An idea hit him like a thunderbolt. This project should be just as much his as it was hers.

He must have looked dumbstruck, because she narrowed her eyes at him and bit her lip. "What are you thinking?"

Del focused back on her. "I'll do it."

"What do you mean you'll do it?"

He chuckled and looked up at the sky. The cornflower-blue sky was as clear as his mind was now. "I don't know why I didn't think of this before." Lowering his head, he met her wide-eyed stare head-on. There was no doubt what he was about to say was the equivalent to a declaration of war.

"The contractor I choose is *Property Ace*."

When Del arrived at the Center Street Deli the next day, the lunchtime rush was starting but the place was still fairly quiet. He spotted Teri at a small table in the back and muttered a thank you under his breath. Billy, the deli owner, was taking an order from a young lady but caught Del's eye and lifted his chin in greeting. Del responded in kind and kept walking toward the table.

"I saw a coffee shop on my way into town. Why didn't we meet there?" Teri asked, never looking up from her phone, her thumbs flying across the screen.

"Hello to you, too." Del pulled out the chair and sat across from his producer. "My sister owns it. If we went there, we'd never get any work done. Amelia's quite the talker. Besides, I'm starving."

Teri tilted her head and the purple streaks in her brown hair made an appearance under the fluorescent lights. She set her phone on the tablet sitting on the table, focusing on him. "Interesting. You said your whole family was here, right?"

Del nodded. "Yeah, most of them stayed around here. But I'm not meeting with you to talk about my family."

Teri rolled her eyes and lifted a laminated menu from the holder at the center of the table. "Fine, whatever, Ace. I'm starving, too, and you're buying."

"Works for me." Whatever would keep her off his back about his family and the town. Del knew it was a risk, bringing his last show back to his hometown. He liked to keep his family out of the spotlight as much as possible. He'd made the choice to be in it, but they didn't. He wanted to shield them as much as possible from the darker side of fame.

And he preferred to keep his past where it belonged. But he was doing what he had to do.

A hearty slap on the shoulder sent shooting pains down Del's arm. Son of a mother lover, when did pain become a constant for him?

"Hey, man. Glad to have you home." A smile split Billy's broad face and his forehead shone. His Brooklyn accent was still as strong as it was the day he bought the deli over twenty years ago. Del always thought Billy looked like a shorter, wider Mr. Clean. He even wore all white, except Billy's white apron was smeared in various places with remnants of sandwich condiments.

Del smiled back, the pain subsiding to a dull roar. "Hey there, Billy. Good to be back."

"How long has it been?" the older man asked, crossing his arms over his large girth.

Del thought back for a minute. "I was here a few months ago for Emma's engagement party."

Billy nodded. "Glad to see her settle down. That Shane boy is good people." He glanced over at Teri, his eyes appraising her. "Who's your friend?"

"This is Teri, my show producer."

Teri extended her hand toward Billy. "Nice to meet you, Billy."

Billy took hers and shook it once before pulling his hand away. "Likewise." He glanced toward the front of the store. "Hate to cut it short, but I wanted to come over and say hey. You eatin'?"

"You still make monster club sandwiches?" Del asked. At the thought of the meats and cheese, his stomach made its presence known.

Billy scoffed. "Am I still breathin'?" He turned to Teri. "What'll ya have?"

She tapped her index finger on her chin. "Let me have a Reuben with the fruit and a Pellegrino."

The elder man nodded. "You got it. Be up shortly." He clapped Del's shoulder again as he passed. "See ya soon, Ace."

Del smiled at the nickname he'd acquired when he became the host of *Property Ace*. "Take care, Billy." When he lifted his gaze, he found Teri's shrewd stare on him. "What?" he asked, his tone more defensive than he cared for it to be.

"You really do know most people in town, don't you?"

The muscles in Del's shoulders tightened. "I've been away awhile. It's a small town but it doesn't mean I know everyone." Actually, it did, but he wasn't going to let her know. "I'd appreciate it if we kept my past and my family out of it. Okay?"

She pursed her lips but nodded. "I understand."

A young woman brought Teri's water and Del's sweet tea. A small smile played on Del's lips. Billy never missed a trick.

He sipped his drink. "So, what's the story? Did the network go for my idea?"

She nodded and leaned forward in her seat. "Del, they loved it. A homecoming as your last episode? Genius. They're going to make it a two-hour special."

Del bit back a sigh of relief. "That's great news. Because I need to make this project work." *For more than just getting out of my contract.*

She narrowed her eyes. "And you already have a location picked out? How the hell did you do it so fast?"

Teri was a great producer and most of the time they got along fine. Other times she was a royal pain in his ass. She'd been even worse since he broke the news he was leaving the show. It meant she had to find a new job, but his sources told him she had a new contract with a show—all she had to do was sign.

In reality she wasn't really doing anything wrong. He just didn't want a lot of questions. He had no desire to air his dirty laundry out for the gossip rags to write about. On the other hand, Teri would skin his ass if someone caught wind of it and she was caught off guard. His mind raced as to how much he wanted to tell Teri. He trusted her. At least as much as he trusted anyone in Hollywood, which wasn't saying much.

He wrapped his hand around the glass in front of him, the condensation from the glass cooling off his overheated skin. "Okay, I'm going to tell you, but I would appreciate it if you would keep it on the down low. Got it?"

She nodded and leaned forward. "What's the story?"

"To start with, it's one of the original homes in the area. I know this because one of my ancestors built it two hundred years ago." He held up a finger, anticipating her questions before she started. "Hold all questions until I'm done."

She rolled her eyes but waved her hand in a "go ahead" motion.

"Anyway, several years back, my father and his business partner, Stephen Davenport, purchased it. Their plan was to make it into a historic museum. The Davenports and the Reynolds were the founding families of Madison Ridge." He blew out a breath while his stomach pitched. "Long story short, my dad died, leaving Stephen the house. A couple months ago, Stephen was killed in a plane crash, leaving the estate to his daughter, Addison Davenport."

What the fuck. Just saying her name made his body tighten.

Del continued. "Stephen made a deal with the town to renovate and have the museum done by the bicentennial anniversary celebration this year."

"And you know the daughter well enough to pitch it and for her to go for it?"

He closed his eyes and pinched the bridge of his nose, letting out a self-deprecating chuckle.

"Yeah, you could say I know her well enough. She's my ex-fiancée."

Teri was stunned into silence as the waitress came up to the table. "Who had the Reuben?" Del gestured to his producer, who still sat silent. Once the server moved away, Teri finally found her voice.

"Holy. Shit. And she agreed to it?"

He rubbed the back of his neck. The more he thought about it, the more guilt wound its way into his chest. He'd backed her into a corner, hadn't he? "Well, let's just say she had few choices."

Teri raised a brow. "There's a story there. But you know what? I don't want to know." She was quiet again as she ate, a rarity for her. That could only mean she was trying to figure out her next move. Del couldn't blame her. She had a show to get produced—and a successful one at that. It was coming to an unfortunate end sooner than either of them had planned.

Teri chewed her sandwich and swallowed before leaning back in her chair. "What if Addison refuses to work with us on this?"

Del shook his head. "Not an issue, but if it is, I'll turn on the Reynolds charm and convince her otherwise." He sighed. "I'm not going to lie. It's going to be an uphill battle with her. Addison doesn't hold grudges for petty shit and the way we left things doesn't fall in the petty shit category."

"Well, Ace, I hate to be the bearer of bad news, but you're going to have to make sure it works. The network wants this for your final episode."

He shoved his plate of food away when the coffee he had finished off lurched in his belly and threatened to make another appearance. "I'll make it work," he said through gritted teeth.

Teri looked him in the eye. "If you say so."

Having the network back his idea was exactly what he wanted, but on his own terms not backed into a corner. But he had no choice, either, when it came down to it. Not only would he legally be in breach of contract, they would sue him for millions he'd have to pay back. Unfortunately, there was no wording that would let him out under medical duress—which he was in—only death. When he'd signed the contract years ago, Del never figured he would be ending his contract early. Much less for a medical condition that would bring his career to an early end.

Ahh…karma was a real bitch.

CHAPTER FOUR

an awkward truce

"MURPHY, STOP STARING AT ME."

The large chocolate lab laid his head on the bed and sighed a long-suffering sigh. Addison stared at the ceiling, just as she had for the last several hours, until Murphy sighed again. Her lips twitched in a smile.

Rolling on her side, she ended up nose to snout with her patient-for-the-moment canine. As soon as she said, "wanna go out?", he'd jump in circles and act like he'd never heard anything better in his life. Of course, when one needs to pee, it was the truth.

"We're not going running today. I need more sleep. I need sleep, period." She glanced over at the clock. "It's only seven. Why are you up so early?"

Murphy's only movement was to blink his eyes as he waited for her to give the command it was time to go out. Addison reached up and rubbed his soft head, which was slightly warm from the early morning sun that streamed through the windows of her bedroom.

Most mornings, Addison was up and well on her way by this time. Murphy didn't usually have to prod her along in his silent dog way as he did this morning. It was evident he believed if he stared at her long enough, she would get out of bed. It was an effective plan because she found herself kicking off the covers and stumbling her way into the bathroom. "Me first."

When she came out a few minutes later, his ears perked up, but he stayed seated, awaiting her command. His large tail wagging, his broad body vibrated.

She couldn't keep the grin off her face. "Ok, Murph, time to go." He galloped out of the room ahead of her and clambered down the stairs, sounding like a herd of elephants.

When Addison caught up to him, he was sitting at the back door, waiting for her to open it. Releasing the latch, she pulled open the door and he used his head to nudge the screen door wide open, taking off like a rocket across the back deck and down to the fenced yard. When he watered more than one bush, she shook her head and walked into the kitchen to start the much-needed coffee.

Sleep had been elusive, and she'd become besties with her ceiling and her walls. To keep herself from thinking about Del, she'd thought of all the colors she could paint those walls and watched the tree shadows dance off and on through the night. It reminded her of the dancing fountains in Vegas and she started singing offbeat tunes. It was at that point she feared delirium had clearly set in.

Seeing Del unexpectedly and the effect he still had on her really irked the shit out of her. Over the last ten years he'd been gone, she'd rarely thought of him.

You big fat liar. You thought of him quite often.

She rolled her eyes at her conscience that never left her alone. Okay, sure. She'd thought of him all the time after he'd left. And every time she dated a new guy, she'd immediately compare him to Del. And that's probably why she didn't date. Well, and the fact she had a business to run, especially now. She needed to focus on her business and making sure she didn't taint the family name. The town would be watching to see if she was going to screw up her father's legacy.

The fact Del had come up with that insane plan to be the contractor for the house was not the best way to get started.

Jesus, Dad. What were you thinking?

The doorbell rang before she could fall down *that* particular rabbit hole. When she opened the front door, the man monopolizing her thoughts stood on her porch, balancing a tray of coffee and a pale blue box in one hand and a ginormous rawhide with the other.

"Good morning." Del smiled. "I come bearing gifts."

"I see." Manners told her to let him in, so she stepped aside so he could walk through. She nodded toward the bone. "How did you know I have a dog?" Her manners kicked in and she relieved him of the coffee tray.

Del shot her that panty-melting grin. "I have my sources."

Addison rolled her eyes and shut the front door. "He's on the back porch." She walked toward the kitchen and sat the coffee tray down before opening the back door "Murph, I got a treat for you," she called out.

Del stepped out onto the back porch as the large dog clambered up the stairs and, traitor that he was, happily took the bone and the scratch behind the ears Del gave him before going to the other end of the porch and flopping down in his dog bed. Del chuckled then turned to her.

It wouldn't have bothered her one bit if the earth opened up and swallowed her. She wore nothing but sleep shorts, a tank top (sans bra), and hair she was sure looked like a bird did a tap dance in.

Del, on the other hand, looked mouth-watering and sinfully appealing with his five o'clock shadow, faded blue jeans, and a white T-shirt that showed off his sun-kissed skin all too well. And of course, heat rushed to the pit of her stomach. What the hell was wrong with her? She shouldn't be reacting to him this way after so long?

She frowned and smoothed back her hair before crossing her arms over her chest in hopes of feeling less exposed. Straightening her spine, she hoped to regain some sort of decorum. "Del, what are you doing here?"

"Coffee, doughnuts." He raised a brow with a silent question of *"can I come back in?"*

She sighed when manners got the better of her and, with one arm still across her chest, she pushed open the screen door and stepped aside to let him through. As he walked by, the enticing aroma of the doughnuts and coffee mingled together and caused her stomach to rumble. The scent of his cologne caused her thighs to clench.

Dear God, please help me. She closed her eyes briefly before letting the screen door slap shut behind her.

Del had set the box of baked goods on the kitchen island and glanced around the room. His stare found hers. "This place has changed a bit since I was here last."

She crossed her arms over her chest again and leaned against the counter on the opposite side of him. "A lot has changed since you were last here."

He pursed his lips and averted his eyes to the counter. Had she detected a shadow of pain in his eyes? Nah, he was the one who never came back. He gestured toward the box. "I hope you still eat dough-nuts. I seem to recall you had a thing for chocolate with sprinkles." He raised his eyes back to her. "And mocha lattes."

Addison narrowed her eyes at him. "What's going on in that brain?"

He slid his hands into the front pockets of his jeans. "Peace offering. I shouldn't have blindsided you yesterday. I—" He blew out a breath and ran a hand over his dark blond buzz cut. "Can we sit and talk a minute?"

Addison paused a moment before nodding. "Sure. Let's go on the back porch. You grab the coffee; I'm taking the doughnuts."

They went out to the large screened back porch, greeted with the warmth of a spring day. Addison settled onto a cushioned loveseat and Del dropped down on a matching armchair across from her.

"May I?" she gestured toward the doughnuts.

"Go ahead. I bought them for you."

She ignored the "awww" that came from the vicinity of her heart (especially when she spied the chocolate-covered ones with sprinkles) and plucked up a piece of the fried sugary goodness. She bit into it and nearly moaned with pleasure. Foodgasms were the only sort of plea-sure she'd received as of late.

With the faint sounds of birdsong and the breeze blowing through the magnolia trees in her backyard, it should have been a peaceful scene. But being so close to Del had tension tight in her chest. Espe-cially as his eyes watched her mouth as she polished off the doughnut.

"So what did you want to talk about?"

When she asked, Del just stared at her intently for a moment. "The renovation." He paused. "I may have gone about it all wrong yesterday, but the truth is we need each other."

Addison bobbled the coffee cup that was on its way to her mouth. "Shit," she muttered and did her best not to jump when some landed in her lap, the drops spreading on the fabric of her shirt, warming her skin underneath.

"Here."

Her stomach pitched as she settled back down on the chair and looked over at Del, who was holding out some napkins. "Thanks." When their hands brushed, she jerked hers back as though she'd been burned.

She hadn't *needed* a man in years. It's why she had a vibrator. "I don't follow," she said, brushing at the coffee stains.

He leaned forward, his forearms on his thighs, pinning her with the bright blue stare she'd been known to get lost in. "You need me to pick the contractor, per your dad's wishes. And I need one last show to fulfill my contract."

Say what? She tilted her head. "What contract? Your show contract?"

He nodded. "I didn't renew it. The regular season is over, but I'm obligated to do one last TV special before I can be officially released."

The pieces were beginning to fall in place. "And you want to use the remodel of my house and museum opening as your final TV special?"

Something was off. When he nodded, she shook her head, as though trying to break something loose. "I don't understand. Why are you leaving the show? You love doing it." *So much so you left me behind for it.* While the knife twisted in her gut right nicely, she pushed the pain away and focused on his answer.

He turned his head and looked out into the yard. Her heart thumped against her chest in anticipation of his answer. She needed to know why now? Why was he quitting, ending the thing that ended them?

Maybe she should be over him for leaving her ten years ago. But the truth of the matter was, she wasn't. He'd been her best friend as much as her lover. When he left, he'd taken her heart with him, but also left a void in her that missed his friendship. It was a betrayal that cut deep.

When he brought his gaze back to her, the shadows were definitely there. "It's just time." He paused, his eyes roaming her face. "Can we work together for the short term?"

It wasn't the answer Addison expected. It definitely didn't answer any of her burning questions. It made her look at him with a new perspective. He was being cryptic and it was a different side to him. She wasn't sure she liked it.

She didn't want to feel anything for him, nothing at all. Not even anger. This man had received so many of her emotions over the years she wasn't sure she had any more to give. But to her dismay, the stupid organ in her chest ached for him at the way sadness seemed to envelop him suddenly, as his shoulders slumped and he stared into his empty hands.

He was right. They needed each other. She had a house to renovate and was running out of time. He needed to fulfill a contract obligation. And knowing Del, once he was finished, he'd leave Madison Ridge behind until the occasional obligatory holiday visits. He'd said "short term" anyway.

The sooner the house was done, the sooner her world could go back to normal. Well, a new normal anyway since she had an empire to run now. She didn't have time for ex-fiancés and drama. The family name was at stake.

Addison sipped her now-cooled coffee before answering. "Yeah. I'm in." Not that she'd really had much of a choice, but she'd give it to Del that he made it seem like she did. "In regard to the show, how does this work?"

"Well, as the owner of the home, you'll be interviewed by Teri and that will be filmed. Then we will film together at certain intervals. When big problems arise, we will film that as well."

Addison nodded. "Okay. Will I need to be there every day?"

Del shook his head. "No, but you're more than welcome to be there whenever you want. It's your house." One side of his mouth tilted up.

"But to be honest, things go better when we can just work. As your contractor, I will send you daily reports."

"I understand. Stay away." He frowned at that, but she stood, ready to walk him out the door. There were things she needed to think about.

"There's something else I want to say." He lifted his head to capture her gaze.

For the life of her, she wanted to refuse him. Send him along. Keep it professional. Instead, she sat back down and waited for what he had to say next.

His stare was steady and fierce on her. "We've known each other for a long time, Addie. We're family of sorts. And we were friends before we were…more than friends." He paused and cleared his throat. "I've given you plenty of reasons to hate me. But I want us to be friendly again."

Addison stared at him for a couple of beats. She wanted *so badly* to continue the cold front she'd put up for him when he'd blown back into her life yesterday. But less than twenty-four hours in and she was already beginning to cave.

No. She couldn't let him do it anymore.

"I don't know about friends, Del. But I will be civil and professional with you. You can count on it. We both have a lot at stake and need each other in the short term, just like you said." She shook her head. "But I can't make any promises on being friends with you."

A small nod. "Understood." This time he stood, signaling the end of his visit. "Well, thanks for taking the time to talk to me."

She set her drink on the table and stood. "Thanks for bringing breakfast." They made their way back into the house, toward the front door, Murphy hot on their heels, his nails clacking on the hardwoods. Once inside he sprawled out on the kitchen floor and sighed.

"Looks like the rawhide wore him out," Del said.

Addison rolled her eyes with a smile. "He's a drama king is what he is."

Del chuckled and saluted the dog. "Enjoy the rest of the bone, buddy."

Murphy didn't raise his head, just wagged his tail in acknowledgement. "Lazy," Addison chided.

At the front door, Del opened it and then turned back to her, standing on the threshold, the sunshine streaming over him.

"I know we have a tight deadline, so I'll email you the timeline I mapped out. I'll have my assistant send over the details about filming and the contracts to be signed. I'll start demo as soon as permits are updated if you'll let me know when they're ready. Work for you?"

For a moment she was lightheaded trying to keep up with what he said. So much to do, so little time. "Yeah. Works for me. Oh," she snapped her fingers. "I guess you'll need a key to the place."

She walked back into the kitchen and grabbed the extra set of keys to the estate that hung on the wall with her other keys. Her eyes slid closed as butterflies set up camp in her belly. *Dad, what are you doing to me here?* She inhaled and exhaled deeply before palming the keys and heading back to the foyer.

He smiled and Addison swore the temperature in the room rose a few degrees. "Thanks." His smile dropped a bit, his gaze narrowed onto her mouth. "You've got some chocolate on your lip." His voice was deep and rough. The sound of it started a warming sensation low in her gut.

She stood frozen to the spot when his thumb grazed across her bottom lip. Her breath hitched at the contact. Their stares clashed when her tongue inadvertently darted out and brushed his thumb.

Neither of them said anything for several moments, just stood there staring at each other. Memories of him touching her in all sorts of places crashed into her so hard, she swayed toward him.

"I think I got it."

More than you realized. She fought to regain terra firma but it was wishful thinking when he brought the pad of his thumb to his mouth and sucked. His grin was wicked. "Sweet."

Before she could unscramble her brain, he was gone.

family affairs

DEL PULLED the pickup truck he'd recently purchased into the circular driveway of the house that once belonged in the Reynolds family. His cousin Emma had sold it to Shane Kavanaugh, the new winery owner—and now her fiancé—a few months ago when she was unable to keep up with the mortgage. It was currently being renovated into an updated version of the bed and breakfast it had once been as an extension to the new winery and vineyard.

He stepped out of the truck and thought he'd been dropped into the middle of a busy anthill. Workers were all over the place, moving wood and hammering. He heard the whirring of screwdrivers and, underneath it all, the thump of rock music. A smile curved his lips, and anticipation filled his chest. He couldn't wait to get back to work on a site. His only holdup was the permits Addison said she'd handle.

There was another pressure in his chest thinking about her, but it was one he was more than willing to ignore.

He jogged up the wide front steps and walked through the open front door, taking his sunglasses off when the light around him dimmed. The smell of sawdust filled the air, and the sounds of construction were louder in the large space that had once been the living area. Some of the walls had been knocked down to open the space and make it bigger and brighter. The old hardwood and carpeting had been pulled up, and there was no doubt in his mind Noah would be putting down the best of the best real hardwood in its place.

Shane would spare no expense, not only because he could afford it, but also in honor of making his soon-to-be bride's family home top notch.

"Del!"

He turned when he heard his name to find Noah waving him over from across the large open room. Del started toward where he stood with Wyatt Davis, one of Reynolds Construction's contractors.

"Hey, guys," he said as he approached. He held out a hand to Wyatt. "Davis, good to see you, man."

Wyatt grinned and returned the handshake. "Hey, Property Ace. How the hell are ya? In town for long?"

Del planted his hands on his hips and looked around. "Yeah, for a little while. Working on a project." He gestured toward Wyatt. "How about you? You still moonlighting at the Silver Moon?"

Wyatt chuckled. "Of course, how else do you think I hold up my playboy reputation? Trying to keep up with you, you know."

Del looked at the ground a moment, smile still in place, even though his gut ached. "Don't believe everything you read."

He hoped like hell Addison didn't.

Eager to change the subject, Del asked, "How's your mom?"

The slightest of shadows crossed Wyatt's face, but it was gone as quick as it came, and he rubbed a hand over his strong jaw. "She's hanging in there. Starting another round of chemo next week."

"Shit, I'm sorry. I didn't realize the cancer had come back."

Wyatt tapped the tablet in his hand against his thigh and looked away for a moment. "Yeah, but she's a fighter and she's beaten it before. We can do it again."

He brought his gaze back to Del's and sent him a smile, but it didn't quite reach his eyes. "Anyway, I gotta get back to work. It was good to see you, Del." He turned to Noah. "I'll take care of the issue."

Noah nodded and clapped Wyatt on the shoulder. "Thanks, I appreciate it."

Wyatt gave a jaunty salute and walked off, tapping something into the tablet.

Del had the uneasy feeling he'd stepped in shit and hadn't realized it until the stench hit his nose. "Damn, I feel like a heel. I didn't know his mom was sick again."

Noah's sigh was long. "Yeah. Wyatt doesn't say much about it. Hell, if you'd just met him, you'd never know. He's damn good at what he does, with stone and wood especially, so I've been giving him as much work as I can. It's the only way I can help him. He won't take help any other way."

Del hated to hear the situation. Maybe he could hire Wyatt on the renovation project. He wanted to help his friend out.

He looked around the room, noting all the work that was done. "Looking good, big bro."

Noah folded his arms over his chest and gazed around. "Yeah," he said with a sigh. "It's getting there. The best thing about this project is the budget. Shane has one, of course, but it's healthy, and he's aware of how much things cost." He grinned. "Gotta love when you work with a repeat client who knows his shit."

Del slid his hands into the front pocket of his jeans. "I like the layout here now. Knocked out that wall. It's a great space now."

"Shane's idea. Like I said, he knows his shit and what he wants."

"Well, I try."

Del turned to find Shane Kavanaugh strolling toward them. The man ran a multi-billion-dollar international wine empire, but it would be hard to tell. Today, he wore jeans, work boots, and a navy T-shirt, and if the dirt on his boots was any indication, he'd spent some time in the vineyards recently.

"Shane, how the hell are ya?" He put out a hand, and Shane shook it and clapped his shoulder with his other hand.

"Can't complain."

"My cousin driving you crazy yet?"

Shane grinned. "Oh yeah, but I'll take it any day of the week."

Noah gave him the side-eye and gestured between him and Del. "Don't forget, we're watching you."

Shane chuckled and held up his hands. "I know, I know. But trust me, Emmaline handles herself just fine."

Del liked how Shane used Emma's full name a lot of the time. She was in no danger of being anything but loved by the man standing next to him.

Not to mention, Shane would be a bitch to take down. He was a tall, broad-chested motherfucker that wouldn't go down easy.

"How's business?" Del asked.

Shane blew out a breath. "Busy as hell. There's still a lot of jobs to fill at the winery to get everything up and running the way I want it. And I'm still trying to get my bearings with running the company."

Del frowned. "I'm sorry about your father, man. Alan was a great guy. How's your brother doing?"

Shane nodded and his smile was sad. "Thanks." He sighed. "Colin's doing well. Now that he's off becoming a tech king, I'm trying to fill his position and some others so I don't have to travel quite so much. I finally found an office for my home base. I'd like to spend some time in the building I bought."

"So, you went with the one Addie showed you?" Noah asked.

Del's stomach took a nosedive. "Addie? As in my Addie?"

When both Shane and Noah raised a brow in his direction, he wanted to kick his own ass. *What the fuck? She hasn't been your Addie in years, and all indications say she never will be again.*

Still…what did Addie have to do with Shane? He cleared his throat. "I mean, I didn't realize she was in real estate."

Shane nodded. "Yeah, Addison was instrumental in helping me find the right space I wanted. She's one of the best brokers I've worked with. Knows her shit for sure."

"How's Lindsey liking Addison's business class?"

"She loves it. Emma encouraged her to do it, and I think it was a great idea."

What the hell were they talking about? Addison teaches business? There was a boatload of confusion winging its way around Del's brain, trying to keep up with what these two were talking about.

"Well, Addison always had a good business head about her," Del said, though his voice was tinged with something akin to awe mixed with a bit of regret.

Shane's smile was rueful. "She knows how to handle a deal. She worked me over pretty good as Emma's agent." He shrugged, then glanced around the room. "I would have paid anything to get this house and make my woman whole."

Del was happy Emma and Shane had found each other. Addiction had nearly ruined both of their lives. Still, Del's crudely mended heart panged just a little hearing Shane talk about the woman he loved.

It also occurred to Del he didn't know much about what Addison did anymore. He knew she had worked with her father in some capacity but didn't realize what it was. Even when he and Jackson spoke, there was a silent, mutual understanding that Addison wasn't brought up in conversation. Since Jackson had nothing to do with the family business—he owned his own law firm in Atlanta—Del could only assume Stephen had left Addison in control of his company.

As much as he didn't want to feel it, pride swelled in his chest for Addison. And as much as he didn't want to acknowledge it, he would always care for her even if they could never be together again.

He shook off the melancholy. "I'm sure she learned from her father, who besides my own father, was one of the sharpest businessmen around." He eyed Shane. "You and your father remind me a lot of Stephen and Paul. Which is probably why I admire your handsome ass so much."

Shane rolled his eyes but chuckled. "Okay, Hollywood." His smile faded and he lowered his voice. "Look, I don't know what went down between you and Addison. But whatever it is, or was, I have a feeling you guys will be fine working together on the renovation of the museum. You're both consummate professionals. Whatever you do, though,"—he pointed a finger at Del—"don't run off my new broker."

Del shook his head. "Don't worry about me. I'm only here for the renovation, to fulfill a contract, and figure out my next move."

Noah coughed out "bullshit" under his breath, and Shane gave him a "yeah, right" look. But before Del could defend himself, Shane's phone rang from his back pocket. He glanced at the display and nodded his head. "Sorry, guys. I need to take this. Let's grab a beer before you leave town." They shook hands, and Shane walked away, talking into his phone.

Del turned to Noah. "Is that why you called me out here? To bust my balls?"

Noah laughed and shoved at his brother's shoulder. "No, but it's fun." He started to walk toward the back of the house. "Let's go take a walk. I can't hear myself think in here."

Del followed Noah out through the house and down into the field stretched out behind it. The smell of grass mingled with the blooming trees from around the property, kicked up by the breeze. The sun was hiding behind a wall of gray clouds, giving the day a sort of gloomy feel. It matched Del's mood at the moment. He was still sorting out all the things said about Addison. It made him realize how much had changed. What else had he missed?

Noah led them down toward the large pond and sat down on an old, abandoned bench. Del followed suit and stretched his arm across the back, waiting for Noah to get on with whatever it was he wanted.

"You've piqued my curiosity, Noah. Bringing me out here with no one around. If it were anyone else but you, I'd think you were about to confess a crime to me."

Noah smiled and leaned forward, his forearms on his thighs. "Nah. I just wanted to be able to talk freely, and I know you're still keeping your illness on the down low."

Del's grin faded. "I appreciate that. Because yeah, not ready to tell the world just yet. Addison doesn't know, and I'd like to keep it that way, okay? I want to be able to tell her myself."

Noah nodded. "It's not my story to tell, so no one will hear about it from me." He looked out over the pond and to the land beyond. "You've been away awhile, Del, but you also know this family and how we work. We haven't changed that much. If anyone hears about it, it will be from your doctor in LA or agent. Because you know Doc won't say anything."

He wasn't worried about Doc. The man was not only his uncle, but he also took being a doctor seriously and had for over thirty years. Doc didn't mess around with the doctor patient privilege thing.

"My agent doesn't even know. And my doctor won't say anything.

And I *do* know this family. Nothing's changed." Del shoved at Noah's shoulder. "Except you. You're a bit longer in the tooth."

"Ha. Smartass. Anyway,"—he cleared his throat—"what are your intentions when your contract is up? Are you planning to stay in the business?"

Del let out a long, groaning sigh. "The million-dollar question. My agent told me about a new series the network wants me for. It would be less physical work, more money. I'm excited about it; it sounds like what I need." He blew out a breath when Noah remained quiet. "You know me, Noah. I'm going to need something to do. For as long as I can, anyway."

"What are you doing about a neurologist? Doc could recommend one."

"Keeping mine in LA for the time being."

"Treatment going okay otherwise?" Noah asked. His voice was a mixture of concern and authority. Del may have been the one to take off to LA, make his living on TV, and lead a production company, but make no mistake, Noah was the head of the family. Being the oldest, it was a job he'd taken over when their father died too soon and one he took seriously. In some cases, too seriously, but that was a subject Del wasn't going to broach with him. All it did was shut Noah down.

Instead, Del took one for the team and talked about his own trigger that made him want to run. "Yeah, it's fine." He leaned forward to mimic his brother's stance but turned his head toward him. "What are you driving at, Noah?"

He met Del's stare head-on. "Once you're finished with your contract, I want you to come work for the family business."

For a moment the only sounds were the gentle breeze and the faint sounds of saws and hammering coming from the house. A coldness hit Del's chest, surprise and dread a nasty mix behind his breastbone. He swallowed hard, his tongue unable to form words.

Noah raised a brow and looked away. "I see I've shocked you into silence." He smirked. "Finally."

Del blew out a sigh and shook his head. "I can't. And you know it."

Noah narrowed his eyes. "Why? Not enough glitz and glamour for you?"

Anger surged in Del's blood. He clenched his fists and prayed he wouldn't hit his brother. It'd been a while since they'd had a fistfight. And they were both too old for that shit now. "Fuck you. When we made that video and sent it in, the network wanted both of us. You had the opportunity to come with me. You chose not to, even encouraged me to go. So don't pull that shit on me now."

Noah rubbed the back of his neck. "You're right. I'm happy for your success." Del scoffed. "I *am*. But now it's coming to an end, and with your condition, it would be nice to have you back here. I could use the help, and Mom would be thrilled."

Del covered his heart in mock pain. "Low blow using Mom in your pitch."

Noah shrugged. "Low blow be damned. It's true."

Del leaned back, crossing his arms over his chest. He kicked his long, jean-clad legs in front of him. "I know, but there are several reasons I can't. One of them being my condition. I mean, it isn't cancer or anything like that, but it is career ending for me and it isn't curable. That's why I can't continue with *Property Ace*. The physical part of the job is something I can't do."

"We can get around that. I've got some things coming down the pipeline that I could use your expert eye on when it comes to renovation." Noah shrugged. "Hell, I hardly ever do the physical labor myself anymore."

Damn Noah and making sense. Still… "There's also the whole being in the same…" He waved his hand as a wave of mortification hit him. "Never mind." Nope, nope, nope. Not telling Noah that Addison was another reason he couldn't stay.

But Noah being Noah, he'd already figured it out. "I know, being in the same town as Addie. I get it." Noah was quiet for a moment, before a caustic smile quirked his lips. "I'm lucky. My ex didn't like Madison Ridge anyway, so she's not underfoot all the time."

"I didn't mean it like that."

Noah shrugged. "It's fine. Sara's happy now and so am I."

Del raised a brow. "Sure about that? When was the last time you got laid?"

Noah rolled his eyes. "Can we get back to the subject at hand?"

"That long, huh?"

"Asshole," Noah muttered under his breath, causing Del to laugh.

"Okay, I'll think about it. I'm going to be here for a while anyway."

Noah straightened and clapped Del on the back. "That's all I can ask for." He stood and pulled his phone out of his back pocket. "I better head back before they call out a search party for me. This thing's been vibrating the entire time we've been out here." He mocked throwing the phone in the pond. "That's what I feel like doing on days like today. See why I need you?" Waving, Noah walked back through the field toward the house.

Del stayed seated and smiled, but the weight in his chest made it hard to breathe. And he was pretty certain it wasn't his medical condition causing it.

Madison Ridge may have grown in his absence, but it still wasn't big enough for him and the torch he carried for Addison Davenport. She was a fixture in town, just like her father had been. She'd made it clear they would get along to complete her father's last wish, but that was it. He had no desire to live that way the rest of his life. If he stayed, he'd want to win her back, and there were so many reasons that was a shitty plan, the least of which was his health.

No, Delaney Reynolds had one goal right now. Finish his contract and get the hell out of town. He'd figure out the rest later.

CHAPTER SIX
ten year ache

"OKAY, I think that's it, everyone." Addison closed the notebook in front of her and folded her hands over it with a smile. "Are you guys set?" She directed her question to the conference phone in the center of the table.

A chorus of "we're set" and other affirmations came from the regional managers that had called in for the meeting.

"Great. And again, if you need anything or have any questions, text, email, or call me. I'm available."

Nods and thanks echoed around the conference table as the handful of men and women who now worked for her gathered their things and left the room, their conversations leaving the room quiet in their wake. She blew out a breath and leaned down for her tote bag.

This was her third staff meeting since she'd taken over the company. One would think she'd be a natural at it since she'd sat in the same meetings herself for the last ten years. As head of the real estate side of the business, she'd been required to be at the monthly department head meetings her dad held. She knew how the meetings were run like the back of her hand. Had even run one or two in his absence over the years. But it was different when you were running it as the head of the company, instead of in lieu of the head of the company.

Fortunately, she had a good set of people who had been with Davenport Enterprises for years. She knew them well and they knew how hard she worked. But that had been as coworkers, not as their new boss. So far, so good with everyone, but Addison was just waiting for the shoe to drop and for drama to ensue.

Which reminded her, she needed to get a regional director in place as soon as possible. There was no way she could keep up with the various managers scattered all over the Southeast. She groaned as the to-do list in her head continued to get longer.

"Hey, Addison." Jane, her inherited assistant, poked her head into the conference room.

"Hey, Jane." She slid her notebook and planner into her tote and looked up. "What's up?"

Jane lifted a pink piece of paper and read off it. "Wendy from zoning called and said your permits for the museum are ready."

And that's why she didn't need drama at work. The damn museum her father left her to finish—with her ex-fiancé no less—was enough drama to last her to the end of days. But the sooner they got started and finished the better. "It only took them two weeks? I'm impressed." She checked the time on her phone. Twenty minutes until closing time for the zoning office. "Then that's where I'm headed. Can you lock up for me tonight?"

Jane nodded. "Absolutely."

"Thanks." She stood and followed Jane out of the conference room. "See you tomorrow."

She hustled out the door and was pulling her car into a spot at the government building on the hill five minutes later. As she pulled open the door, a small smile curved her lips. What was it about these old buildings that made them all smell the same? The musty smell reminded her of the old elementary school she'd attended just down the street. The kids these days had a shiny new school with electronic white boards and tablets in every classroom. She was sure it smelled more like new paint than old paperback books. It was a shame they didn't get that experience. The city had turned the old school into an annex building for the local university where she taught her business classes in the outreach program.

And she laid the blame squarely on Delaney Reynolds's head for all the nostalgic feelings lately. Memory lane was best left closed down.

"Good afternoon, Wendy." Addison smiled at the clerk behind the counter at the zoning and permitting office.

"Hey, Addison. How are you?"

"I'm doing well, thanks." She drummed her fingers on the counter. "Jane said the permits were ready to go?"

Wendy stood and nodded. "Hold on one sec," she said before walking over to a file cabinet behind her. Addison dropped her chin into her hand and waited while Wendy flipped through a folder in the top drawer.

"You must be excited about getting started on the museum," Wendy said.

Not exactly the word I'd use. Addison measured her words before she spoke but plastered a smile on her face. "Very excited. I'm honored to be fulfilling my father's last wish and giving the town such a gift."

"Ah-ha. Found it." Wendy pulled out the papers and shoved the drawer closed, the metal on metal sound ringing like a bell. She read over the document in front of her as she walked back to the counter. She grinned then slid the paperwork across to Addison. "I'm sure you are, especially since you're working with Del. He was here yesterday getting his filming permit." She looked around and leaned closer to Addison, who automatically followed suit. Wendy lowered her voice as though they were sharing a huge secret. "How is it possible for one man to be that hot?" She fanned herself and a wistful look filled her eyes. "All of those Reynolds men are too handsome for their own good. But Del has something special."

Addison's heart twisted in her chest. She was no stranger to how special Del was and it wasn't because he was "hot." Sure, he had it all going on with that dark blond hair, bright blue eyes, all-American *Varsity Blues* look. Enough people had made the comparison to the blond star of the football and car racing movies. And yeah, he had broad shoulders and six pack abs and sex appeal that went on for days. But he was also smart, creative, kind, and generous. He had an adventurous soul, one she'd overlooked and thought she could change. Alas, it had blown up in her face.

Addison laughed a little too long and too high-pitched. She cleared her throat before speaking and wanted to smack herself for acting so silly. "Yes, he does. But that's not why I'm excited about this project."

Wendy rolled her eyes at her. "I've lived here all my life and even though I was a couple of years behind you in school, everyone knew the Addison and Delaney story. You guys were legendary."

"Legend…now that's just ridiculous."

Wendy tilted her head. "Maybe so, but it's the truth, nonetheless. And he's been gone for quite some time. But now he's back." Her smile was sly. "Think you guys will hook back up?"

Oh, for fuck's sake. "Um, no. There will be no 'hooking up.' Besides he's not back for good. Just for this project."

"Be that as it may, don't try to tell me you're not excited about being around him every day, especially looking like that." Wendy fanned herself again. The woman acted like she was in the middle of having a series of hot flashes.

"Yeah, I guess so." Addison needed to get out of there pronto. If Wendy started in with asking how she could have let him go, blah, blah, blah, and fanned herself one more time, Addison would scream. The truth was she needed to play in the sandbox like a good girl with the zoning people and Wendy was a zoning person, albeit a chatty one.

Once again, she plastered on her best smile and dropped the permits into her tote. "Well, it was great chatting with you, but I gotta run."

Wendy glanced at her watch. "Well look at that, it's quittin' time anyway."

Addison waved as she left the office and let the smile drop from her face once she settled in her car. God forbid she run into anyone else who knew her life's story between the front door and the safety of her Mini Cooper.

After Del left it had taken some time, but after a year or two—and some bust-ass hard work—Addison could finally show her face around town without getting the "bless your heart" pity expressions from everyone she knew. And it did no good to explain what really went down between them. Not to mention it wasn't any of their business.

But now Delaney was back on her turf—hey, he gave it up a long time ago—but it was like she was starting all over again. And that wasn't somewhere she ever wanted to be again. She'd learned one solid truth over the years: men she loved left her behind. She wouldn't fall prey to that again, no matter how well Delaney Reynolds filled out his snug T-shirts.

Sighing, she started her car and pointed it in the direction of the estate. The sooner she posted the permits, the sooner Del could round up his crew and get started. If she left now, she wouldn't cross paths with him.

He would be back in his swanky beach house in California before the summer was over. And that's what she wanted. To get back to normal.

Right?

As she turned onto the side street off the square that lead to the estate, she shook her head. Why was it even a debate? She needed to get started and get this museum project done. She only had a couple of months to restore the historic home and fulfill a contract with the city her dad had started years before. He was gone now, and it was on her shoulders to live up to his promise. Davenports never welched on a deal—they always kept their word. She wasn't going to be the one to break that record.

She pulled into the driveway that ran down the side, leading to the back of the large house. Her foot stomped on the brake, surprised when a black pickup she didn't recognize was already occupying most of the parking area.

Her brow furrowed. The truck had dealer plates on it from a place in Atlanta. Who the hell would go all the way…?

No, no, no.

Del couldn't technically start demolition until he had the permits displayed, so what the hell was he doing here? She walked up the sidewalk to the front door and a turn of the knob found it to be unlocked, the door opening without hesitation.

"Hello?" She was greeted with the sound of faint blues music and a whirring sound at regular intervals. She walked toward the odd combination of sultry music and power tool.

The farther she walked into the house, the louder the noise became. She moved toward the back corner of the house to the room once used as a library. In the back corner of the room, Del stood with his back to her and she froze, jaw dropping.

He was sans shirt, and she had an unobstructed view of his muscles bunching and releasing when he moved pieces of two by fours around and drilled into them. She didn't know what he was doing and didn't really care. His broad shoulders tapered down to a long, beautifully sculpted back. Her eyes trailed down his spine to where jeans and a tool belt rode low on lean hips.

Yeah, Delaney Reynolds had always been a good-looking guy. But the young Del had nothing on the grown-up Del. Wendy was right.

The man was smoking hot.

With the slinky, sultry music surrounding them, Addison had to remember to breathe. God, it had been a long time since she'd had a man. The problem was that she didn't want just any man. She wanted the man standing in front of her with every fiber of her being. But there was no way in hell that was happening again.

Then who's going to scratch this itch, my friend?

Uh, no one. Leave me alone.

She was going crazy. It was official. Straightening her spine, she knocked on the doorframe as though she'd just arrived. *You're a fraud, Addie.*

He pivoted and smiled at her. "Hey."

She waved, unsure she could speak, but somehow found her voice. "Hey."

He turned fully and walked toward her, sliding the drill into a loop on his tool belt. It reminded Addison of a holster for a gun.

"What's up?"

She swallowed hard before speaking and it took all she had to tear her eyes away from the chiseled, tanned chest, the rock-hard six pack abs. When the hell did it get so hot in here?

"Uh, the permits were ready, so I was bringing them by to post." The more she talked, the more confidence built in her chest and her brain seemed to come back online. She walked into the room and folded her arms over her chest, the echo of her heels in the large room a reminder they were alone. Her mouth may be working but she still couldn't look at him. It would be like looking at the sun. "What are you doing here?"

"Building a table to use in the room when we film. This is going to be ground zero so to speak." As though she were prey in his predator sights, his eyes tracked her every move. The burn of his stare was warm on her skin and it was all she could do not to fan herself the way chatty Wendy had.

"Oh." Seriously? That's all she could say? Yes, because her mouth was as dry as the desert with no oasis in sight. She turned away from him under the pretense of looking at the walls. "Um, are these walls coming down?"

"Addison."

She froze when she realized he was right behind her. And the wall was in front of her. *Shit.* How the hell had she managed to literally back herself into a corner?

With a silent deep breath, she drew herself up to her full height before turning to face him, effectively putting them toe to toe. If she took a really deep breath, her boobs would graze his bare chest. Right, no more deep breaths. "Delaney." She tried like hell to sound unaffected.

Even at a respectable five foot eight plus heels, she still had to look up at him. The heat of his body and the faint scent of his aftershave surrounded her. It was intoxicating and she wanted to wrap herself around him.

"I don't know. Are those walls coming down?"

She closed her eyes for a moment and shook her head. Her brain was hazy, and she couldn't decipher if they were talking about the same walls. When she opened her eyes, his intense navy-blue stare pinned her where she stood. It was all she could see.

Jesus, she'd missed him. Missed the lover, missed the friend. The thought of how much was gut-wrenching. There was no going back to the way things used to be. Too much water under the bridge and shit.

A flush of heat started in her core and worked its way through her body. Her limbs were heavy. Breathing was difficult. The heat generating between them combined with the heat trapped in the house from the warm May afternoon had a small trickle of sweat running down Addison's spine.

If she wasn't careful, she'd start panting. "I," she croaked then cleared her throat and licked her lips, trying again. "I remember now. I've seen the plans." Could she sound anymore of an idiot right now?

His eyes darted to her mouth and a dark part of her did a gleeful happy dance. Del lifted a hand and lightly outlined her lips with a fingertip. Her eyes slid closed. It was a gesture he'd done so many times before and to her dismay she was unable to stop him. She could only breathe out and in small puffs of air.

"How is it possible you're more beautiful now than you were before?" His voice was husky and soft.

She opened her eyes and met his heated stare with one of her own. Just as she was about to say *to hell with it all* and launch herself at him, he blinked, breaking the spell.

Del took a step back, physically and figuratively putting distance between them, and shoved his hands into his jeans pockets. "If you'll leave the permits here, I'll put them in the box in the morning. We're going to start demo on Monday."

Bringing it back to work and the job they had to do was as effective as dousing her in cold water. She pasted on the fake smile she'd given too many times to count today. "Great. The sooner we can get started, the better." *For both of us, I'm sure.* "Let me get them from my car."

Del looked down at the floor and nodded. "I'll walk you out."

Outside, she walked ahead of him, gulping breaths of the late afternoon air. There was a breeze that she hoped would cool off her overheated body. It helped he'd covered up that beautiful, impressive chest with a T-shirt. She wasn't sure how much longer she could look but not touch.

When she got to her car, she pulled open the driver's side door and grabbed the permits. "Thanks for doing that. I appreciate it," she said, handing them to him.

His smile was close-lipped and formal as he took the papers from her. "Sure, no problem. I'll keep you posted on how things go." It shouldn't have bothered her that he was acting so formal, but it did. She followed his lead and kept it professional.

Addison nodded and leaned against the open car door. "When does filming start?"

"Monday morning. But probably for only about half a day. Some of the crew members are wrapping up another show."

She nodded like she understood his world that was so foreign to her. "That's good."

"Yeah." He rocked back on his heels and looked away for a moment with a sigh before looking back her direction and giving her a half smile. "Well, good night, Addie. Drive safe."

He backed away, signaling she should get in her car and head home. It was the safest and smartest thing to do for both of them. She didn't want to be heartbroken again and he would leave her once the project was over. Staying professional was the only option. It's what would keep her heart whole.

So why did the ache in her chest feel the same way it did ten years ago?

thank god for demo day

DEL PULLED his truck into the driveway of what he'd dubbed the Davenrey project, waving at the cop standing guard. Women stood in groups along the brick half-wall and wrought iron fencing that circled the perimeter of the property. They screamed his name and waved, many holding signs proposing to him, saying hi, and a variety of other things to try to get his attention. He shook his head with a wry smile. It still amazed him how some people acted around a celebrity.

When he stopped the truck, he got out and stood in front of the large historic estate, swiping at the sheen of sweat on his forehead. The sun had only been up a few hours and the air was already still and thick. Mid-May in Madison Ridge was hotter than Del remembered. But even the wet-blanket, humid air couldn't dampen the excitement coursing through Del's blood, making him feel alive. It was demo day.

It was the same with every project he worked on and it never got old. But this project? This project was by far the closest to his heart. Even with Noah's blessing, he harbored some guilt at leaving his brother behind to pursue Hollywood.

Truth be told, there was a void in the pit of his stomach as well. His father had been dead a couple of years by the time he left Madison Ridge, but he'd always had this nagging feeling his father would have been disappointed at the choices he'd made. The feeling had left him torn between wanting to stay away and to say "fuck it all" and run home.

He hoped once the project was over he would be able to find closure with his dad's ghost. But he would also be without a known path in his life. His professional life was at a crossroads. His health was at the forefront of his mind on a daily basis, one area of his life he had admittedly taken for granted. His personal life…well, that was one area that reminded him of quicksand. He had no desire to get tangled up in a relationship right now. With his newly diagnosed disorder and life in general disarray, he didn't see that changing. He shook his head to dislodge the image of Addie that popped into his mind.

The completion of the museum was the end of an era for Del.

The sounds of hammering and wood splintering that greeted him as he walked into the fray were a symphony to Del's ears and a grin split his face. The local crew he'd hired had arrived ahead of him and was already at work. Right on schedule. Using the noise to guide him, Del made his way to the kitchen, where a crew worked tearing the cabinets off the walls. He leaned against the doorjamb, watching the guys work. Particles of dust and who knows what else filled the air, dancing in the sunbeams streaming through the window.

This was his favorite part. Smashing shit apart. But he also knew parts of it would have to be saved for when the camera crew showed up so they could film the demolition.

"Morning, fellas. Can I get one of those masks?" he asked, raising his voice over the hammers bashing.

Work stopped for a moment and greetings were made all around. He tried to remember all the names thrown at him. A couple of them were relatives of some classmates he'd gone to school with and satisfaction filled his chest with the thought he was helping out a few friends in some way.

"Good to meet you all. I'm just going to take this with me." He grinned and picked up a sledgehammer leaning against the wall and left the guys to do their job in the kitchen.

Del made his way into the parlor where a wall needed to come down to open the space for more memorabilia. He glanced at his watch and smiled. Perfect. He had about twenty minutes before the film crew showed. Plenty of time to let out some frustration binding him up.

Yeah, thinking about the source of said frustration and the way her hair fell down her back was bad for his mojo. He picked up the sledge-hammer ready to slam it into the wall.

"Mornin', boss!"

The muscles in Del's arms flexed as he dropped the hammer to the floor and put a smile on his face. "Hey, Tommy."

Tommy Richards might look like he belonged in a big rig and talk with a Southern accent thick as molasses, but the guy knew construction management inside and out. He came highly recommended by Noah, who'd gone to school with him and worked with Tommy's crews quite often. Tommy knew the best vendors and contractors in a hundred-mile radius. Del had hired Tommy as the super for the job to oversee the work when he couldn't be there.

He nodded his head toward the kitchen. "Your boys are making great progress in there."

Tommy nodded. "Yeah, they were ready to get started early. I chose my best guys. Professionals, each one of them." He grinned. "But I'd be lyin' if I said they weren't acting like schoolgirls getting to dance with the hottest boy in school."

Del laughed. "Glad I could make their day."

"Day?" Tommy snorted. "You made their whole year."

With his hands jammed on his hips, Del continued to laugh. "Just make sure they keep those badges on so the guard will let them through. At least for the first week or so." He looked around the room. "Got a can of spray paint?"

The older man scratched at his chin and shoved at his ball cap. "Yep, think there's one around somewhere."

"It doesn't matter what color. I just need to section off the area in here I'm going to save for filming."

While Tommy walked off to another room, Del inspected the one he stood in. It was going to be a great space and he couldn't wait to see it all come to life.

"Here you go." The balls in the can clattered as Tommy shook it before handing it over to Del.

"Thanks." Popping the top off, Del shook it hard once before spraying a large neon orange X over the section of drywall still intact. "When the filming crew gets here, we'll let the guys loose on it." He narrowed his eyes at it. "I may help them with it, too."

Tommy nodded once and touched the bill of his hat. "Got it."

"Hey, Tommy! I gotta question," one of the workers called out.

"Let me go see what's going on over there. Talk later, boss."

"Thanks, man." Del clapped him on the shoulder as Tommy passed him. He fit the mask over his face, then hefted the large hammer again, ignoring the protesting muscles in his arms and shoulders, drove the sledgehammer home. The vibration of the hammer creating a large hole in the wall ran up his arms and down into his back, but it was a comforting pain. He repeated the process over and over, until sweat ran down his face.

When the wall was demolished, he stepped back and set the hammerhead on the floor, leaning on the handle. He was in good shape, worked out several times a week, but this hammering had him winded.

"I see you've been practicing."

Teri walking into the room, followed by some of the cameramen and lighting guys. He nodded in their direction. "Hey guys. We ready to get filming?" he asked Teri.

She gave him a side glance before her gaze went back to the area where the wall once stood. "Yeah. Did you leave any wall to use for filming?"

He pointed toward the wall with the orange X. "Over there."

"Perfect." She rubbed her hands together and looked him over and crossed her arms over her chest. "You're all sweaty. The makeup crew is out front. I need that pretty Delaney Reynolds face for the camera."

He ran a hand over his damp forehead and wiped it on her arm. "Ew! Gross, Del." She rubbed her arm on her jeans.

"What, you don't want any of the Property Ace's sweat? Some women would love it in a bottle." He'd had some graphic and rather perverted fan mail once or twice that involved his sweat. It still made him shudder to think about it.

"You're worse than a kid. Get away from me, you nasty man."

Del laughed and leaned his sledgehammer against the wall. "I'm just getting you started. Before this day is out, you'll be just as nasty as me." He laughed again at her grimace.

The next few hours were spent in front of the camera, hitting his marks and walking through the house telling the audience some of the history and what the plans were for the rooms. He was also able to work out more of his frustration by tearing some old cabinetry off the walls with a crowbar. Inwardly, he was disappointed he wasn't able to keep working on the actual demolition, but on the outside, he flashed that million-dollar smile for the camera and moved on.

Around lunchtime, Teri yelled cut, "that's a wrap for today," and handed out call sheets while she thanked the crew. Del's face ached from so much smiling into the camera and he rolled his shoulders. "Thank God," he muttered under his breath.

Teri came up to him and stood close to him. "Are you okay, Del?" she asked, her voice low.

With one hand massaging his opposite shoulder, he looked down at her. Teri gave him shit and rode his ass during filming usually, but she was damn good at her job. Her eyes were earnest and more friend than ball-busting show producer right now. "I'm good, T. Just some soreness."

She narrowed her eyes at him, skepticism lining her features. Eventually he would tell her the reasons he was quitting the show even while it was at the top of its game. But for now, he was keeping those reasons to a small circle of people who didn't make their living in Hollywood.

"Fine. Don't tell me." She sighed and looked away before bringing her gaze back to him. "You did a great job today. Being back home seems to agree with you."

One side of his mouth quirked up. "Maybe."

Teri rolled her eyes and shoved at him. "Cryptic as always."

Del put an arm around her shoulders and pulled her in to place a loud smacking kiss on the top of her head like he did with his sisters. "Aw, I'll miss you too, ballbuster."

"Delaney, are you here?"

Teri raised a brow and pulled back to look at him. "Who the hell is that? How did they get past security?"

"I'm back here," he called out and shook his head with a grin. "That would be my mother. And everyone knows my mother, especially the cop out front. He works with my brother."

Del dropped his arm from Teri's shoulder as his mother, Stella, his sister, Grace, and Addison filed into the room. Stella and Grace had genuine smiles on their faces, but the same couldn't be said for Addison. There was a smile on those perfect, full lips of hers, but knowing her like he did, the curve of her lips was forced by the manners ingrained in her. Those green eyes of hers were apropos for the situation, too.

He couldn't help the small shot of triumph in his gut that made him grin. Del walked toward his mother and kissed her cheek, then leaned over to do the same with Grace. No doubt Addie would be less than thrilled if he tried it, so he stepped back, shoving his hands into the back pockets of his jeans. "What are you ladies doing here?"

"A welcome wagon of sorts courtesy of the Chamber of Commerce," Stella said. "We have a bunch of food out in my SUV."

Del put a hand over his heart. "Whew. You saved me from dealing with a rowdy bunch of hungry men." He waved a thumb toward Teri. "Miser here only got breakfast catered in today."

"Hey!" Teri shoved at his shoulder. "I knew we were only working until lunch. There was no point."

"Yeah, yeah." Del chuckled when she stuck out her tongue at him. "Let me introduce you to this beautiful woman, my mom, Stella. Her look-alike here is my sister, Grace." His gaze slid over to Addison. "And this is Addison Davenport, owner of the place. Ladies, this is my show producer, Teri Andrews."

Addison's smile dipped for half a second, so quick most wouldn't notice it or the tiniest of narrowing of her eyes, before giving her full attention to the woman in front of her. Addie moved forward with her arm outstretched. "Teri, so nice to meet you."

Teri returned the handshake. "Addison, it's a pleasure to finally meet you. I've heard a lot about you. The house is a work of art."

Addison nodded, her smile still in place. "Thank you." She put an arm around Stella's shoulders. "I think my dad and Paul would be ecstatic to see all the work being done."

Stella's smile widened as she looked over at Addison. "Yes, they would." She shifted her focus to Teri. "I'm so glad to meet the person who keeps Del in line on a daily basis."

"Well, it's a chore for sure, but someone has to do it," she replied, her eyes seeking out Del's. The messages she was sending were of the "what the fuck, Del?" kind.

Grace snorted a laugh. "A chore is one way to put it." She punched him lightly in the gut. "We love him anyway."

Teri blew out a breath. "It is a full-time job. Well, I gotta run. We had a short filming day, so I'm off to start some editing." She nodded to the other women in the room. "It was a pleasure meeting you all." Teri turned to Del. "Same time tomorrow."

When Teri walked away, Stella frowned at him. "You're done for the day? We brought lunch for you and the crew. I was hoping to get to see you filming."

He leaned against a stud, arms crossed over his chest. "We're done filming what we needed today, but there's plenty left to go. You'll have plenty to see."

A smile lit up Stella's face. Her smile was just one of the reasons he needed to be back home for a while. It made him feel happy like a child. He'd missed her. "Good. Now come on, I'm sure your crew is hungry." She shooed him away. "Go round them up and we'll get the food ready. Come on, ladies, let's set up."

Addison moved past him but never looked his direction. Her body heat reached out and yanked him by the neck. His eyes followed her long jean-encased legs out the room.

Snug, looked-as-though-they-were-painted-on jeans…damn. It didn't bode well for him that the woman could wear a paper bag and look hot as fuck.

"Son of a bitch." He blew out a breath, trying to get his hormones under control. Just being in the same room with her sent his body into overdrive like it always had. It was a phenomenon he couldn't explain. And how the hell was he going to work with her daily if she looked like that?

By the time Del gathered his wits about him, a group of six women, including his mom, Grace, and Addison had set up tables under a large canopy. Each table was filled with food including double-decker sandwiches, potato salad, fruit, chips, and a large plate of cookies Del would bet his next paycheck were made by his sister, Amelia.

"Eat up, ladies and gentlemen!" Stella called out.

"Mom, what is all this?" Del walked up and stood next to her, the workers congregating at the tables like bees on honey.

"It's just a token of our appreciation, courtesy of the Chamber, Madison Ridge's Historic Revitalization Committee, the Sweet Spot, and Center Street Deli."

Del ran a hand through his hair. "Mom, that's great. Thank you."

Stella waved her hand. "It's nothing. The town is happy to pitch in." She clasped her hands in front of her and leaned over to him. "We take care of our own, Delaney. Always have." She turned her head toward Addison and his gaze followed. "Even when we think we don't want to."

He jammed his hands on his hips and shook his head. He didn't even want to know how Stella was able to wrangle the townspeople. The woman had superpowers that scared him sometimes.

He hugged her. "Thanks, Mom."

"You're welcome, son." She cupped his face in her hands. "I'm glad you're home," she whispered.

He nodded, not trusting himself to speak. She patted his face gently and looked over his shoulder. "I better get more cookies out. Amelia's going to love all this free advertisement."

Del chuckled. "She'll be impossible to live with now."

Stella rolled her eyes. "Oh, honey. You've been gone too long. She's still hell on wheels to live with. Lucky for me, she has her own place." Stella winked and walked around him. "Margie," she called out as she strode away, "put out some more cookies. They're eating them two at a time."

Del smiled and his gaze landed on Addison across the clearing. She was smiling and nodding at something Eve, his makeup artist, said. Her strawberry-blonde hair glinted like golden flames in the sunshine. While the skirt and blouse ensemble she wore most of the time was sexy as hell in an executive sort of way, the skinny jeans and fitted black T-shirt she wore today made his heart pound in his ears.

She walked under the tent and started chatting with Tommy who was busily eating a bag of chips. He offered her some, which she declined with a shake of her head and a smile. Stars shone in the tall, burly man's eyes when Addison was around. Not that Del could blame him. He'd been the same way when he'd met Addie. She had that effect on people but had no clue about it. All it did was make her even more attractive in Del's mind.

Addison put more bags of chips in the basket and nodded politely a few times at whatever it was Tommy was chattering about. But the longer she engaged with him, the closer his superintendent got to her.

Del shoved his hands into his pockets and narrowed his eyes. Karma was an evil bitch. That nasty green-eyed beast reared its ugly head causing Del to take a deep breath to beat back the jealousy that whipped through him. Tommy was harmless overall, but he was also a big motherfucker. Del would hate to have his ass kicked in front of his own crew. Talk about a tabloid headline. Shit.

But when she laughed, he'd seen all he needed to see and before he could stop himself, his work boots kicked into gear and he strode toward them.

"Hey bossman," Tommy said when Del approached them. "I was just talking with Addison here about the timeline we're looking at." He crunched the chip that he had just shoved into his mouth, balancing his piled high plate with the other.

Addison turned to Del, her arms crossed over her breasts. "Yes, Tommy was just letting me know how long demo would take and when we would be moving on to rebuilding. It's nice to get some info from someone." Her eyes shot daggers his way and anger radiated off her like rogue waves crashing into a sinking ship.

And he was going down.

Fortunately, Tommy didn't appear to notice the tension that was thick enough to cut through. "Tommy, could you give us a moment, please?"

"Sure, catch ya later." With a wave, he ambled away.

Del turned and leaned against the table in front of them, picking up a grape and popping it in his mouth. "Care to tell me what that was all about?"

She shook her head and looked at the ground. "Some things never change," she muttered under her breath. Her head came up and her eyes drilled into his. "It's about you not letting me know what is going on. You told me that you would send me reports. Look, I know this is your show, but what goes on with the house and when it goes on is something I should know about.

Del eyed her for a moment as realization sunk in. "You're mad you didn't get to smash some things, aren't you?"

Her eyes darted to him for a moment and her lips twitched. Ah yeah, his Addie was still there, feisty little thing.

His Addie? Since when? Not in about a decade, buddy.

He chewed another grape, waiting for her answer. When she glanced back at him, he lifted a brow in question.

She rolled her eyes and huffed out a breath, looking out toward the house. "Okay, fine. Yes, I wanted to bust up some things."

He inched closer to her, close enough to feel her body heat, and the scent that was uniquely Addie wrapped around him like vines. "I can attest to the fact demo day is a great stress reliever," he said, his voice low enough for her ears only. "Some tension you need to let go of, Addie?"

Del knew he was teasing her, but damn, he needed to give some back to her. Just being in the same space as her, especially after a decade of not touching her, was driving him crazy. He glanced down at her arms and found they were covered in goosebumps. He hit his mark.

The wave of victory he thought he would feel never came, though. Interesting.

They stood side by side, a breeze blowing the electric air that crackled around them. He looked down, rolling a grape back and forth between his fingers. Shit, why were things so hard with her now? Once upon a time, it had been so easy.

He cleared his throat. "No, you're right."

She turned her head to him slowly, disbelief alight in her eyes. "I'm sorry, what? Can you repeat that?"

Del smiled and popped the grape in his mouth. He chewed and swallowed before speaking. "Ha ha. I said, you're right. I should have been keeping you in the loop better than I have." He cleared his throat and looked into her stormy green eyes. "This project has a special meaning to me, too, Addie. Our fathers started this together. It's a legacy of sorts. But," he shrugged a shoulder, "it's still a job for me. Both as a contractor and as my television show. And I admit I haven't given you the same respect communicating with you as I would someone I don't know. That was wrong and I'm sorry."

Addison narrowed her eyes and lifted her chin. The wheels were turning in her mind and she studied him for a moment. No doubt waiting to see where the fissure in his apology lay.

"I'll be more in touch when you aren't here. You'll hear from me so often you'll be sick of me." He raised three fingers close together. "Scout's honor."

A small smile lifted one edge of her lips. "Apology accepted."

He nodded once. "Thank you."

She turned her body to him and opened her mouth, but was interrupted by Tommy, who called out to her. "Hey, Addison. When's the next softball game? When will we get to defend ourselves against those rat bastards from Briarcliff Lakes?"

Del looked over his shoulder and narrowed his eyes at Tommy. "Softball?"

Addison chuckled. "I'll have to look at the schedule, but I think we play them once more before playoffs. If we can pull it off again this year."

Del looked back at Addison, who was smiling at Tommy. "Softball?"

Addison tilted her head. "Careful there, Ace. You're starting to sound like a parrot."

"Smartass," he muttered, causing her smile to widen. If that's all it took to make her smile, he'd call her a smartass all day long.

Del pointed at Addison but addressed Tommy. "Are you sure you have the right person by asking her?"

Tommy frowned and tugged on his ear. "Yeah, I think so. Addison is our captain."

Del wasn't sure why, but all he could do was laugh. Addison folded her arms over her chest and raised her chin. "What the hell are you laughing about, Delaney?"

His laughter trailed off. "Addie, you've never played a sport in your life." He shrugged. "Unless you count cheerleading."

"Cheerleading is a sport and so is gymnastics, you jerk." She put her hands on her hips and straightened her spine. The motion pressed her breasts out against the thin material of the T-shirt. His gaze inadvertently drew down to her chest, causing him to bite back a groan.

He raised his hands in surrender. "My bad. I forgot about the gymnastics." At least he tried to, anyway. Addison had been quite flexible back in the day and Del had thanked the gymnastics gods every time they'd had sex when they were younger.

"I'll have you know I've been playing softball for years now. I'm pretty damn good, actually."

Tommy nodded. "She kicks ass. Our best home-run hitter," he said around a mouthful of chips. "She's also the fastest runner on the team."

Del's eyes widened. "Huh. I wasn't aware of that."

Addison gave him the side-eye. "Yeah, well, there's not a lot we know about each other anymore, is there?"

Del sighed. Shit, he'd walked right into that, hadn't he? But her tone was more sad than angry, catching him off guard. "I guess not." He shoved off the table, an idea brewing in his mind. "But I guarantee there's one thing that hasn't changed."

She cocked her head. "What's that?" Del couldn't help but grin at her, she was so damn cute. Her eyes narrowed. She *should* be suspicious of him.

He grinned and the two of them faced off against each other. "I challenge you to a softball game."

"Really, now?" She took a step toward him, her hands on her hips. "You got a team?"

"Sure, my show crew here is always up for some shenanigans. They'll love this."

She crossed her arms over her chest and Del had to work hard to keep his eyes from wandering down to her breasts. Again. Shit, it was turning into a full-time job. "What are the stakes?"

Del raised his eyes to the sky. "Let's see." A thought struck him and it was priceless. "If we win, you guys will have to sit in the makeup chair and let Eve paint your faces in whatever way we see fit. And then for posterity, we're going to film a segment for the show."

Addison's lips twitched. "That's the deal?"

"That's the deal." He moved in a little closer, closing the space between them, where he could smell her lavender and vanilla scent from what he suspected to be her shampoo. It had always driven him insane in the best way possible. "How about a side bet? Just between me and you?"

She raised her eyes to him, and he was close enough to see her pupils dilate and the pulse in her neck kick up a notch. "What do you have in mind?"

Del did his best to keep his excitement at her not flat-out saying no in check. "If I win, you go to dinner with me. If I lose, I'll take a full page ad out in The Ridge Herald and tell the whole town how about how I had the slightest case of performance anxiety the night of senior prom."

Her eyes went wide before they turned to a smolder. "I had forgotten that. But if I recall though, you got over that real quick."

He shrugged and ignored the X-rated memories parading through his mind. "Yeah, but I won't mention that."

She eyed him. "Will you put it in the town Facebook group?"

His jaw dropped. "We have a Facebook group?"

She smirked and nodded. "Yep. A couple of them. But the secret one is for the gossipy locals only."

Okay, now he had to win the game. There was no way he was really going to rehash the embarrassing few moments of performance anxiety he had with her at senior prom. She'd just been so damn beautiful he couldn't think. He had redeemed himself and then some later that night, but he'd take one for the team if he had to. "Hell..." He rubbed a hand on the back of his neck. "Yeah. I'll put it in the Facebook group." His grin reappeared. "Wanna counter this offer?"

A confident smile spread across her lips. "Nah, I like my odds." She tilted her head to one side. "You sure you want to do that?"

"Oh yeah," he said, with a smile that matched hers. "You might recall I had a baseball scholarship."

She took another step forward. "You mean the one you didn't take? I didn't forget. But that was a long time ago, my friend."

They were nearly chest to chest and the people around them fell away. "I haven't changed that much, Addie," he said, his voice barely above a whisper. He shoved his hands in his back pockets to keep from touching her. His palms itched to caress her cheek.

The muscles in her neck moved when she swallowed, her stare on his. "Yeah, well. You've changed enough," she said in a low voice. She stepped back and raised her voice. "You want a game? Challenge accepted, Ace. Be at Pine Street Park, Thursday night. Seven o'clock."

"We'll be there. With bells on, Starshine."

Addison pursed her lips at the old nickname, and Del considered it a victory when she didn't correct him. "Show us what ya got. We'll be ready for you." She turned and walked away. Del would swear on the Good Book the little minx added a sway to her hips.

He blew out a breath. "Oh boy. I'm in deep shit," he muttered to himself. He turned and stomped back into the house. There was only one way to combat the sexual frustration plaguing him.

Thank God for demo day.

locals vs the out-of-towners

"LOOKS LIKE YOU DREW QUITE A CROWD."

Addison raised her head to find Grace standing on the other side of the fence. "Well, we do have a celebrity among us." She glanced around at the aluminum stands that stood behind the dugouts on either side of the field. "Even the outfield stands are seeing some action."

Grace's eyes narrowed. "Why the hell is Tara the terror here?"

Addison turned toward where Grace's death stare landed and wrinkled her nose. "Ugh, did she really dress like that for a baseball game?"

Tara Moore was the town floozie who tried to desperately hold on to the high school days when she was fresh-faced, pretty, and popular. Before all the bitterness of her life going nowhere set in. Tara would tell anyone who would listen that since she wasn't a Reynolds or Davenport, she never won homecoming or prom queen.

Her goal in life was to try and land a Reynolds man—which was never going to happen—or some other rich guy like Shane. Tara's big mouth had almost managed to destroy Emma and Shane's relationship earlier in the year. There was little to tear the two of them apart now, but Tara had tried.

The woman seemed to hate everything the Reynoldses and Davenports represented in the town. You know, tradition and class.

Case in point, tonight Tara's copper-red pixie haircut was spiky and the makeup caked on like she was headed out to the bars. Knowing Tara, she'd be hitting the Silver Moon after this looking for the guy that would be her ticket out of Madison Ridge. Especially given that she teetered along the clay in at least four-inch platform sandals, cutoffs that barely managed to cover her ass cheeks, and a bright blue skintight tank top.

As she came closer to where Addison and Grace stood, her mouth curled into what was more sneer than smile. "Well, well. It's the goody-two-shoes club."

Grace gave Tara a feral smile. "What are you doing here, Tara? Trolling for dates again since you've already slept your way through the guys at the Silver Moon? Except for your cousin Wyatt, of course."

Tara's lips flattened, and her cheeks flushed red. "You might be a Reynolds, but you don't own this town, Grace. It's a free country, you know."

She turned her hateful green-eyed stare to Addison. "I see you're still pining after Delaney. Even though he left your ass in this stupid town." She tilted her head. "You really think he'd want you now that he's had a taste of all those supermodels and actresses?"

If Addison didn't know Tara's MO, her words might have landed a hard blow to Addison's ego. But Tara was always looking for a dig, and while it had been a thought Addison had once or twice, it wasn't something she thought about anymore. Tara had no idea what she and Del had, then or now.

Hell, she didn't even know what they had now.

She simply smiled at Tara and held up a hand to keep the normally mild-mannered Grace from launching herself at the desperate woman in front of them. She mimicked Tara's tilted head. "Hey, you're still renting that duplex just outside of town, right? That nice little one that's so well maintained, where the rent hasn't gone up in the three years you lived there?"

Tara narrowed her eyes and popped a hip out. "Yeah. What of it?"

Addison moved closer and lowered her voice to where only Tara could hear her. "I've also heard about some things that go on there. You'd hate for all that to get back to, oh, I don't know, your landlord? Who just so happens to be Noah? You know, Grace's brother?" She glanced up and tapped a finger on her chin. "Or maybe a certain deputy? Who's *also* Grace's brother?"

She looked back down at Tara. "You don't need that kind of complication in your life, do you?"

Now Tara's face was as red as a tomato. "You're a bitch, Addison. Always thinking you're better than everyone else. You and those Reynoldses." She stomped off toward the stands, toward where a group of guys from town were calling her name.

Addison sighed and leaned back against the fence.

"What the hell did you say to her?" Grace asked.

"Oh, just reminding her to show some respect."

"Well, it worked."

"Yeah, we'll see about that." Addison brought her gaze back to Grace and raised a brow. "Should I be talking to you? Whose side are you on tonight?"

Grace put a hand over her heart and frowned. "Now, that hurts, Addie. You're my best friend. You know I'm on your side."

Addison shrugged. "Well, he is your brother after all."

Grace rolled her eyes and shoved a strand of hair that escaped her bun behind her ear. "Exactly. Always been a big pain in my ass. Besides,"—her blue eyes gleamed with mischief—"this is like the locals versus the out-of-towners, and I'm a local. It's going to be fun."

"Even more fun when we kick their asses."

Grace whooped, and they fist-bumped against the fencing before laughing. "Alright, I'm going to go get some popcorn and find a seat. Good luck, girl!"

Addison turned to find some of the other players filing into the dugout with her. As she picked up the clipboard with the lineup attached, she caught a glimpse of Del on the other side of the field in the dugout talking to his teammates. She clenched her jaw. He still had baseball pants? Damn showoff.

Her annoyance had nothing to do with the fact he still filled out a pair of baseball pants quite well with his long legs and tight ass. She'd spent many a hot afternoon on this very field watching him play in high school. Del the boy was something to see, but Del the man was driving her crazy.

She squeezed her eyes shut and rubbed her forehead. Maybe if she rubbed hard enough, she could get the old memories out of her head. As though he could hear her thoughts, he turned his head and looked right at her. A slow smile spread across his face, and the son of a bitch had the audacity to wink at her before turning back to the guy standing beside him.

Addison grimaced and turned her attention back to the lineup in her hand. A few minutes later she faced off with Del as the captains of each team with the umpire between them flipping a coin.

"Heads," Addison called out when the coin glinted in the park lights. When it hit the ground, a puff of dirt had to settle before they could see who won.

"Heads," the umpire said. "Del, that makes you the visitors, so you're up first."

She nodded and jogged back over to the dugout. "Let's go, guys!"

For the first couple of innings, the game went quick, three up, three down on both sides. Del was on his game, of course, pitching for the Hollywood Aces, as they'd dubbed themselves. By the end of the third inning, the score was still zero, zero when Addison stepped up to the plate. Bent at the waist, Del stood on the mound in position to pitch the ball to her, the bill of his ball cap putting his eyes and part of his face in shadow.

She swung the bat back and forth in front of her before settling it above her shoulder. He pitched, and she swung for the fences, missing it by a mile. Her chest tightened, and a blush warmed her skin. She wouldn't mind a sinkhole opening right up under her at this moment. She cast a furtive glance toward Del, expecting to see a smirk or grin of some sort on his handsome face, but found his face was set. He was all business, no emotion on his face whatsoever.

It kind of took the wind out of her I-really-want-to-hate-him sails. Another pitch, another swing, another miss.

"Damn it all to hell," she muttered under her breath, stepping out of the box. She smacked the top of her helmet and let the noise of the crowd and the cheers of her team wash over her and settle her down. The fact Del was pitching had her off her game. Literally.

Addison stepped back into the box and settled into her stance. This time when the ball came her way, she was ready. There was a *thwack* as the ball hit the aluminum bat, and the vibration from the connection ran down her arms. The ball sailed through the air, gaining more height and speed. A grin formed on her lips when she realized the ball was headed to the fences. A quick glance at Del told her he had come to the same realization.

She casually tossed the bat to the ground and started the jog around the bases, not even trying to hide her laughter. When she got to home plate, she jumped and landed with both feet on the plate, causing the crowd to applaud louder. She glanced back over at Del who stood on the mound shaking his head, but a smile split his face. She pushed away the desire, and another emotion she didn't want to acknowledge set up camp in her chest when she looked at him.

The team greeted her at the opening to the dugout with high fives and accolades. By the end of the inning, the Madison Tigers were up by four runs. It was a decent lead, but Addison wasn't comfortable with it. Del was capable of pulling out crazy plays and getting a leg up on the competition. It was the first time she'd been on the opposing side against Delaney Reynolds, and she didn't like it one bit.

"Come on, let's go! Get your defensive game faces on!" She clapped her hands and jogged out to her spot at third base with her team. Her motivation was as much for her as it was for her team.

The next inning, the first two hitters struck out, and while Addison wanted to relax a little, an itch set up between her shoulder blades when Del's tall form walked up to the plate. She grimaced and squatted into position. For a pitcher, Del was no stranger to the business end of the bat. He could either knock them out of the park or hit ground balls that shot through the infield, so they needed to be ready for anything. Some of the players on her team had played against Del back in high school. She just hoped they remembered he was the opposition and not the town golden boy for this game.

Whistles and calls for him to knock it out of the park drifted on the wind and onto the field. If Del noticed, he never let on. He stepped into the box and into position. On the first pitch, he swung, and the ball shot between first and second where Tommy ran up to meet it, as Del rounded first base on his way to second.

"Throw it!" Addison yelled, her heart racing. Tommy threw the ball to second base where Del was called safe, and the crowd went wild.

"Traitors," she muttered under her breath, slamming her fist into her gloved palm. She crouched down, with Del in her peripheral vision. Instinct—and knowing how the man operated—told her if he had a chance, he would steal third base. Out of the corner of her eye, Del edged his way off second base toward third.

"Tommy, be ready for him." She nodded toward Del. Her teammate nodded and looked over at Del. Teri was up at the plate, and Addison studied her stance. It didn't appear this was a comfort zone for the woman with purple-streaked hair. Addison could sympathize. She'd been the same way years ago when Grace talked her into playing on the local team as a way to get her out of the crater-sized hole she wallowed in daily, no thanks to the man who stood less than ninety feet away from her. But Del was right—she'd never done anything athletic that wasn't cheerleading or gymnastics. At least up until that point.

She pushed down the thoughts that started to creep into her mind and the despair that wanted to claw at her throat. Addison Davenport was no longer a heartbroken twenty-four-year-old who'd lost every-thing that meant anything to her. Nope, she was now the owner of one of the largest land development and real estate brokerage firms in Georgia. She was well respected in the community both professionally and personally and was at the precipice of cementing her family's name in the history of Madison Ridge. So what if she was thirty-five years old and never married? After Del had left her behind, she said who, when, and how she managed her love life, and she was doing just fine, thank you very much.

Keep telling yourself that, spinster.

Shut up, bitch.

She shook her head slightly to get the nasty little voices in her head to both shut the hell up and focused back on the game. It was fortuitous timing. Teri got a piece of the ball on her second swing, and Del took off.

"Come on, come on," she muttered under her breath. One of the young guys on Tommy's crew played outfield and had a damn good arm. He threw it toward Addison, and as it sailed toward her, she extended her gloved hand to catch it. Out of the corner of her eye, Del barreled toward her, and her body tensed, bracing for impact of the ball in her glove. It struck her hand, making it sing, the instant before Del's foot hit the bag.

"Out!" called out the field umpire. Addison's victory was short-lived, though. Del had too much momentum going and collided into her, knocking them both to the ground. But Del's reflexes were quick. When she hit the ground, the impact was buffered by his strong arms. His hand was warm against the back of her head, cradling it from hitting the ground.

"Holy shit, are you okay?" he asked, breathless.

She tried to gulp deep breaths, but the realization of why she couldn't took hold. Del's long, muscular body lay on top of hers in a way her body remembered. Their eyes met, and his bright blue concerned gaze darkened to a navy blue. It was only seconds, but to Addison their stares held for an eternity. The shouts and general crowd noise fell away. All she heard was their breathing that had synced up, and all she could feel was the weight of his body on hers. Her body was a traitorous bitch, wanting to arch up against him like a cat looking to be rubbed. Her dry spell of almost a year was rearing its ugly head in the middle of the damn softball field.

Still, it was hard to tell if her racing heart was because of the man on top of her or her acute mortification.

She closed her eyes a moment. "Yes, I'm fine. Help me up." Her eyes opened to find Del's face still inches from her own. If he shifted just half an inch...

Nope, nope, nope. Those thoughts needed to get off at the next exit before she ended up finding herself in Brokenheartsville again.

Or in jail for indecent exposure.

Del lifted up off her like he was doing a push-up and got to his feet. He reached a hand down to help her off the ground. When he pulled her up, she slammed into his hard chest. Her palms lay flat against his chest, but she couldn't look into his eyes. It was too much. She shoved lightly at him so he would release her. "I'm good, thanks."

"Are you sure?"

Addison brushed off her clothes and picked up her glove from the ground. With an overly bright smile, she turned to him. "Yep, I'm great. That was the third out, Ace." She jogged away from him and all that sexiness he exuded, joining the rest of the team in the dugout.

For the rest of the game, she did her best not to look at Del unless it was necessary to play the game. That was the easy part. The not-so-easy part was having to choke down the fact that Del's team of Hollywood misfits were better at the game than they let on and her team lost by two runs. When the game was over, the teams met in the middle of the field and shook hands, "good game" tossed back and forth between the teams.

Del whistled loudly enough to get the attention of the players. "Okay, guys. Since the Hollywood Aces defeated the Madison Tigers, it's time for the losers to learn their fate." He grinned and rubbed his hands together as groans went through the crowd. "On the last day of filming, each of you are going to come to the job site and lovely Eve here"—he waved his hand in the direction of one of his teammates, who raised her hands above her head—"will make up your face however we see fit. Then we will film scenes for some of the commercials used for the final episode."

"We have to be on television with makeup on?" Tommy asked, his voice an unusually high pitch.

Del nodded. "You got it."

Addison had to admit it was creative, and even though she was on the losing end, she held back the laughter bubbling up in her chest. The looks on the guys' faces on her team ranged from disgust to humor, but the women on the team looked eager to be on television. In the end they would all end up having a blast with it. That's just the way her team rolled.

"Come on, team, we can do this, right?" Addison called out. Her question was met with a mix of grunts, agreements, and curses.

Del laughed. "I tell you what, I'll sweeten the pot. You guys wear makeup on television, I'll donate money to the Parks and Rec Department to overhaul the ballfields here." That got a rousing cheer and "hell yeahs."

He clapped twice. "That's more like it. Okay, I'm starving. Who's up for pizza and beer?" A cheer went up among the crowd gathered on the field. "Eve, can you call The Ridge Pizzeria and let them know we're headed that way?"

As she walked off to the dugout, shock ricocheted around in her head regarding the donation to the ballfields. Not that he would have trouble affording it, but she figured it would be no small amount given the shape of the fields. And he was buying pizza and beer for everyone. Addison didn't want to recognize the emotion that welled in her chest thinking about his good deed. Del had always been the giving type.

Except for that night ten years ago. *Right, easier to hate him if I keep that tidbit in mind.*

Addison shook her head and began to gather her items. Other players started milling around with their equipment, chatting, and calling out about who was riding with whom. A few people still dotted the stands, no doubt hoping to get an autograph from their resident celebrity if the crowd of mostly women gathered at the fence was any indication.

She was aware he was popular, especially among the ladies, but anytime crowds surrounded him, she was always taken aback. To her, he was simply Delaney Reynolds. The boy she'd grown up with, been best friends with, fallen in love with, and had planned to spend the rest of her life with until he decided to walk out.

When she glanced over, Del was signing a piece of paper thrust at him and, with a smile, waved at the crowd. They started to disperse, and she looked away, shoving her glove into her bag.

"Hey, need a ride to The Ridge?"

Addison glanced up to find the man of the hour at the opening of the dugout. His arms were raised over his head, gripping the metal bar above him. The muscles in his biceps and forearms bunched and relaxed every time he gripped and released the bar. The tail of his jersey played peekaboo with his lower abs. The memories of his happy trail and that sexy V he sported slammed into her and made her skin flush. He'd turned his ball cap backward so his strong jaw and too-handsome face were clearly visible. Those crystal-blue eyes stared at her with an emotion akin to wonder.

She stood taller, in spite of the flip-flop of her stomach. She hated the fact he blocked her only way out. He stood between her and the open space she needed. Between the wall of his body and the thick, humid late-spring air, suffocation was in the realm of possibility. Still, she feigned a bored tone.

"No, I've got some work to do at home."

He was quiet long enough that if she hadn't felt his presence, she would have thought he'd walked away.

"You never cease to amaze me," he said.

"What are you talking about, Del?"

"You're a helluva ball player for someone who was always a bystander with it."

"You did play on a boys' team," she replied with a wry smile. "Being a bystander was all I could do."

He grinned and lowered his head to look at the ground. "Fair enough. But Madison Ridge has had coed teams for years. You never played."

She shrugged. There was no way in hell she was admitting to him that he was the catalyst to her playing. "Grace got me into it. I wanted to broaden my horizons, get some exercise, and have some fun."

"Hmmm...well, it's just something I never thought I'd see you do."

She rolled her eyes and turned back to finish packing her bag. "Jeez, Del. You make me sound like some fragile little princess."

"Starshine, you're anything but a fragile little princess." The heat of his body reached her just before he spoke, his breath blowing the tendrils of her hair at her neck exposed by her ponytail. "So, you free tomorrow night?"

She closed her eyes for a moment and took a silent breath before turning to face him. He was close enough they shared the same air. For the second time that night, the thought crossed her mind that if she shifted just slightly, their mouths would align and she could see if all the heat and need that ran through her blood was real or just nostalgia. But she couldn't find out right now. Or ever. It just wasn't a great idea.

Kinda like the ridiculous side bet she'd agreed to if Del won. What the hell had she been thinking?

Oh, that's right. That she'd win. Shit.

But a bet was a bet, and she didn't welch on a deal.

She blew out a breath and averted her gaze from his pointed stare for a moment to collect herself. "Yeah, I'm free."

His smile was slow and sexy and would be the death of her, she was sure of it. "Alright then. I'll pick you up at seven."

"Where are we going?"

He tsked her and wagged a finger. "That's a surprise."

She huffed. "Well, I need to know what to wear. Is it fancy or casual?"

"It won't be fancy. That's the only clue I'm giving you." He reached out and laced the fingers of one hand through the fence behind her, effectively trapping her against him and the fence wall. "But I can promise you, you will enjoy yourself."

Addison swallowed hard and held his gaze. The air thickened around them until she could barely breathe. He moved close enough for their bodies to touch. Of their own volition, her eyes fluttered closed as his mouth descended on hers.

"Hey, Del? You over here?"

They jumped apart when a female voice called his name. He ran a hand through his hair and answered. "I'm here, Eve."

The young blonde appeared in the opening of the dugout with a phone to her ear. "There you are. I've got Sal on the phone. He wants to know how many he's cooking for."

"Give me a second and I'll talk to him."

Eve nodded and left, talking into the phone as she walked away.

Addison pulled her keys out of the bag and lifted it onto her shoulder. "Sounds like you're needed. And I have work waiting for me."

Del nodded, his gaze on the ground. He lifted his head, a crooked smile curving his lips. "Sure I can't interest you in pizza and beer?"

"No, I'm good, thanks."

"Can I take your bag for you?"

She shook her head. "I got it." She walked past him and stopped at the opening, turning her head to him. There were things to say, but she just couldn't say them. Instead, she went with the easy, the polite. "Have a good night. Be safe."

CHAPTER NINE

second first date

HE WAS FRETTING, for God's sake.

Del paced the length of the living room at his family's old lake house where he currently lived. He glanced up at the large decorative clock hanging above the fireplace. Two minutes since the last time he looked. He was making progress from looking every minute.

It would take him ten minutes to get to her house, if he drove slowly. And here he was, ready to go at six thirty.

He drummed his fingers on the thigh of his jean-clad legs. The last thing he wanted to do was look too eager and scare Addison off. Of course, he wasn't fool enough to think she would have gone out with him anyway. Hence, the whole little bet thing. He was a lucky son of a bitch for winning that game.

His mind drifted down memory lane to a time where he'd pushed her before, trying to convince her to go to California with him. She'd fought back and when it came to matters of the heart, Del had been the biggest loser.

It only took him ten years to figure it out.

But he had and it was in his nature to push forward and try something, even if he didn't know the outcome. Backing down from a challenge just wasn't something he did. And winning back Addison's trust was the biggest challenge he'd faced so far. One with the highest stakes and greatest reward.

Del relished the challenge.

Another glance at the clock again and he smiled. Showtime.

Keys, wallet, and he was out the door. On the back side of the main house sat a solitary building that was once his father's workshop but had been turned into a garage of sorts after he died. Del opened the large, wide carriage doors to reveal the gleaming Harley. Every time he saw it, he grinned. Of all the property he owned, his Harley was the one piece he didn't want to part with until he absolutely had to sell it. One day his illness would probably keep him from riding it, but until that point, he was going to enjoy the hell out of it. He hoped Addison would as well.

He attached the extra helmet he'd brought to the back of the bike and put on his own. Within minutes, he was cruising down Main Street toward Addison's house. The air warmed his skin and plastered the white T-shirt against his body. The hum of the powerful bike under him lulled him into a contented, relaxed mood. Beneath the helmet, he smiled. It'd been too long.

But soon, nerves found him when he stood on the porch spanning the front of Addison's craftsman-style home. He silently cursed himself when the thought that he should have brought her flowers crossed his mind, but he dismissed it. There weren't too many places for delicate flowers to survive on his bike.

Son of a bitch, his palms were sweaty and his heart raced. With one last effort to calm down, he blew out a breath and he leaned forward to ring the doorbell. He heard the faint sound of the chimes followed by loud, deep barking. He smiled at the sound of the scary bark. Murphy was just like Addie's old dog, Jax. All bark and no bite. The worst an intruder would get is a face full of dog slobber.

"Murphy, get back." Del grinned picturing Addison trying to move the eighty-plus-pound solid body of her chocolate lab. The deadbolt turned and the door opened.

Addison smiled. "Hi."

Del forgot how to speak. Her long strawberry-blonde hair was pulled into a ponytail that swept her bare shoulders when she moved.

The dress she wore reminded him of mermaids for some reason with its green color and flowing material. It tied behind her neck and scooped just above her breasts in the front. It stopped just above her knee, and with her platform sandals her long, tanned legs looked never-ending.

She was summer casual and stunning.

"Hey," he replied after what felt like an eternity.

"Want to come in? I'll just be a minute." She stepped aside to allow him access.

When Murphy saw him cross the threshold, he came bounding over full throttle, a tennis ball in his mouth. Del had just a second to protect the family jewels before Murphy leaped.

"Murphy, get down!" Addison scolded.

Del chuckled and rubbed the dog's ears. "He's okay."

"I'm so sorry. He wants you to play fetch."

Del wrestled the ball from Murphy's jaw and gave it a light toss. Del grunted when Murphy pushed off him and scampered after the ball, his nails clicking across the wood.

They chuckled when Murphy lost his footing and he slid into the wall. Not to be deterred, he gained his footing and bounded back to Del, dropping the ball at his feet.

"Well, since you boys seem to be entertained, I'll just finish up." Addison walked down the hall and up the stairs. He couldn't help it if his gaze followed her up the stairs, especially given the fact the sexy little sundress she wore was backless. Del figured he looked much like the dog with his tongue hanging out at that moment.

He looked down at Murphy, who stood looking in the direction Addison had gone before swinging his large, brown head back toward Del, his dark, doggie eyes intent on him.

"What? My intentions are good, I promise. I'll take care of her, okay?" Murphy wagged his tail and walked over to Del, bumping into his legs before sitting at his feet.

A few minutes later, Addison came down smelling of sunshine and lavender, pulling a light sweater around her shoulders. "I'm ready. Sorry about that."

"No worries." He turned and opened the front door for her. "After you." When she walked past him, her arm brushed against his chest, setting the areas she touched on fire.

In through the nose, out through the mouth. That fucking yoga retreat he'd been roped into once upon a time had turned out to be good for something.

When he closed the door, she locked it behind him. With her head down, she put her keys in a small wrist bag. He stepped in front of her, bringing her up short. She lifted her head with a questioning look in her eyes.

"You look..." Beautiful, stunning, heart stopping. "Amazing. I just wanted you to know that."

The muscles in the long column of her throat moved under her skin, her eyes wide on his. "Thank you."

"You're welcome." He held out his arm. "Shall we?"

She wrapped her arm through his and smiled up at him. "We shall."

They held gazes for a moment as they walked across the porch. When she looked away, her steps halted.

"What is that?"

Del tore his gaze away from her to follow hers to his Harley. He grinned. "My motorcycle. Isn't she beautiful?"

Addison rolled her eyes. "I know what it is. What I meant was, why is it here?"

Aw, shit. Bad call, dude. Still he forged ahead.

"I figured it's a beautiful evening. I thought it would be fun." He paused a moment, trying to gauge her reaction but he couldn't read her. "Not so much, huh?"

He dropped down to stand on the step in front of her, bringing them eye to eye. "I can go get my truck if you'd rather not ride the bike. It's up to you."

After a moment, a grin with a hint of wickedness to it curved those beautiful lips. "Let's go."

He tilted his head. "Are you sure?"

The sassy head tilt and smile she gave him nearly brought him to his knees. "Got a helmet for me? And where can I put this?" She held up a small wrist thing that looked like a small purse.

He nodded. "I brought a helmet. For your purse thingy, I have a pocket for it."

"Confidence has never been an issue for you," she said, with a wry smile.

They walked down the sidewalk to the bike, Addison's eyes bright with excitement. Del lifted a helmet off the back and held it out to her.

"I wasn't sure you would ride with me, but I took my chances. When I saw this one, I thought of you instantly."

She ran her hand over the smooth surface of the helmet, the dark red sparkling in the dying sunlight. "You remembered my favorite color."

"I remember a lot of things, Addison. Even when I tried to forget."

She raised her head and a mix of emotions swirled in her eyes. Del couldn't decipher what they were before the moment passed and she looked back down.

Del eased back and tried to get ahold of the emotions battering him. "Ready to go?"

She nodded and put the helmet over her head. After a couple of attempts to adjust the chin strap, she growled in frustration.

"Here, let me help you." While he worked the strap, his knuckles brushed at her neck and she bit her lip to keep from smiling.

"I know, you're ticklish there." He wanted to forget but she was making it damn hard. "That better?"

Addison gave him a thumbs-up and he smiled, pulling his helmet over his head. She stepped back so he could swing a leg over the bike and balance it before she got on. She squirmed for a minute before settling down, but her hesitation came off her in waves.

He turned his head and lifted the visor. "Everything okay?"

"Yeah, it's just…"

"You'll have to hold on to me."

"Yeah, I know. We rode together before, but this is different."

"Addie, I don't want to do anything to make you uncomfortable tonight. I'll go get my truck. It's not a big deal."

With the helmet covering her head and the visor covering her eyes, Del couldn't tell what she was thinking. She paused for a moment, then leaned forward and wrapped her arms around his waist, pressing her body to his.

"No, I'm good."

He swallowed hard. With her hands resting just above the waistband of his jeans, he closed his eyes, counting to ten, willing his dick to behave.

Del started the engine and it roared to life. He revved it a couple of times before letting it idle. With a glance over his shoulder he leaned back. "Are you ready?" he shouted over the noise. Another thumbs-up from her and he pulled away from the curb.

Through the streets of Madison Ridge, they rode as one, leaning into curves and turns together, the ride at once exciting yet smooth. Addison's body was warm and molded against his back. The sensations of her snuggled up behind him, mixed with the cool wind and the hum of the bike beneath him, had all his senses on high alert. With his heart racing, it had been a long time since he'd felt so alive.

Addison sighed and interlaced her fingers into a fist on his belly. He didn't dare look down or cover her hand with his own. Not only was it dangerous for the ride, it was dangerous for his heart.

"Where are we going?" she shouted when they stopped for a red light.

"We're almost there," he shouted back. He'd almost blown it with the motorcycle; he hoped he hadn't fucked up with the place he'd chosen for them to go.

A few minutes later, they passed through the historic square area and were on a side road leading up into the hills, toward the vineyards and the lake. The sun continued its slow descent into the horizon causing the air around them to darken, giving the feeling that they were out in the middle of nowhere.

They slowed and made a right-hand turn into an unmarked, hard packed dirt parking lot, dust swirling around them. There were several cars parked in the makeshift lot, which had been sectioned off with ropes. They rode down toward the oversized tiki bar-looking building with a weathered sign welcoming patrons to Dusty's Low Country Boil.

Del eased the bike into an area along the side of the wood structure and shut off the engine. When he engaged the kickstand, Addison managed to get off the bike without flashing anyone and he shook his head with a smile. The woman was a class act down to her bones.

After taking off the helmet, she smoothed her hair down and finger combed her ponytail, then stopped.

"Oh my God," Addison said looking around. Del took her helmet and attached it to the bike before she dropped it on her soft pink-painted toes.

"What?" Yeah, okay. He was playing it dumb a bit here, but he had to ride it out. See if she remembered like he did.

"You brought us to Dusty's." It wasn't a question as it was a stated fact.

He nodded once and leaned on the seat of his bike. "Yes, I did."

Addison met his stare. "This is where we had our—"

"First date," they said in unison.

CHAPTER TEN
impossible to hate

DEL SLIPPED his hand into hers, breaking the sudden tension surrounding them. With a soft smile, he said, "Follow me."

"Where are we going?"

He walked to the back side of the building that wasn't made up of plastic roll-up windows and stopped at a metal door.

"Dusty closed off one of the back areas so we wouldn't be interrupted."

In the past when they'd gone out, Del had always garnered looks. The man looked like a movie star even before he went to Tinseltown. But now, he was plastered all over the television and gossip magazines. Hell, just last year, *People Magazine* had profiled him and his gorgeous Malibu home. Going out with him now was an odd dynamic for Addison and she wasn't sure it sat right with her.

He banged on the door with his fist three times, waited a few seconds, and banged another three times.

"Is that some kind of code?" Addison asked, laughter in her voice.

Del grinned at her. "Dusty's idea."

"Of course."

A few moments later, the door swung open and a tall, muscular man filled the entrance. A smile as bright as his white hair split his square Nordic face.

"Delaney, Addison!" His voice, still thick with a Norwegian accent even though he'd been in Madison Ridge for more than thirty years, boomed into the night air.

"How's it going?" Del asked, holding out a hand.

Dusty clasped it in his large, beefy one and pulled Del into a hug, clapping him on the back with the other. "You're finally home!" He pulled back. "Your mother is ecstatic." Dusty pointed to his head. "This is a fact."

Del laughed and rolled his shoulders. "Yep, she's a happy mama."

"Good to see you both. Come in." He moved aside to let them into an area that opened into a hectic, bustling kitchen. Once the door slammed shut behind them, Dusty wrapped his arms around Addison and picked her up in a bear hug, causing her to squeal. Once he'd put her down, he pointed at her.

"I know why this one doesn't come to see me. But you, little girl? It's been too long."

She nodded and her face heated. "You're right, it *has* been too long. I'll do better."

Dusty turned to Del. "And you..." His blond eyebrows drew together. "You fly all over, but you need to come home more. I know you miss my food."

Del glanced at her. *Help me here.* She bit her lip to keep from laughing at the look of desperation on his face.

You're on your own, buddy.

"I'll do better," Del said, echoing Addison's words.

Dusty nodded, puffing out his chest. "Good. Come with me. I set you up nicely."

He herded them through the kitchen, where no one even bothered to pay attention to them. Out in the large, open-air dining area, the floor and the walls were oak-colored, and a breeze came through the windows lining the walls.

Several long cafeteria-type tables were lined up in the center of the building from the front to the back. Every table was packed to capacity with families and couples, young and old. Waitresses took drink orders and refilled others, while some left large bowls of mixed greens and cole slaw at other tables. Young men carried enormous steaming, stainless pots, occasionally stopping to dump the contents on a table.

It was a hectic scene and in spite of the voices carrying outside, there was a din of noise and mix of steam and savory spices settled over the room.

It might have been a while since she'd been there, but it hadn't changed a bit.

Dusty ushered them to a small table in an empty back room that could be closed off by large, sliding barn doors. "Here we go. A table for two of my favorite—albeit absentee—customers." He waited for them to sit down before proceeding. "What's to drink?"

Del gestured to her to go ahead. "What do you have for bottled beer?" she asked.

Dusty gave her a quick rundown of the dozen or so beers, some local, that he kept stocked, and she ordered a local light brew.

"Perfect," he said. "What about you, Ace? We got some tasty local brews."

Dusty laughed when Del made a face at the use of his TV name. "Thanks. I'm good. Sweet tea, please."

The large man nodded once. "Sure thing. Dinner will be out shortly." Given the only item on the menu was a steaming pot of seafood, potatoes, sausage, and corn, there wasn't much of a wait to eat.

When Dusty walked away, he closed the barn doors behind him. The noise level of the room dropped several decibels, leaving nothing more than the sounds of nature filtering in through the open windows.

Del looked at her with a raised brow. "Aren't you more of a wine drinker? Since when do you drink beer?"

She returned the raised brow with one of her own. "Since when *don't* you drink beer?"

He shrugged and shifted back in his chair. "I'm driving."

Addison pursed her lips. "Fair enough. I started branching out the last couple of years. Grace, Amelia, and I started taste testing some local microbrews and we enjoyed them."

Del's eyes widened. "Oh Lord. You, Grace, and Ame out on the town drinking? Who got arrested? Wait, don't tell me. Ame."

Addison laughed but swatted at his arm. "No. She's better than she used to be. Not nearly as wild." She straightened her back. "Besides, she's an upstanding business owner now. It wouldn't look good for her to be caught getting drunk and stupid."

"At least not at the same time."

Addison covered her mouth and giggled. "That's not nice. But it's true." She waved her hand. "Besides the fact that Dusty doesn't have wine on the menu, I'm a wine snob now. I pretty much only drink Kavanaugh wines now."

Del laughed. "Lucky you know the owner, huh?"

The door slid open and Dusty walked up to the table with their drinks in one hand and a stack of white butcher paper under his arm. "Gotta prep your table," he said, setting down the stack on the end of the table.

Once he finished and left them alone again, they each sipped their drinks. Addison savored the bite of the cold carbonation sliding down her throat. Her finger tapped on the bottle as the silence between them stretched out.

She leaned forward on her elbows. "So, what made you choose this place?"

He smiled but didn't respond or meet her gaze. Instead he lifted his head and gazed at the ceiling. "The only thing different about this place is there are maybe a few more dollar bills pinned to the wall. Hard to tell though since it was wallpapered in dollar bills twenty years ago."

Addison followed his gaze. "Hey, you haven't truly been to Dusty's if you haven't left your signature on a dollar. You know that." She lowered her head and took in his form. What was the man thinking in that sharp brain of his?

He gestured toward her bottle with his plastic glass. "How's the brew?"

"Delicious. Has a citrus flavor to it. Sounds weird but it's good." She ran her fingertip along the rim of the bottle. Just when she was about to think the date was a bad idea and awkward didn't even begin to cover it, Del leaned forward and mimicked her stance.

Del sighed. "I chose this place because it holds a special place in my heart. I missed it." He raised his eyes to hers. The blue in them glinted like a gas flame. "I missed you, Addie. And I'm sorry for the way we left things."

An apology was not what she expected. Addison's belly fluttered and her lips parted. She wanted to look away, but managed to hold his stare. She blew out an unsteady breath and said the only thing she could at that moment. "I missed you, too."

He held out a hand, palm up and she laid hers inside it. It was warm and strong when he squeezed gently. "I don't expect anything from you. I royally fucked up. I know that." His gaze was intense on hers. "But I'd like us to start over as friends. Can we do that?"

She wanted so badly to be back where they once were. Friends, lovers, confidants, everything. It had taken her so long to put herself back together after he left, and while she'd never truly be who she was before he left, she'd become a version of herself she liked and was proud of most of the time.

Reluctance was just the beginning of the myriad of emotions in her mind. Still, she'd agreed to the crazy-ass bet that had her sitting across from him in a place that swung the door wide open to memory lane. What the hell did that mean?

She cleared her throat and looked away from his intense blue stare for a moment. Her back straightened when she looked back at him. "I'm here, aren't I?"

A slow smile curved his lips. "Yeah, yeah you are."

The low din of conversation outside the room filtered in as Dusty came in with two workers behind him. The young man dumped a large stock pot of steaming food onto the newspaper on the table and the young lady set large bowls of greens, slaw, and black-eyed peas along with plates and flatware. After a few minutes of chitchat and assuring Dusty they were fine, they were left alone again.

"Oh my God, this would feed a small army," Addison said, her eyes wide. She tilted her head and looked over the pile of steaming food at Del. "Was there always this much food?"

"Hell if I know. I was always too busy looking at you to pay too much attention to the food."

A blush crept up her neck and into her cheeks and she unrolled her silverware. She didn't have a clue how she wanted to respond to that. So she didn't. But the next words out of her mouth stirred up a mix of heartbreak and curiosity, causing a tightness in her chest. "So, tell me about what's going on with your show."

A shadow passed over his face and was gone before she could figure out why. "You sure?"

She nodded and scooped up some of the side onto a plate and handed it to him. "Absolutely." It shocked the shit out of her to realize it was true.

"Well, my contract is up. Time to move on. The museum is my swan song so to speak."

She tilted her head. "But you've made a brand out of Property Ace."

He shrugged a shoulder and bit into a shrimp, swallowing before he continued. "True. But my agent has a lead on a new show. Better hours, better money, and I'm still Property Ace."

Addison sipped her beer and stared at him. The tightening of the shoulders, the set of his jaw...there was more to him moving on to another show. She knew how the man ticked. She bit her lip. Well, she used to know what made the man tick.

She pasted a smile on her face. "Well, that sounds like a win-win to me. Will that start soon?"

He nodded and returned her smile. "If all goes well with negotiations, I'll have to be back in Hollywood right after the reveal. I'm looking forward to a new adventure."

Her stomach clenched. Of course, he was excited. That was Del's MO in life. At least this time around when he left, she wouldn't be on the receiving end of a broken heart.

She raised her beer bottle. "To new adventures."

He raised his water glass and clinked it to hers, his smile just this side of wary.

"Now, I want to hear some behind the scenes antics. I know you had to have them," she said, needing to steer the conversation in a new direction.

"You sure?"

She nodded and scooped up some of the sides onto a plate and handed it to him. "Absolutely." It shocked the shit out of her to realize it was true.

As they feasted on steamed shrimp, crawfish, sausage, and potatoes, Del told her stories of some of his more bizarre moments in television and things that never made it into the show. Addison couldn't remember the last time she'd laughed so hard or enjoyed a man's company. It was something she didn't want to analyze too closely because she could take three guesses as to when the last time it was and who it involved.

"Rumor is you teach some business classes for women at Hardiman." Del cracked the shell of a crawfish and met her gaze.

Her eyes widened. "How did you know that?" *That* was a stupid question. The grapevine moved in small towns quicker than a flash of lightning during a summer storm.

With a half grin, he shrugged a broad shoulder. "I have my sources," he said, pulling the white meat out of the shell and popping it in his mouth. Before she could respond, he swallowed and leaned forward. "Hey, I think it's an amazing thing you're doing."

Addison tilted her head. "Really?"

"Why does that surprise you?" Del asked, wiping his hands and leaning back in his chair. He studied her face with a guarded expression.

She looked away and shifted in her chair. Why indeed? Del was raised by a strong woman and had never shown anything but support to her or his sisters over the years. "I don't know. It just does."

I want his validation, but I also want to show him I have moved on. That wasn't a thought she was comfortable with sharing, so she continued down the path of blissful ignorance.

His gaze roamed her face for a moment before a smile tugged at his mouth. "So tell me about it."

Addison couldn't hold back the grin. "After a few years working with my dad and dealing with clients, I realized that even with all of the opportunities women have, there are still some things we're not all that welcomed in. Not like we should be."

She sipped her beer, the cold carbonation wetting her throat and fortifying her. "Anyway, I wanted to help younger women—those that may not be able to afford online college or attend Hardiman as an official student—learn some business basics. Business plans, budgets, marketing strategies, in a face-to-face, safe environment. So that's what I do. They have homework, we have mock board meetings, all those kinds of things."

His smile was slow and seductive and started a burn low in her belly. "You've just upped your amazing factor."

She swallowed hard and fiddled with the edge of her napkin. "I understand how lucky I am, I was," she amended with a gnawing in her stomach. "My father was brilliant. I went to college but most of what I know in business, I learned from him. I just want to pass it along."

When she hazarded a glance back at him, a mix of desire and something else she couldn't place swirled in those deep blue eyes of his. The low burn became an inferno that left her damp between clenched thighs with warmth spreading through her limbs.

Or it could have been the beer.

"I was wrong. You're not amazing. You're phenomenal." His voice was low and rough and seemed to caress her flushed skin. Nope, not the beer.

Addison really didn't want to feel anything at all. She was all whole and healthy now, stronger than the day he left. Even stronger than the day she told him she was letting him go. His being in Madison Ridge was temporary. She could handle it and then some.

But man, she had a sneaking suspicion she was going to become BFFs with her shower nozzle and cold water while he was here.

He cleared his throat. "You ready to get out of here?" She nodded mutely and stood.

After Del paid, Dusty walked them through the open dining room quickly. Del's hand rested along the small of her back and even though he barely touched her, the heat of his skin seared through the thin fabric of her dress.

They went through the kitchen to go out the way they came in, but when Dusty opened the door, Del and Addison were greeted with a group of women waiting right outside it.

"It *is* him!"

"Did you get a pic?"

"He's even better looking in person."

Addison stood frozen to the spot, shocked by the conversations from grown women and how they seemed to move as one to get closer. It was like a wave of women coming at them.

"Shit!" Dusty exclaimed. "What the hell?" He hollered for one of his workers to help control the crowd starting to form. "Del, I'm so sorry. I don't know how this happened, but I'll find out."

Del smiled but spoke under his breath. "Call Aidan just in case this gets out of hand."

The warmth of his hand disappeared as he stepped forward and, right before her eyes, turned on the Hollywood persona. The smile, the stance, the laid-back drawl in his voice. But someone that didn't know him better would've missed the tightness of his smile and broad shoulders. "Hey, ladies. How are you?" He gave a slight wave.

A chorus of "Can I get your autograph?" rang out and napkins and other papers were shoved at him. He scrawled what she supposed passed as his signature on as many as he could keep up with.

Addison stood back and waited, an uneasiness settling in her stomach. Women, young and old, had formed a line that seemed to grow by the second. Del smiled at each and every one, signed napkins and random pieces of paper, posed for what seemed to be a hundred pictures, and was that all-around kind man she'd fallen so hard for years ago. But tension in his smile and body language never left. Just like the women in the line.

It was a stark reminder that things could never be how they once were for them. He wasn't here to stay. Getting involved with him past friendship would only break her heart again.

And this time, she wasn't sure she'd recover.

A white pickup truck pulled up behind the crowd and stopped just before a blue light came on, flashing strobe lighting into the night air around them.

Sheriff Aidan Reynolds walked around the hood of the truck and toward the crowd with a megaphone. "Ladies, break it up, please. Return inside or to your cars. Give Mr. Reynolds his space."

Aidan's tall form split the crowd like the parting of the Red Sea. Del grabbed Addison's hand and pulled her behind him down the path that his brother's presence created. "Thanks, man," Del murmured as they walked by the sheriff toward the motorcycle.

"Anytime, bro," Aidan said with a grin. "It's a hard-knock life, man."

Del mouthed "fuck you" causing Aidan to chuckle. "Back up, ma'am." He waved a brave onlooker back.

"I like a man in uniform. Are you single?" she asked, her words slightly slurred.

Seriously? Addison didn't hear Aidan's response if he even had one.

Within minutes, they rode through the humid night air on his bike, heading in the direction of her house. A rumble of thunder and a couple of flashes of lightning had Del pushing the bike, if the vibration under her ass was any indication. When he idled to a stop and shut off the bike in front of her house, the rain fell in a steady sheet. They made a run for it to her front porch, both soaking wet once they got under cover.

"Damn, that happened quick," Del said, running a hand over his hair to dry it.

"Where did that come from?" She sluiced water down her arm and pulled her dress that was plastered to her skin away from her body. "Do you want to come in for coffee?" *What the hell, Addie? What are you doing?*

Shut up, bitch. I got this.

Her warring sides were going to be the death of her.

Del's brows met his hairline. "You're inviting me in?"

She shrugged. "Well, yeah. We're friends, right? And you can't leave in this weather anyway."

"Yeah, I'd love some coffee."

When she unlocked the door, Murphy met them with happy barks as he ran in circles, excited to see his mistress. "Hey, boy. Calm down." She walked in and turned on the lamp by the door. "I'll be right back. I've got to let him out."

Murphy watered two bushes in record time and ran back in through the back door she held open. He shook his coat out and went off to flop down on his bed. She went into the laundry area and retrieved two towels.

"Here you go," she said, walking into the kitchen.

"Thanks." He took the towel from her and started to dry off.

After rubbing a towel over her own body, she went through the process of getting mugs from the cabinet to keep her mind off him standing so close. Which was ridiculous since she had just been plastered to his back on the bike. *But that had been for safety reasons.*

"That was crazy back there with the crowd of women. Is it always like that?" She laughed. "Poor Dusty. I'm guessing he is dealing with some unhappy females right about now."

Del chuckled before letting out a deep sigh of resignation as he leaned against the counter next to her. "More than likely. I'm going to have to make it up to him. It isn't his fault. He did the best he could, but there's always someone who leaks things. I should have known better for both him and you." He paused. "And no, it isn't always like that. Sometimes it's better, sometimes worse. It just depends."

Worse? How the hell did he deal with that? She shook her head, dropping a pod into the machine, and pushed the brew button. "Well, I admired the way you handled it. You were so kind, even though I could tell you were irritated."

He crossed his arms over his chest and rubbed his chin with one hand. His gaze wandered over her face. "How could you tell? I thought I did a pretty good job at hiding it."

She shrugged. "Your shoulders were tight and your mouth," she pointed to the side of hers, "gets these fine lines right here."

"Huh. No one has ever pointed that out before."

"At least not to your face, anyway." She slid the full mug over to him and started another one for herself. "Cream, sugar?"

"Nah, black's fine." He smiled and looked over at her. "But since we're friends, we can do that kind of thing. Be honest and all."

Her heart galloped in her chest. "Right." She needed to lighten the mood and fast. Before she found herself leaning over and kissing the hell out of him. That would be a bit *too* friendly.

She stood next to him and bumped his shoulder with her own. "Did you see that one lady all in black with red feathers in her hat? I swear she was panting to get to you. The woman was pissed Aidan broke it up." She elbowed him in the ribs with a sly smile. "I wonder what she would have done once she got to you."

Del shivered visibly. "I saw her. It doesn't bear thinking about. She scared me."

Addison laughed at his expression. "It was quite the flock of women. There was another lady that was ninety if she was a day. She was practically bouncing with her walker."

"Now for her? I would've given her a kiss."

Addison glanced at him sideways and nodded, taking her cup from under the machine and wrapping her hands around it. "You know what? I do believe you would have."

"You know, I thought about the recognition thing. It's why I talked to Dusty about closing off the room. He was happy to do it. But it was a precaution. I didn't really think it would be an issue." Del rubbed the back of his neck and frustration colored his voice. "I've been in the Hollywood cocoon for too long."

"Was it ever an issue on location?" Addison asked, sipping from her mug.

"Not really. The home becomes a closed set of sorts. If they can, they clear out the street right around it, food is brought to you. There's usually a guard out front." He looked over at her with a wry grin. "I don't get out much honestly. Not exactly the glamorous, playboy lifestyle the tabloids make it out to be."

"Ha, yeah right." Addison worked hard to sound friendly and light, even though her chest burned. Del had been free to do his own thing for nearly a decade and that wasn't going to change now or ever. No expectations, no strings. It was the way it had started with them years ago. And that's the way it needed to stay. They had jobs to do. He had a show to film, she had a museum to open.

Del set his mug down on the counter behind him and turned to stand in front of her. He didn't box her in, but she was effectively trapped between the hard wall of his body and the counter behind her. His eyes were that impossible blue flame color and locked on hers. "I might have to take my chances with this storm."

"Why?"

He reached out and brushed a lock of hair off her forehead. "I always loved the look of your wet hair. It's like ropes of gold streaming down your back. Reminds me of a beautiful siren-like mermaid." He toyed with the ends of her hair that fell just above her breasts.

Her breath caught in her throat. He wasn't even touching her skin, but it was on fire through the wet fabric of her dress. She half expected it to disintegrate under his long fingers. His stare hypnotized her, and she had to swallow hard before she spoke.

"Please, I…" She trailed off, her voice barely above a whisper.

He curled the lock of hair around his finger. "What?" His voice was low, deep, and touched off sparks low in her belly.

Please, I need you to kiss me, hold me, make me whole again.

Nope. That was a dangerous line of thinking. One she simply couldn't do.

Her gaze drifted away, and she cleared her throat. "I can't have you leave in this weather. You're out at the lake house, right?" He nodded and she continued. "Okay, so it isn't far, but you could get into an accident, catch a cold." Okay, maybe the last one was bogus, but he really could have a serious accident. "Sleep on my couch. Because it doesn't sound like it's going to stop any time soon."

When she looked back at him, his eyes continued their intense stare. After a few tense seconds passed, he released the hair from his finger and smiled. "I appreciate the concern."

Addison let out a breath, the ground a bit more even now that he wasn't touching her. "I can dry your clothes for you. Jackson left some clothes here."

Del shoved his hands into his back pockets. "Works for me."

"I'll be right back." She walked through the living room and ran upstairs. In the guest room, she rummaged through the dresser until she found a pair of Jackson's black basketball shorts, but no shirt.

"Damn. I can*not* have him shirtless around me," she muttered to herself. She closed the drawer and walked out of the room, drawing up short when a thought hit her. Yeah, she had something he could wear, and it was folded in her dresser drawer.

A few minutes later, she jogged back downstairs with the clothes, a blanket, and a pillow. Del stood in front of the fireplace looking at her pictures. "I found something for you."

He turned and took the shorts and T-shirt when she held them out to him.

She dropped the pillow and blanket onto the couch and gestured to the shirt. "That's yours anyway."

He held up the soft, black UGA T-shirt, his eyes wide. "You kept it? I figured after I left you'd pretty much burned anything of mine."

She shifted her feet, not looking him in the eye. "Well, I wanted to, but I love that shirt. It reminds me of my first day on campus. You were wearing it when you stopped by my dorm."

"I remember that." He lowered the shirt and met her gaze, a faraway smile on his lips. "You had on a green tank top that made your eyes look like emeralds. Cutoff shorts. You looked like you'd just come off the beach." He chuckled. "I wanted nothing more than to kiss you senseless, but with your parents and Jackson standing there, I decided against it."

She smiled and bit her lip. "Good call."

His smile turned into a wicked grin that had heat flaring in her core. "If I recall, I did more than kiss you senseless later that night."

Addison swallowed hard as desire, nostalgia, and common sense waged war in her mind, heart, and body. But for the life of her, she couldn't tear her gaze away from his midnight-blue eyes. "It was a memorable night." She met his grin with a soft smile. "One of many in that uncomfortable dorm bed."

Seconds ticked by while they stared at one another. Her pounding heart broke her out of her trance. "There's a bathroom down the hall." She gestured over her shoulder. "Need anything else?"

"No, I'm good. Thanks. I appreciate you letting me stay."

Addison rubbed her hands down her dress and smiled brightly. "Of course, that's what friends do, right?"

He nodded slowly. "Yeah, that's what friends do."

"Good night, Del." She turned and made it to the bottom stair before he stopped her.

"Addison." His raspy voice caused her nerves to dance along her skin.

Damn it, when he used her whole name, she nearly came undone. "Yeah?" She couldn't look at him. The battle would be lost.

"I..." He paused. "I'm glad we're friends again."

She nodded, unable to speak for a moment. "Me too."

"Good night."

She raced up the stairs like the hounds of hell were nipping at her heels.

The next morning, the sun shone bright and burned off the remaining clouds left from the sudden storm. When she came downstairs dressed to go walking, she rounded the corner and knew she'd find the couch empty. The rumble of his motorcycle in the early morning hours and the stillness of the room told her he'd been gone for a while. Her breath hitched. He'd folded the blanket and left a note on top. She walked over and picked it up, her hands shaking lightly, much to her dismay.

I took Murphy out and made coffee in a to go cup I found.

There were no chocolate donuts, but I left you a banana for breakfast on the counter.

Be sure you eat it.

— Del

P.S. Last night was the best night I've had in years. Let's do it again sometime, friend.

She sighed and flopped down on the couch. Her heart skipped a beat and realization set in.

Del made it impossible for her to do anything but love him.

only a matter of time

THWACK!

Del grunted when the sledgehammer hit drywall, sending vibrations down his arms. He'd left Addison's house as the sun came up. The quiet, peaceful ride through town out to the lake helped clear his head. He was there just long enough to change clothes, take his meds, and head to the job site. Arriving before the rest of the demo crew, he went to work.

Although her couch was comfy and his body was more than tired, he'd been wide awake when the sky outside the front windows became a mix of gray and orange, signaling the impending sunrise. He needed to leave. Horniness was going to be a chronic condition for him if he kept hanging around Addison in little, wet sundresses with her long reddish-blonde hair and curvy body pressed against his back. What the hell had he been thinking?

Maybe delusional thoughts should be listed as a side effect of his medication.

His muscles protested as he continued to pound the wall into pieces. Destroying some more shit should help. What was for damn sure was he was cranky, horny, and—honestly?— fucking lovesick. He worked through the worst of the tension that had him on edge and ignored the heaviness in his arms and the shooting pains down his back.

The sound of tires on gravel followed by the shuffle of boots over bare wood floors signaled his alone time was over. It was just as well. If he didn't stop now, his body would make him stop and he'd miss filming. With a gloved hand, he swiped at the river of sweat running down his temple.

"Morning." Tommy stood in what was left of the doorway to the kitchen. "You're here early." He held out a cardboard tray with disposable coffee cups jammed into it. "Coffee?"

The sledgehammer dropped to the floor with a thud and Del pulled off his gloves. "Yeah, thanks."

If Tommy noticed the mess he'd made, he had the good sense not to mention it. "So, where do you want us to start?"

Del gulped the steaming cup of coffee, burning his tongue in the process. Good. It would give him something to focus on other than a pair of green eyes and a soft smile. His fingers tightened on the cup briefly.

"How many crews you got?"

"Three. Four men on each crew."

Del nodded. "Perfect. Let's pull them together and show them what needs to be done."

Tommy nodded and walked back toward the house. With an ear-splitting whistle, Tommy's crew gathered around him and Del, waiting for instructions.

Within the hour, the crews were in full swing tearing down walls on the first and second floors. As he stood outside in front of the house, the sound of hammers banging, walls falling, and the overall sound of work lifted a weight from Del's shoulders. As much as he loved his work, there was always an anticipation that came with beginning a new project. This particular project was not only daunting in size and tight timeline but meant more to him than any other. Addison might own it, but it was a legacy to the Reynolds family as well.

Tommy jogged down the front steps and strode over to Del. "Hey, boss. Got a question for you about the balcony on the back."

The sound of a vehicle coming up the driveway had the two men turning. When Del saw the tiny, sassy red sports car, his gut clenched.

"She wasn't kidding about wanting to be in on the status of things." Tommy chuckled and rubbed at his brow.

"No, she wasn't," Del murmured under his breath. "Tommy, can you give us a minute?"

"Sure." Tommy ambled off, but Del caught the grin on his face as he turned to leave.

Del walked toward her, his gait slow as she alighted from the car and he stopped a few steps from her. She leaned against the car, her arms crossed over her chest. His mouth watered as his gaze raked over her from head to toe. The workout pants and matching jacket covered her with not even a peekaboo of skin. But the pants formed to her legs, leaving nothing to the imagination but lots of danger signs flashing in his head. He'd never been good at heeding warning signs and it appeared he wasn't about to start if the blood pounding in his ears was any indication of sanity.

"Good morning," she said with a smile.

"Morning, beautiful. Been out for a walk?"

She nodded, the blush coloring her cheeks only making her beauty more breathtaking. She kicked a rock with the toe of her sneaker. "Thanks for breakfast. I don't usually eat anything. But I think it put some pep in my step this morning. My walk time was better than normal."

Del shrugged. "It was just a banana." He stepped toward her until they were toe to toe. His hands rested on either side of her hips, the metal of the car cool beneath his hands, a contrast to the heat of his skin. He leaned forward ever so slightly, caging her against the car. Addison leaned her head back and it delighted him to see he could read her again. Caution and desire warred in her eyes. "Maybe some morning I can cook a real breakfast for you."

"You cook now? Once upon a time you couldn't boil water." She kept a straight face, but those expressive green eyes twinkled with humor underneath the desire and wiped away the wariness.

His lips curved. "Ha ha. I picked up a few things along the way." He moved his hands up to her hips. She didn't move, didn't protest.

The only acknowledgment she gave was the darkening of her eyes and the slight shift of her feet, causing her body to brush against his. He tightened his grip on her hips and desire shot through him. He inched closer until their lips were just a breath apart. "I can make you anything your heart desires."

"I might just let you." Her lips parted and eyes slid closed as he leaned in to close the space between them.

The sound of a vehicle coming up the drive stopped him from capturing her mouth with his. Her eyes flew open and met his.

"Want to help me bury a body? Because I'm going to kill whoever this is." She giggled and he looked up with a frown. "Damn it. Building inspector. I forgot he was due out here today." With a heavy sigh, he stepped away from her and shoved his hands in his pockets.

Addison stood up straight and smoothed a hand over her ponytail. "I guess I'll be going then."

"Hold on, you came by for a reason, didn't you?"

"Yeah, I wanted to see how things were coming along. I mean, I read the daily reports you send. Thanks, by the way."

He nodded once. "You're welcome."

"But it's been a while since I've seen it myself. But now that he's here," she nodded her head toward the white truck parking in the roped-off area, "I'll come back."

"You sure?"

"Positive."

Del huffed out a breath, frustration building steam in his chest. "Okay, I'll call you tonight. Maybe we can try dinner again somewhere not so public."

"Um, yeah." She turned to get in the car but stopped and faced him again. "Oh, hey. Will you be coming to the Honoring America parade Memorial Weekend?" Her body sagged and her lips pursed. "Probably not, though, after last night's debacle."

He narrowed his eyes at her and quirked up one side of his mouth. "Do you want me there?"

She flung a hand out to her side. "I mean, it's a public—"

Del grinned. "I'll be there."

She nodded once and her lips twitched with a restrained smile.

"Okay, then." Her wave was awkward and fucking adorable. Damn, he had it bad for her. Again.

He blew out a breath as she drove away. He brought his hormones —and his anger at the interruption—under control before he faced the inspector, but it was a Herculean effort.

It was going to be a long day.

It turned out to be a long week and a half.

There were issues with some of the filming and the renovations, and he spent two days back in California meeting with his agent and publicist who'd begged him to meet with them in person. It wasn't a trip he enjoyed. Although he trusted both of them, he wasn't ready to tell them just yet about his illness and how that would play into his future, both jobwise and image-wise. Hell, he didn't even know what his future held for him.

Right now, all he cared about was his immediate future and getting to see Addison, who was never far from his mind any time of day.

In his baseball cap, flip-flops, T-shirt, and board shorts, he looked like any other tourist milling around and as such, was able to come out and enjoy the festivities. Del walked around taking it all in, soaking up the scenery. Fortunately, the locals knew him and hadn't made a big fuss about him. So far, if anyone recognized him, they hadn't said anything.

It had been years since Del had been to an "Honoring America" parade. The parade drew large crowds each year and this one was no exception. While the locals turned out in full force, the summer tourists showed up as well, lining the streets and filling the stores of the relatively quiet mountain college town.

He wasn't looking for Addison. He hadn't come out to the parade hours before it started just to see her. Nope, not at all. His mother was chairwoman of the Chamber of Commerce and, as the sponsor of the parade, he came out to support her. Being a good son was all he was doing. If he happened to see Addison while he was here, it would make his day. But she wasn't the reason he was here.

Yeah, right. Whatever gets you down the river of denial fastest, Ace.

It was just luck he'd found her on a ladder, hanging streamers from the top of the announcer's booth. With a smile on his lips, he walked over to the ladder and looked up. He tilted his head in appreciation of the view. His body tightened at the way she filled out the shorts she was wearing. Yep, it was fair to say Addison Davenport was all woman.

Shit. He needed to get his head out of the gutter and act like the grown-ass man he was, not like some horny teenager in heat. He shook his head to clear out the naughty thoughts. "Hey, there. Need any help?"

She looked down and her smile gave the sun a run for its money. "Hey! Hang on. I'm coming down."

Her sneakered feet maneuvered the steps like a graceful cat and at the bottom, she jumped off the second rung to the ground. It took all he had not to reach out to wrap an arm around her waist and haul her to his chest.

He managed, but barely. His hands fisted inside his pockets.

Addison looked up at him, with the smile that set his world on fire. "You made it. I wasn't sure if I'd see you."

Before coherent thought crossed his mind, he closed the space between them, taking her face in his hands. "What the hell was I thinking ever leaving you?"

Her eyes widened momentarily before she slapped a hand to his chest. "What are you doing?"

"I'm going to kiss you now, Addie. Okay?"

His mouth was just a breath away from hers. But he waited while a flurry of emotions played out in her eyes.

"Okay," she whispered and her eyes slid closed as he lowered his mouth to hers in a searing kiss.

The whistles of people around them sounded hollow in his ears, but Addison's scent surrounded him and he was lost. His tongue swept her lower lip with lazy strokes until her mouth softened and opened under his. His shirt tightened around his chest when she curled the fabric into her fists.

With reluctance, he broke off the kiss. His eyes opened and found Addison's were drowsy and dark with desire. He smiled and gently rubbed his thumbs along her cheekbones, making her lids flutter closed.

"We'll finish this later. You know, when we aren't in public," he said low enough that only she could hear.

She nodded and opened her eyes. "That's a good idea because my thoughts would get us arrested for sure." Her fingers uncurled from his shirt and she licked her lips.

He groaned and laid his fingertips over her soft pink mouth. "Don't do that. I'm having enough trouble with blood flow as it is." Her chuckle was cut short when the sound of a throat clearing came from behind him.

Del welcomed the interruption this time around. When he turned, a gray-haired gentleman in a white-and-navy-pinstriped seersucker suit stood grinning at him.

"Mayor Samson," he said in greeting and held out his hand. "Happy Memorial Day."

The mayor, who was once his history teacher, returned his handshake. "Delaney. It's good to see you. I'd heard you were back home. I apologize for not getting out to your set sooner. I was out of town for a bit."

"Don't worry about it. How's the family?"

Samson's smile fell a notch. "Ah, well. Betty's doing well and my boys have busy lives down in Atlanta. But my mother's been sick and she lives in Florida now, so I've been spending a lot of time down there."

"I'm so sorry to hear that. Is there anything we can do to help?" Addison asked.

He gave her a sad smile. "Thanks, but for now we're good." He gazed around at the decorations. "The chamber did a fantastic job on the parade and festival."

Addison smiled and nodded. "Thank you, sir. You know Stella."

"Yeah, I do. Del, your mother is a powerhouse."

"Yes, sir. She's pretty amazing."

"The town loves her." Pride filled Del's chest while regret churned in his gut. What all had he missed?

Rick Samson smiled his mayoral smile at him, bringing his focus back to the conversation. "Are you staying for the parade?"

"I wouldn't miss it. It was a staple growing up. Glad to see it still happens every year." He grinned at the mayor. "When did you decide to trade in teaching government for being part of the government?"

The older man laughed. "I retired around the same time Mayor Thomas passed away. So I threw my hat in the ring and decided to go for it."

"Well, the high school lost a great teacher, but the town gained a great leader."

"Thank you, Del." He cocked his head. "Though, from what I remember of you being in my class, you wouldn't know if I was a great teacher or not. If I recall, you were a bit distracted in those days."

Del chuckled. "True enough."

The mayor looked over Addison's shoulder and nodded. "Looks like the First Lady is beckoning me. Enjoy your day and support your local merchants!" With a salute, he ambled away, crossing the street.

Del looked down at Addison. "Anything I can do to help you? Since I kind of distracted you."

Addison looked around then back at him. "Well, I need to finish setting up and decorating the booth here."

Del clapped and rubbed his hands together. "Alright, let's get started."

Working together, they finished the task with about an hour to spare before the announcers would be there. When they were finished, Del placed the box of extra decorations and toolbox on the hand truck and walked with Addison to the city pickup she'd parked about a block off the closed-off square.

"Thanks for your help."

"It was my pleasure." He lifted the boxes and hand truck into the bed before slamming the tailgate shut.

Addison wiped her brow with her forearm then fanned herself. "God, it's already sweltering."

His eyes tracked a bead of sweat that ran down her neck and pooled in the hollow at the base of her neck. The formfitting, navy T-shirt she wore clung to her torso in various spots where moisture had gathered.

Small gold and red tendrils escaped her ponytail and curled around her face. The apple of her cheeks held a faint pink tone. Visions of her hot and sweaty in his bed, calling out his name, assaulted his brain, tightening his body with desire. He tried to think about anything else. Anything at all would be good right about now.

She pulled her phone from the back pocket of her short white denim shorts and looked at the screen. "The parade will be starting soon. I know the perfect spot to watch it and it's shaded." Her smile was smug and her tone conspiratorial.

He held out a bent elbow. "Lead the way, Ms. Davenport."

After watching the parade from the balcony of the historic courthouse she had access to, they stayed seated in the rocking chairs while the crowds cleared out.

Addison sighed as she rocked. "Ah, it feels good up here. And see?" She waved a hand in front of her. "We can see everything going on in the square from here."

"It really is the best seat in the house." He pushed off the ground and let his chair rock in time with hers.

She nodded once. "I think so."

He rubbed a finger along the wide arm rest of the white painted wood. Why the hell was he so nervous to ask her about the family barbecue? It wasn't like she'd never been, never met his family. Hell, they'd just tangled tongues not long ago and went out on a date of sorts—okay, they needed a redo and soon—a couple of weeks before.

Damn, grow a pair, man. She's not going to turn you down anyway.

"Hey, Addie. You got any plans Monday afternoon?"

"Actually," she said with a twinkle in her eye, "I do."

Not going to turn me down, my ass. "Oh, okay."

She pulled one leg up into the chair and shifted to face him. "Why do you ask?"

He waved her off. "No reason. You're busy, that's cool."

Addison leaned an elbow on the armrest of her rocker and dropped her chin in her hand. "Delaney Reynolds, were you going to ask me to the barbecue?"

His brow furrowed. "How did you know?"

She tilted her head, resting it on the lattice back of the chair, and laughed. "Oh, Del. Honey, you really have been gone too long. I've been going to the annual Reynolds Memorial Day party for years. Jackson usually comes up, too. He should be on his way." Her smile dropped away. "My parents went every year, too."

There was so much to unpack there. The fact she'd slipped and used the endearment she'd always called him when they were together. The fact he didn't know the Davenport family still turned out to the family party every year, in spite of the loss of his father years ago and his and Addison's broken engagement.

Her gaze was unfocused and her mouth tilted up slightly. "They did enjoy a good party."

"Threw some damn good ones if I recall."

She shook her head and the shadows in her eyes cleared. The slight smile on her lips grew. "Yes, they did. It broke mine and Jackson's heart to sell the family house." She shrugged. "But neither of us could keep it up or needed it. He doesn't live here and it's just...me here." Her eyes cast down and she picked at the paint with a fingernail. "It was time for another family to make some memories there." She looked up at him, tears pooled in her eyes. "You know? It was time."

Curled up in the rocker like she was, Addison looked like a forlorn child who'd just realized she was an orphan. The heartbreaking part about it was that she was. He held out a hand. "Come here." His voice was rough and low and his heart aching.

Without hesitation, Addison stood and sat in his lap, leaning her head on his shoulder. They rocked in silence for a few moments before the dam broke. She buried her face in his neck, her body racked with sobs. He brought his arms up and around her torso. He held the back of her head with one hand and stroked her back with the other, trying to soothe her.

He didn't say a word, just rocked and let her cry it out for who knows how long. And he didn't give a shit how long it took. There was no other place he'd rather be than right there holding all he'd ever wanted in his arms.

After a while, she lifted her head and sniffled. He released the hold he had on her so she could lean back. She swiped at her eyes and looked down at her lap. "I'm sorry." Her voice came out as a low mumble, but he heard her mortification loud and clear.

"Hey," he lifted her chin with his index finger. "No need to apologize. I recall a time when I lost my dad and needed a friend. I'm just returning the favor. Okay?"

"Yeah, but—"

"No buts, Addie. There's nowhere else I'd rather be than right here with you." He kissed her, soft and quick, banking back the passion for her that ran constantly under his skin. Right now, she needed him as a friend, not as a man who wanted to be her lover again. "Better?" He rubbed a hand along her upper thigh in a comforting gesture.

Nodding, she gave him a wobbly smile. "Yeah." She slid off his lap and stood, blowing out a breath. "Wow, I needed that." Her voice was strong again, maybe even stronger than before. Her gaze took in the town below them. "Looks like most of the crowd has cleared out. We should be able to get away now. I need to get the truck back to the city yard anyway."

"Good." Del stood and put his hand on the small of her back. "I'll walk you to the truck."

The walk back was quiet, punctuated with the sounds of the crowds around them and occasional greetings as they weaved their way back to where the city pickup truck sat.

She opened the door and turned to face him. "Thanks for helping me out today. With the parade stuff and…you know." Uncomfortable was not something he was used to seeing Addison try on, but it was endearing.

He leaned his forearm against the top of the door and leaned on it. Fatigue was beginning to be a constant companion, seeping into his muscles. "Just helping out a friend."

Addison opened her mouth and then closed it without another word. She just shook her head. "Well, thanks, friend."

"Hey, since you're going to the party and I'm going to the party, what if I pick you up, say three o'clock?"

She rolled her eyes. "Del, I can drive myself. You live where the party is going to be."

He grinned. "Yeah, I know. But this way I can get out of any prep work."

"Oh, I see. So I'd be helping out a friend? Right?"

"Absolutely."

"Well," she shrugged. "Can't say no to that."

He paused, running times through his head. "Two thirty work?"

"I'll be ready."

"See you then." He pushed himself off the truck so she could boost herself up into the cab. When she slammed the door shut, he leaned on the door. She started the engine, rolled down the window, and gave a little wave. "Bye."

He reached in the cab and cupped the back of her neck, bringing her to him for another taste of her. This time, though, his lips barely grazed hers and he rubbed gently. Before either of them could take the kiss deeper, he released her. "It's custom for lovers to kiss goodbye."

Her already pink cheeks deepened a shade. "But...we're not lovers."

A slow smile spread across his face. "We'll always be lovers, Addison. It's only a matter of time."

Before he could do anything that could get them arrested, like taking her right there in broad daylight in the cab of a city-owned truck, he turned and walked away.

He meant what he had said to her. It was only a matter of time.

A matter of time before he lost the grip on his sanity.

CHAPTER TWELVE
get a grip, hormones

"THERE." Addison dropped the last sliced strawberry in the bowl. She stepped back and eyed her work. The strawberry, blueberry, and whipped topping trifle was quick, easy, and festive.

"What do you think, Murph?" She spun the pedestal dish, inspecting the layers through the glass. Murphy let out a long sigh and rolled over onto his side.

"Sorry, I interrupted nap time. I'll keep it down." She shook her head with a smile.

This was the first time she'd been in charge of bringing a dessert. It had always been her mom's thing. Addison frowned. Her little trifle dish would have to do, but it seemed sad compared to some of the beautiful desserts her mother had always made. Since taking over the business, her chamber duties, and now trying to keep up with the renovation project, cooking fell way, way down the list. Takeout was her new best friend these days. That and her assistant who was a saint and made sure she ate during the day.

Thinking about the renovation inevitably made her think about Del. Her skin tingled thinking back to how he'd held her when she *finally* broke down and cried. It had been a little more than six months and it was the first time she'd let go. Jackson had his own issues at home and was more than two hours away. So the day of the parade was the first time she'd been around someone she trusted enough to let down her guard and let out her heartache over the loss of her parents.

Addison wasn't sure when things changed with Del and when she had started considering him someone she trusted again, but she would be forever grateful to him for being her friend again and helping her through her grief. Since then, there was a lightness in her heart when she thought of her parents now.

But before she'd broken down, he'd kissed the fuck out of her. Like he used to do when they'd obliterated the line between friends and lovers years ago. What had he been thinking kissing her on the street like that?

What had she been thinking kissing him back? And wanting more than to just kiss him right there? When his lips were on hers, the whole world had fallen away. There was nothing more than his touch on her skin. The heat had radiated from him, the firm planes of his body against her softer ones, his hard length pressing against her thigh. Her mind may want to forget about how he made her feel, but her body had no trouble at all remembering the feel of Del's skin against hers, the fullness of him when he was inside her.

The tingles of desire became an all-out throb and she clenched her thighs together. No question, between her yearlong sex drought and the only man who'd ever made her feel that much desire and passion being in such close proximity lately, she was losing control of her body.

After today, she needed to keep her time spent with Del strictly to the work on the house. If she didn't, she'd surely make a fool of herself.

Murphy's ears perked up and he took off for the front door, barking as he looked out the window in the dining room.

Addison glanced at the clock to find Del would be there in five minutes. And she was still in her robe from her shower.

"Shit!" she exclaimed. She slid off the stool and crossed the kitchen to the fridge. Practically ripping the door off the hinges in her haste, she opened the fridge door then slid the trifle in. As she slammed it closed with her foot, the doorbell pealed, a harmony with Murphy's high-pitched barks.

Where the hell had the time gone? Had she really daydreamed about the man on the other side of this door for that long?

Murphy whined and spun in circles in the foyer. Even though she knew who it would be before she looked, she checked the peephole of the door to find Del standing on the other side. When she opened the door, her mouth went dry. All thoughts she had left her brain, never to be found again.

The navy polo shirt stretched across his broad chest and darkened his already impossibly blue eyes, which traveled down her body and back to her face. She wanted to place a kiss in the V opening of his shirt, knowing his skin would be warm. The short sleeves showed off his muscular, tanned forearms, and along with his khaki shorts and boat shoes, he looked cool, confident, and sexy as hell, which is exactly what he was.

She wanted to wrap herself up in whatever cologne he was wearing. It was crisp with pine undertones, both sharp and subtle, but not sweet.

She needed to get a damn grip on her hormones.

"I know I'm early," Del began.

Waving him off, she stepped aside to let him into the foyer. "No worries. I'll just be a minute."

"Take your time," he drawled, his voice low and rough.

The husky tone to his voice danced across her skin. Without looking into his stare again, she hightailed it upstairs.

A few minutes later, she walked down the stairs, dressed, and her nerves balanced out. When she rounded the corner from the stairs into the living room, she was brought up short by the picture the dog and the man made in front of her. "Awww…"

Del's hand was on top of Murphy's head, which laid in Del's lap. Her dog noticed her and moved his head ever so slightly, but the man was out cold. Del's head leaned back against the pillows and his chest moved up and down in a rhythm that told her he'd dropped off into a good sleep.

She moved closer and tilted her head. Had she been upstairs long enough he'd fallen into such a deep sleep? She didn't think so. But she also knew he was working his ass off on the house, judging by the daily reports. Add filming to the mix and it couldn't be an easy job. No wonder he was exhausted.

Addison shook his shoulder gently. "Del, wake up. I'm ready."

He moaned and turned his head to face her. His eyes fluttered open and for a moment it looked like his eyelids were drooping. Concern pricked her skin. "Hey, are you okay? Do your eyes hurt?"

"Hmmm..." He leaned forward and rubbed his eyes with the heels of his hands. "What?"

Her eyes narrowed on his face. "I said, do your eyes hurt?"

Del shook his head. "No. No, they're fine. Can I get some water?"

"Absolutely." She paused. His movements were unsteady and not characteristic of his usually smooth nature. "You sure you're okay?"

He nodded. "Yeah."

Something seemed off but she went into the kitchen and pulled out a bottle of water and took it to him. "Here ya go." She smoothed her dress under her legs and sat beside him on the couch, her hands in her lap. "Exhausted, aren't you?"

He took a long pull from the bottle of water before answering. "Yeah, I guess I am. I just sat down and the next thing I know, you're waking me up."

"You looked peaceful. I hated to wake you."

He smiled and capped the bottle. "We should get going before my mother starts to think I'm staying away on purpose."

They stood together and she walked in front of him toward the kitchen.

"Holy hell, Addison."

She stopped and turned back to him. "What?"

His hot blue gaze set off little hot spots of fire all over her body. "Nothing. Let's go get your dessert contribution."

While her attire wouldn't draw any scandalous comments, Addison also knew the short, cotton strapless dress showed off more skin than she normally showed. She'd be a liar if she said she didn't like the fact Del seemed to appreciate her formfitting, summery dress.

Addison pulled open the fridge door and slid out her dish. She turned to set it on the island and found him there, hands out.

"I'll take that for you." Before she could answer, his hands covered hers before lifting the glass dish out of her hands.

"Thanks." It came out as a croak. Although it was a simple handoff of a dish, a hot ball of desire formed in her lower belly when his hands covered hers in what she swore was a caress.

He didn't move away, just stood there cradling her hands between his warm ones and the cold glass. His eyes took a lazy route from the top of her dress, down to her platform sandals and back up. A wicked smile formed on his lips. "Nice dress," he murmured.

The grin and the desire in his eyes left her breathless.

He bent his head softly, brushing his lips against hers. It was a soft kiss, his lips cold from the water he'd just drunk. Her fingers tightened on the bowl to keep from grabbing him and taking him up to her bedroom. She didn't know how much more of this she could take.

He lifted his head, smile still in place. "Shall we?"

She nodded without a word and walked ahead of him, moving her feet as quick as was polite. Just today. She just had to keep her hormones in check for the rest of the day.

Easier said than done.

challenge accepted

WHEN THEY ARRIVED at the Reynolds's family lakefront home, the party was in full swing. A badminton net and croquet course had been set up in the large wide front yard. A few children ran around playing tag and hide-and-seek.

Del led Addison around the side of the house and into the backyard where they were greeted by the smells of grilling hamburgers and hot dogs. Laughter, music, and voices of friendship—the soundtrack of summer backyard cookouts—wafted toward them on the breeze.

Addison sighed. "I've always loved your house."

Del took in the grassy yard leading down to a dock and the deepwater lake beyond it. The backyard of his childhood. "Yeah, me too. I've missed it."

She made a noncommittal sound and turned toward him. "Do you know where I should put this?"

He rubbed a hand over his chin. "Let's take it to the deck where all the tables are set up. I'm sure Mom has a place for it." He laid a hand on the small of her back and guided her toward the large deck, where he had no doubt his mother was ruling with an iron fist.

As they approached the large decking and porch area, Del was assaulted with memories. He and his brothers helped their father build that deck one summer over twenty years before. It had been hot as hell that summer, too, he recalled. His mother had insisted that if they were going to build something that big, she wanted to be able to sit on it without getting "eaten up by bugs." It had taken an extra week to screen in one end of the large area. But the look on his mother's face when they'd finished had been worth all the extra labor working with the screening.

A small pang twisted just under his heart thinking back on that time before his dad died and everything changed. His father's death had been a catalyst to a lot of things that happened in his life—some good, some bad. Funny, he'd never thought of it that way before now.

Addison slowed and put a hand on his arm. "Hey, are you okay?"

Del looked down at her and saw concern swimming in those gorgeous green eyes. His heart somersaulted in his chest just looking at her.

What the fuck had he been thinking ten years ago when he left her here?

He didn't want to take another breath without kissing her. His mouth met hers in a soft kiss that only lasted a couple of seconds, but scrambled his brain nonetheless.

When he lifted his head, he pushed a strand of hair that had escaped her ponytail behind her ear. "I'm fine, baby."

He took her hand and led her up the stairs to where the grill worked hard cooking a small fortune of burgers and dogs. Several tables were weighed down with every food dish known to man.

"There's my long lost son." Stella walked toward them with her arms open, giving him a tight hug.

He chuckled. "Hey, mom. You just saw me thirty minutes ago." Del returned her hug with enthusiasm. He inhaled her hair, the smell of her trademark perfume bringing back a ton of memories on the deck they stood on.

When he released her, she ignored his jab and turned her attention to Addison. "Addie, you look beautiful. I'm so glad you came." Stella wrapped her arms around his girl, minding the glass dish in Addison's hands.

"I wouldn't miss it for the world, Stella." When they drew apart, Addison lifted the dish. "Where should I put this?"

"Oh, you can put it on that table with the other desserts." She pointed to a long table full of other sweet concoctions on the other side of the deck.

When Addison nodded and walked away, Stella turned to Del and wrapped an arm around his. "Come with me, son. I need a minute of your time."

Del's brow furrowed and he shot a glance to Noah, who Stella had tasked with being grill master for the day. His brother shrugged and slapped a burger on the grate. The message was loud and clear. You're on our own, buddy.

Stella steered them through the backdoor and into the kitchen, where it was cool and quiet. "Want anything to drink?" she asked, headed to the fridge. Even though Del was the one living there and Stella hadn't lived there in years, she was ever the hostess.

"No, I'm good. What's up, mom?"

She pulled out a bottle of water for herself and closed the fridge door before leaning against it. After taking a drink, she responded to his question. "Rumor has it you and Addie have been spending time together." She twisted the cap onto the bottle. "And I'm not talking about working on the museum together."

"The rumors are true." He nodded and leaned against the counter. "Do you have any objections?"

She shook her head, her dark ponytail sweeping her shoulders, but a frown marred her lips. "Not at all. Have you told her about your condition?"

His mother's pretty face was lined with concern and he hated he'd put it there. Del sighed. "No, but I plan to. Soon. I know I need to tell her, especially if we progress any further."

Stella pursed her lips and looked out the back windows that overlooked the backyard, where it was full of family and friends. After a moment, she met his gaze again. "I don't know what you plans are, Delaney. But you're a smart man. I'm confident you'll make the right decision for yourself. I just want you to be happy, whatever that means for you."

She crossed the kitchen and laid a cool hand on his cheek. "But if you go any further down this path with Addie, you need to tell her sooner than later."

He nodded. "I promise.. I'll tell her as soon as I can."

She smiled and patted his cheek lightly. "That's my boy. I love you, Delaney."

"I love you too, mom." He drew her close and kissed her forehead. "We should probably get out there before Noah burns the burgers."

Stella laughed and led them back outside. When they walked out, she went over to where Addison chatted with Grace. Soon, the three were laughing and chatting like magpies. Del's heart swelled observing his mother and his woman laugh and talk like it was the easiest thing in the world.

His woman? Maybe not yet, but he was trying like hell to change that.

But what are you going to do once you have her, Ace? Now that was the million-dollar question. What indeed? How could he ask her to have a present, much less a future with him, when he didn't know from day to day what his body would do to him? The future of his career would be easier to manage and that was as murky as a swamp. And let's not get started on the fact that he'd had opportunities to tell her, including earlier at her house, and he'd chosen the coward's way out.

But the one thing he did know is that his mother was right. He needed to grow a pair and tell Addison about his condition before they crossed any more lines.

"Mom loves her. Always has," Noah said mildly, handing Del a bottle of water.

Del grunted, taking a swig of the cold liquid. *That makes two of us.*

Wait, what? Del shifted his weight and gripped the plastic bottle tighter, causing it to crackle, and dragged his gaze away from Addison.

"I understand the renovations and filming on the house are coming along nicely," Noah said, one side of his mouth quirked into a smile. He flipped a burger, causing the grill to sizzle and smoke to rise.

"Yeah," Del said, blowing out a breath, thankful Noah changed the subject. They talked shop for a few minutes until Jackson appeared on the deck and walked over to Addison. She hugged him and held on for a minute. She must have asked a question because he gestured out to the yard, then talked with Stella for a few minutes.

When Addison nodded and pointed toward him, Jackson looked up at him with a glint in his eye. Having sisters of his own, Del was familiar with that glint.

Shit.

Jackson made his way through partygoers toward him. Even dressed down in a polo shirt and khaki shorts, he held an air of prestige and power. Their friendship dated back to the cradle. The families were so intertwined, Del never knew a time when Jackson wasn't his friend. Even when he and Addison started dating in high school, he and Jackson were good.

Until Del left. Things had changed after that.

The first time Del came back to the Ridge after he'd left, he'd given Jackson a free shot and Jackson wasted no time in taking it. A few punches, some bruises, and a couple of bloody lips later, they'd shared some beers and got back to the business of being as close as brothers. They also swore they'd never tell Addie.

Things were solid with him and Jackson again. But Del wasn't sure if they would stay solid if—not if, when—he and Addison became involved again.

Jackson stopped next to Del. "Del, Noah. How's it going?"

"Can't complain," Noah replied. "Need a beer?"

"Hell, yeah."

Noah reached back into the cooler and pulled out a long-necked glass bottle, tossing it to Jackson. He caught it handily and twisted off the cap. After taking a long pull, he sighed when he lowered the bottle. "That's good."

Del waited him out. *Sneaky bastard.* Jackson was stalling, to see if he could make Del sweat. It was how his old friend was wired. Patient and calculating.

Hiding a smile, he took a drink from his bottle of water and stayed silent. He continued to watch Addison talk to his mother, before the two went down the stairs and out into the yard.

"Anything we need to talk about, Del?" Jackson asked conversationally.

"Is that your way of asking if I'm putting the moves on your sister?"

"Are you?"

"Yes," Del responded without hesitation.

Jackson grunted, quiet for a few moments. "Will I have to kick your ass again?"

Del chuckled. "For there to be an 'again,' there'd have to be a first time."

"I'm laying bets on Jackson," Noah interjected, with a feral grin. "Sorry, bro."

Del gave him the side-eye before glancing over to Jackson, who waited for a serious answer.

"No. There won't be any ass kicking. Mine or yours."

"Good. I won't interfere. It's her life after all. But if you break her heart again, I won't go easy on you." His voice was calm, even casual as he watched the partygoers milling around in the yard and sipped his beer. But his relaxed tone masked a hint of steel.

Del's body tensed. He wanted to tell Jackson to go fuck himself. Not that it was a possibility, but what if the tables were turned? He'd have not only him but Noah and Aidan to deal with. He'd cut the poor sucker some slack. "Understood. I'd be disappointed if you did." His grin spread across his face and he clapped Jackson on the shoulder.

"Now that we've got all that out of the way, where is this angel I've heard about? I want to meet her," Del asked.

Noah clutched his heart with one hand and scooped up burgers onto a platter with the other. "Ah, Miss Julia. She's a sweet thing."

Jackson's face lit up. "She is, isn't she?" He leaned forward and nodded toward the yard. "There she is. With one of her favorite people."

Del followed Jackson's gaze to where Stella and Del's sisters stood. His heart stopped when his gaze landed on Addison holding a little girl with long blonde hair streaming down her little back. Addison swung her from side to side until the girl grabbed her face in her little hands and rubbed noses with her, causing Addison to throw her head back with laughter.

Something gripped his heart seeing her interact with the little girl. If he hadn't left, would that have been *their* little girl she held?

Shit. There was no doubt in his mind that there would be little Reynolds babies running around with blond hair and Addison's green eyes. The ache in his heart nearly took his breath away. He'd walked away from all he ever wanted. Addison, family, kids.

The thought of going back to LA to a beautiful but soulless beach house and the traveling from town to town, seeing other families come together left him cold. It was no longer want he wanted. He wanted everything he'd left behind.

All the *what ifs* and *could haves* had no place in the now. He'd do well to remember that.

He quickly drained his water, trying to wash away the dry mouth he'd just acquired.

"Come on, I'll introduce you." Jackson's voice was far away, but Del managed to move his feet and follow him down to where the group of women stood.

"Aunt Addie, can you please, please toss me like you used to?"

"Julia, you're a big girl now. Aunt Addie can't toss you anymore," Jackson admonished when they approached the group.

Julia twisted around to look at her father, a pout settled on her tiny rosebud mouth. "Mommy used to do it."

Jackson stiffened next to Del. Addison looked over Julia's head at Jackson, her brow furrowed.

Del didn't know the whole story with Jackson and his ex-wife. All he knew was a year ago Lydia decided motherhood wasn't for her. She'd packed up and left with no forwarding address. No one in the family had heard from her since.

Del stepped forward. "Your Aunt Addie may not be able to toss you, but I bet if you gave me a chance, I could. Wanna try?"

Julia regarded him with suspicion. Del's breath caught. This tiny little thing could easily pass for Addison's daughter. "Who are you?"

He gave her his best Hollywood smile. "I'm Del. Your dad and aunt are friends of mine."

She looked at Addison, then back to Del. "Do you pull Aunt Addie's hair? Because Timmy Jacobs says he's my friend but then pulls my hair all the time when we play on the playground. Then I kick him in the shins."

"Julia!" Addison exclaimed.

"Baby girl, what did we talk about?" Jackson asked, his tone long-suffering.

Del withheld the laughter that bubbled in his chest. He leaned close, eye to eye with the little girl. Davenport green eyes looked back at him.

He didn't recall much about Lydia—other than wondering what Jackson saw in the vapid woman—from the one time he'd met her, but he remembered red hair. It seems little Julia didn't get much from her mother in the looks department.

"No, I don't pull hair, but," he leaned in closer and lowered his voice, "I'd kick Timmy in the shins, too, if I were you." He winked at her and she giggled shyly, leaning her head on Addison's chest.

Del held out his hands. "How about that toss?"

Julia hesitated before lifting her head and looking at Jackson, a questioning look on her face. Del turned his head to Jackson, who nodded his consent.

Julia launched herself at Del, who caught her against his chest. She smelled of sunshine, soap, and faintly of Addison's perfume. With one thin arm wrapped around his neck, Julia pulled back and tilted her head. "How high can you throw me? Because my daddy can toss me pretty high."

Del glanced at Jackson, who looked at the ground to hide a smug smile. "Challenge accepted," Del muttered under his breath. He shot Julia a grin. "Well, he is your dad and dads always toss the best, but I'm pretty good, too." He moved his hands into place under her armpits. "You ready?"

Julia nodded vigorously. "Yeah!"

"On three, okay? One...two..."

"Three!" Julia shouted.

Del tossed her into the air, blonde hair flying, her white dress billowing. Her screaming giggles rent the air. When she came back down, Del was ready to catch her in his arms.

As expected, Julia wasn't satisfied with just one time and the cries of "Again, again!" kept Del and his arms busy for a few minutes. He thanked the Lord above his muscles behaved today and he was able to easily play with the child who somehow had already stolen his heart. How the hell did she do it?

"Alright, Julia. That's enough. Let's give Del a break," Jackson broke in.

Julia pouted when Del set her on her sandal-clad feet. "But Daddy..."

"What do you say to Del?"

She spun around, tips of her long hair brushing his legs. Wrapping her arms around his waist, she looked up at him with big green eyes—eyes he was a complete sucker for—and a sweet smile. "Thank you, Del. You're really good at the tosses. Just like my daddy."

Del's heart melted. Clearing his throat, he smiled and ruffled her hair. "You're welcome."

"I heard Ms. Stella has some homemade ice cream," Jackson said. "We should get some before it's all gone."

Julia's eyes widened and she ran over to Stella, her tiny hands folded under her pointed chin in a pleading stance. "Oh, Ms. Stella, can I have some, please? Is it vanilla?"

His mother leaned down and hugged Julia. "Of course you can. And yes, it's vanilla."

"Yay! Thank you, Ms. Stella." She ran over and grabbed her father's hand, trying to drag him across the yard to the area where a small ice cream bar was set up. "Come on, Daddy!"

Sliding his hands into the front pockets of his shorts, Del turned to Addison with a smile on his face. "That was fun. She's cute as hell."

Addison grinned, watching her brother and niece across the yard. "Jackson has his hands full with her. Julia's totally fearless."

It crossed Del's mind that Julia's aunt liked being tossed in the air when she was a cheerleader in high school. His body tightened at the memory of her in a short, tiny uniform and all the times he'd gotten her out of said uniform. He settled his gaze on her face. "Reminds me of someone else I know."

"Jackson's always been fearless, that's for sure."

"I wasn't talking about Jackson."

She looked back at him before looking away. "I've never been fearless or brave about anything in my life."

The disparaging tone in her voice pissed him off. She didn't have a clue her worth. And his dumb ass had played a part in her believing that lie.

"Hey," he put his index finger under her chin and turned her face toward him. Her green eyes were stark against her skin. "Don't say that. You're one of the strongest women I know. You took over a company after losing your parents, the whole town loves you, you have a say in what happens around here, and you know who did that? You did. All by yourself." He dropped his hand, shoving it back in his pocket. "If that's not brave, I don't know what is. I mean it, Addie. You're amazing."

She stared at him, a stricken look in her eyes. He cursed inwardly and rubbed the back of his neck, not sure what to say next.

He sighed. "Look, I—"

Addison stood on her tiptoes and kissed him. It was a brief, firm kiss, her lips soft under his. It was a simmering heat but held the promise of something more.

When she dropped back down on her feet, she smiled at him, making his knees weak.

"What was that?" he asked, his throat dry as the desert.

"That was for you being my friend," she said softly.

"After all that's happened between us? I don't know why."

"Because you're my friend. Always have been. Even when I hated you."

Her *friend*. In spite of the hot kisses they'd shared, she was still keeping him in the friend zone.

He needed to touch her. He needed to keep her an arm's length away. He had to slow down his pounding heart. He could be her friend. Right?

Right. At least until she realized they would always be more than friends. He could wait her out. Until then...

He tossed an arm around her shoulders and they began to walk across the yard. "On that note, in the spirit of friendly competition, I challenge you to a round of cornhole." He gave her a sidelong glance. "Think you can take me?"

She looked up at him, a gleam in her eye. "Challenge accepted."

looking out for a friend

"SHE'S OUT FOR THE COUNT." The lawn chair next to hers creaked under the weight of Del sitting down. "And you look like you're not far behind."

Addison opened her eyes and looked over at him, her brain hazy. She glanced down at the top of Julia's head. "How long have we been sitting here?" she asked, her voice low.

"Not long."

"Feels like we've been here a while. She's a hotbox." She shifted slightly, trying not to disturb Sleeping Beauty. Angling her head around, she looked through the quickly dispersing crowd. "Where's Jackson?"

"In the john. He's ready to head out and said he'll come relieve you of Julia in a minute." Del reached out and tugged Julia's dress over her bottom, his strong, manly hand a touching dichotomy to the girly dress. Addison's heart clenched beneath her breastbone. It was an almost subconscious move, Del making sure Julia's bottom was covered. But the whole protective nature of it made her heart stutter. It was like seeing a tatted-up biker guy holding a newborn baby on his bare chest. She swore her ovaries just exploded.

The girl didn't move a muscle other than to breathe. "Are you ready to head out? I mean, once Jackson comes out."

She nodded. "Yeah, I'm exhausted."

"Well, you played hard today, Aunt Addie." Stella walked up with a smile and crouched down next to her chair. With a gentle hand, she rubbed Julia's back. "She is so stinking cute. If I didn't know better, I'd say she was your daughter. She looks a lot like her aunt. The Davenport genes are strong with her."

A knot formed in Addison's throat. She longed for children of her own and once had the crazy notion she and Del would have a family. They'd talked about it when they'd made plans to live happily ever after. But that was before life took them in different directions. It was a sweet notion to think love could conquer all, but the reality was it just wasn't true.

She hazarded a glance at him and found him staring at her with his intense blue eyes. His eyes saw right through her and said he knew exactly what she was thinking. He was the one person in the world who could read her like a book.

All she could do was stare back at him. Even after all these years, all the pain and heartache between them, he still stole her breath and cut straight through all of her defenses.

She wanted him with an intensity that shocked her. And yeah, maybe she needed to end her sex drought. But with Del it would be way more than sex. It always had been and her heart told her it always would be. Even though she was going to get her heart broken again, no doubt about it. But the need to connect with him again on a physical level was overwhelming.

Stella cleared her throat and untangled the little girl's arms away from Addison. "Delaney, honey, why don't you go ahead and get Addie home? It's been a fun day. Long but fun and we're all tired. I'll tell Jackson you said good night."

Addison blinked and tore her gaze away from Del's. "Are you sure?"

Stella lifted the child into her arms as she stood, a practiced move by a longtime mother of many babies. "Absolutely." Del stood. With one arm, Stella held the sleeping girl, and with the other, hugged her second born. "Good night, son. I'll see you in the morning."

"Night, Mom." Del returned her hug.

"Night, Addie. Sleep well." Stella's mouth twitched with a grin before she walked away. Apparently an announcement wasn't needed. It was probably written on her forehead.

I want to have mind-blowing sex with my ex-fiancé. Tonight.

And now his mother of all people knew it. Her skin flushed, but was it because his mother knew or because the man in question was looking down at her like he wanted to devour her?

"Ready?" he asked, holding his hands out to help her up.

The one word held multiple meanings for her and she nodded, placing her hands in his. Together, holding hands, they said their good nights to the remaining holdouts at the party. The knowing looks tossed their way by some of the guests told Addison that the town grapevine would be busy tomorrow morning. Hell, knowing this town, it was probably already all over the secret Facebook group.

They drove to her house in silence, the white noise of the truck's air conditioning and the purr of the engine the only sounds between them. They said their good nights to the remaining holdouts at the party and drove to her house in silence, the white noise of the truck's air conditioning and the purr of the engine the only sounds between them.

The air crackled with electricity, causing Addison to shift in her seat. She leaned her head back and closed her eyes, thinking about the seemingly casual touches from him all day long and his intense stare at her moments ago. Her skin heated even in the cool cabin of the vehicle. She was going to need a cold shower when she got home.

The unvarnished truth was she couldn't resist him. She no longer wanted to and no longer cared that he was leaving when the renovation wrapped up. All she wanted was Del in her bed as soon as possible. Ten years older and wiser, she had no expectations from Del this time.

Except for mind blowing orgasms.

She turned her head and studied his profile. The dashboard lights of the truck cast shadows that danced across his straight nose and the five o'clock shadow covering the strong jaw. Her nails dug into the palms of her hands in an effort not to reach over and run her fingertip down the hollow of his cheek.

Del glanced over at her, his eyes bright as a flame in the darkness. One side of his mouth lifted in a smile. "See something you like?"

Everything about you. She turned her head and focused on the passing landscape outside the wide windshield. "I had fun today. Thanks for inviting me."

He tapped a finger on the steering wheel. "I'm glad you came with me."

"Me, too." Needing a distraction from the desire pooling in her belly, she kept talking. "You're pretty good at cornhole. I don't remember you playing like that before."

He grinned as he pulled into her driveway and stopped. "Let's just say I've been practicing over the last few years. It's one of the preferred games on set."

And there it was. A reminder as to why getting involved with Del again was a bad idea.

She nodded, not sure where to go from here. Other than inside. And because even though she wanted him with every fiber of her being and she was trying to be smart, she'd go in alone. Because the need coursing through her blood was about to kill her, she would head straight to the shower. Maybe she should have ordered that vibrator Amelia told her about…

She shook her head to dislodge those thoughts and put her hand on the door latch. "Well, thanks again for the ride and for inviting me. I enjoyed it."

He nodded. "Of course." The truck went silent and the seatbelt slid up his chest when he unlatched it. "I'll walk you to the door."

Hell, no. That was not a good idea.

Except she didn't say anything, just slid out of the pickup and joined him on the sidewalk leading up to her front porch. Climbing the wide steps together, side by side, she was acutely aware of him and every move he made.

At the door, she reached behind a tall flowerpot and pulled out a brass key. As she slid it into the deadbolt, Del's voice was close behind her.

"You know, that's probably not a great idea. Anyone could find that key and break in."

She glanced over her shoulder and rolled her eyes. "Come on, Del. This is the Ridge. Everyone knows everyone. At least I lock up. Many people still leave the doors unlocked around here." She smirked. "Besides, haven't you seen my dog?"

"Oh, you mean the big lab that would lick a robber to death?"

"Ha ha." She turned the key, pushed open the door, and shooed Murphy out the back door. When she came back into the foyer, Del still stood at the threshold. With a hand on her hip, she sighed. Del looked at her with *that* look again, hands casually shoved into his pockets. Warmth spread low in her belly and the air backed up in her lungs. Still, she needed desperately to appear unaffected, so she tossed back her hair and leveled a stare at him.

"Look, you don't need to worry about me. I can handle myself just fine." It occurred to her that she wasn't just talking about crimes against her or her property. Unless, of course, the crime was wanting a man she had to keep in the friend zone or lose herself once again.

Girl, you'll find yourself again. You did it before. Jump him. Now. Damn, her devil side was a horny little bitch.

Del pursed his lips and rocked back on his heels. "I have no doubt you can handle yourself just fine. But there's a lot of tourism up here now. It might be wise to, I don't know," he shrugged, putting the muscles under his shirt into play, "get one of those doorbells with a camera. Lock your doors."

She crossed her arms over her chest. Del's eyes tracked the movement, but she shoved that feeling of glee right off the cliff. He really needed to go. Watching him all day with her niece, playing games with him, and generally forgetting about all the water under the fucking bridge between them was messing with her mind, her heart, and her hormones. The heat between her legs was going to set her body on fire soon if she didn't do something about it. And yet, still she pushed. His body language told her he was playing it cool, but Del's eyes had always told his secrets. He was worked up as well. If she was going to die from unresolved lust, he was going with her.

She tilted her head and narrowed her eyes. "So, I should consider it looking out for a friend?"

CHAPTER FIFTEEN
the best homecoming

ADDISON STOOD IN THE DOORWAY, arms crossed over her shapely tits.

He wanted to peel her out of that little excuse of a dress and drag his tongue over the nipples he could see outlined faintly beneath the stretchy material.

Desire coiled in his belly, begging to spring free. For reasons he could never understand, her sassiness had always been a turn-on.

He had to get the hell out of there and soon.

She tilted her head and shifted her stance, her slender hands dropping to her hips. "So, I should consider it looking out for a friend?"

He couldn't take it anymore. He was tired of fighting her, tired of resisting.

Del closed the gap between them and took her face in his hands. "No, consider it looking out for my lover."

He crushed his lips to hers and took what he'd wanted for weeks. No, check that. Years. Ever since he'd left and made the damn fool decision to stay away. Although they'd shared a kiss a couple of days before, there was a keen, desperate edge to this kiss. It was as though he wouldn't be able to get enough of her.

He feared if he lived to be a hundred years old, he'd never get enough of her.

Moaning, she opened her mouth under his and twined her arms around his neck, pulling him closer. He dropped his arms and wrapped them around her waist. Never breaking the kiss, he picked her up against him, feet dangling, and walked farther into the foyer. He kicked the door shut behind him.

As he released his grip on her waist, little by little her body slid down his, branding his skin beneath his shirt. When her feet touched the floor, he tore his lips away from hers and she let her head fall back, giving him access to her slim neck.

As he nibbled his way down it, the sense of urgency and heat grew between them like wildfire.

He caught her gaze when she lowered her head and held it. Hooking a finger into the cleavage of her dress, he pulled the stretchy fabric away from her skin and ducked his head. He laid an open mouth kiss between the lush curves, pulling a moan and shiver from her.

Del peeled the top of the dress down and was rewarded with her full round breasts in the flesh. He murmured his appreciation and leaned down to take a hard nipple into his mouth.

She cried out with pleasure and grabbed handfuls of his shirt at his shoulders, trying to relieve him of it.

He didn't take much time to pleasure himself with her breasts. All he could think about was getting into her, into her wet heat.

He reached an arm over his head and yanked the shirt over it, dropping it to the floor. She ran her hands over the smooth skin of his torso and moaned her appreciation as her fingertips grazed his chiseled abs.

Bent at the knees, he ran his hands up her thighs, and grabbed her ass. He caressed the soft flesh before hitching her up, where she proceeded to wrap her legs around his waist. He turned toward the living room with all intentions of taking her to the couch, but when she came out with, "Fuck me, Del. Please," the couch was too far away. And who was he to say no?

He lowered her to the floor and pinned her between the carpet and his hard chest. She arched her back and groaned when he slid down her body, alternating kisses and love nips on her skin. As he moved lower, he slid the dress down her body until he grew impatient and slid it down her legs. When it hit her ankles, she kicked it away.

The sounds of their heavy breathing mingled with moans and sounds of passionate kisses. The scent of her arousal had him aching with a primal need from head to toe. She was driving him mad with the way she purred and, son of a bitch, her hands were every-damn-where.

She reached out and her long fingers found the waistband of his shorts where she began to work the button, brushing his crotch beneath the fabric. His vision dimmed and he nearly came in his shorts.

"You can't keep doing that or it will be over before it begins." His voice sounded like he'd swallowed broken glass.

Her response was to moan and defy him. Fuck, he had to be sadistic to think that was such a turn-on. Her hands continued to work his fly until she freed him. Her hand was warm on his cock and she moved it up and down in a smooth rhythm that was nearly killing him. Well, at least he'd go happy.

She looked him in the eye with an air of defiance. "Then you better get down to the business of fucking me, right?"

He grinned. "I missed that dirty mouth of yours. You're a naughty girl, Addison Davenport."

"And you love it."

With a groan, he leaned forward and crushed his lips to hers in another heated kiss. Her lips were swollen under his from the assault he'd subjected them to over and over. Jesus, he couldn't get enough of her.

Her tongue swept across his lower lip when he pulled away slightly. "Condom," he mumbled against her lips. He reached for his wallet in his back pocket and tossed it on the carpet beside them. While he shoved his shorts down his legs, Addison palmed the leather and in record time had the silver foil ripped open.

Seconds later, sheathed and ready to go, he pushed the red silk panties to one side, revealing her slick entrance. He slid the head of his dick against her wet heat. Addison arched up toward him with a loud groan. "Delaney Reynolds, don't you dare tease—"

With one deft stroke, he drove inside, filling her completely. It was the best homecoming in the history of homecomings.

He leaned forward with his elbows on either side of her head, holding his weight off her. For a brief moment, they locked eyes but didn't move. Something shifted in his chest and he almost couldn't breathe. When she contracted around him, he withdrew and slid home again. She lifted a hand up to his beside her head and he locked their fingers together. "Delaney," her whisper was tinged with awe and something else he couldn't define.

He moved again and they fell into a rhythm familiar and yet new. It started slow and built with every thrust. She wrapped her arms around his neck and held on while he thrust into her over and over, her moans of his name spurring him on.

They chased each other to the edge of the cliff and when she wrapped her legs around his waist and lifted her hips to meet his, her pussy clenched around his cock. "That's it, baby. Let go," Del murmured, driving into her hot core, causing her to cry out his name and clench around him again.

The tingling at the base of his spine exploded and when he came inside her, he saw stars. Buried inside her, she pulsed around his cock, milking his orgasm out of him until he felt empty and sated. When they finally stopped coming, they were drenched in sweat and gasping for air.

Del dropped his forehead to hers. "Holy shit," he said between breaths.

"I know."

He chuckled and pulled out of her. "Be right back." A couple of moments later, he walked back into the living room from the bathroom to find Addison laid out like a starfish with her eyes closed and her breathing steady.

With a grin on his face, he picked up his shorts and pulled them on, then grabbed a blanket from the couch. He looked down at her, his fists clenched around the fleece. Her long tresses were fanned out from her head, turning the dark carpet beneath her gold. Her face was relaxed and soft while she snoozed and her long, dark lashes fluttered against her high cheekbones. She shifted her legs and covered her chest with her arms.

Thinking about how those legs were wrapped around his waist and his mouth had covered her nipples with hot kisses mere moments ago made him want to fall into her heat all over again.

And not just because she was stunning in all her long-limbed, golden glory. In his mind, she was a goddess and he was the luckiest bastard in the world to be able to touch her. No, that fact didn't hurt. But it was how she looked playing with her niece, her laugh, her generosity, her loyalty to her family and town, her strength.

Her forgiveness. He didn't deserve her forgiveness. All he deserved was the ass kicking Jackson had given him years ago. After leaving her behind ten years ago, the fact he could be her friend again, much less her lover, blew his mind. But she'd given herself to him again, anyway. Something akin to hope bloomed in his chest.

She moaned softly and her tongue darted out to wet her lips. Her legs pulled into her chest and she shifted onto her side. He squatted down next to her, wrapping the blanket around her, then slid one arm underneath her back and the other under her knees. She curled into him like a child, making his heart ache.

Holding her close, he stood with her in his arms and walked slowly through the shadowy living room and up the stairs to her bedroom.

Moonlight shone through the wall of windows and bathed the bedroom in white light and shadows. Her scent filled the intimate space, warm vanilla mixed with the perfume she'd sprayed on earlier in the day. He crossed to the large four-poster bed and, with her still in his arms, he angled down and yanked back the comforter.

When he laid her on the bed, his arms bracing his weight, her eyes fluttered open, heavy from slumber.

"Delaney." Her voice was raspy. She wiggled one hand from under the fleece blanket and lifted it to stroke his face.

"I'm here, baby." He gripped her hand, bringing it to his lips, kissing her palm.

"Hmmm...that feels good." Her eyes slid closed for a moment before they opened again. "Stay with me."

He looked into her eyes, dark and wide in her face made pale by the moonlight. "I'm not going anywhere. Promise."

The smile she gave him was like a punch in the gut. "Good."

She twined her arms around his neck and pulled him down to her. Desire ran hot in his blood when their lips met in a soft kiss. He wanted to lower his body to hers, slip inside her, and pin her to the bed.

With Herculean effort, he pulled away from her. "Let's get some sleep. You're exhausted."

She frowned slightly, then her pretty rosebud mouth formed an O. "Murphy's still outside."

"I'll go let him in."

Del padded back downstairs, let Murphy in, and gave him a rawhide. "Stay in your bed tonight, buddy. I've got your mistress covered." Murphy wagged his tail and gave his head a shake, his collar rattling like keys. With the rawhide in his mouth, he walked over to his dog bed and plopped down.

Satisfied Addison's canine child was occupied, Del went back upstairs. She gave him a sleepy smile when he came into the room. "Thank you."

"My pleasure." His body tightened when she turned over. Her bare back curved down to the flare of her hips and he wanted to trail a line of hot kisses from her neck all the way down to the top of her ass. She reached behind her and patted the bed. "Take off your clothes and lie with me."

He stretched out beside her and pulled the covers over both of them. With one arm, he wrapped around her slender waist and pulled her against his bare chest. She wiggled against him and he grit his teeth against the growing hard-on he got from having her body up against his. He held his breath until she went still.

Within minutes, her breathing had steadied and she was fast asleep again. He lay there, wrapped around her, when the realization hit him like a two-by-four between his eyes.

He was madly, deeply in love with her. Again.

And he had no idea what he was going to do about it, or how she'd even react to it. With a frown, the realization he had some decisions to make took hold. But not now, not tonight, or even tomorrow.

Closing his eyes, he pulled her closer and joined her in sleep.

CHAPTER SIXTEEN

difficult to breathe

ADDISON BLINKED against the early morning sun that shone through the curtains about the same time she realized a well-muscled arm was roped around her waist. The warm, solid body behind her was a welcome sensation and one she'd missed.

A blush crept up her neck when she thought about the way Del had dragged her to the floor the night before and proceeded to do just as she asked. He also granted her request a couple of times during the night. At the same time, she couldn't wipe the smile off her face. Or keep the warmth from spreading in her lower belly and between her thighs.

His breathing tickled the tendrils of hair around her ear. Her nerves tingled with desire that started to build again and looked for a way to detonate under his touch. Even though it'd been a long time for her, Del had always been able to push her over that edge with ease. Ten years and a heartbreak hadn't dimmed that desire.

What did it say about her that she was as content as a cat lying in the sunshine right now? The fact that she wanted to stay right here in his arms for the foreseeable future was something she didn't want to think about right now. She didn't want to think about the fact that one time with him again made her crave more with each breath.

"Morning, beautiful." Del's voice was deep and rich in her ear, causing the warming in her body to turn to a full-on furnace.

"Good morning." With a smile playing on her lips, she pushed her hips back slightly against the erection that was like warm steel along her backside.

He moaned, rubbing the tip of his nose along the back of her neck. He shifted his hips to meet hers. "Hmmm…God, you're sweet," he whispered. "I've missed the smell of your skin,"—his hand slid up and caressed her breast—"your smooth, silky skin."

"I missed you too," she replied breathlessly, hooking an arm around his neck and arching to be as close as she could.

A shrill ring shattered the moment.

Ignore it.

"Fuck. That's mine," Del said darkly. "Someone better be dead."

When he rolled over to the edge of the bed, the cool air raised goosebumps all over her skin. She whimpered at the loss of contact and squeezed her eyes shut. Damn it all to hell. Not a good sign.

The bed jostled with his movement. "Shit, I'm sorry. I have to take this. Hey, Teri, what's up?"

Addison rolled over and levered up on one elbow. His back was a thing of beauty, all long lines and sinewy muscles rippling under his skin as he moved. Flames of desire licked at the edges of her sanity. She needed her hands on him again. Needed him to feel the near-frenzied lust that threatened to swallow her whole.

She needed to turn the tables on him a bit.

Let's see how well he can concentrate.

A smile played on her lips as she slid across the bed and moved up behind him. At the base of his neck, she laid a featherlight kiss on his warm skin. He jolted, his spine straightening. The fingers wrapped around the phone tightened, but he didn't break stride in the conversation. When he relaxed again, she kissed him again, a couple of inches lower from the first kiss.

She drew a line down the center of his back, her touch light and slow. Her mouth followed the path her finger drew, her lips playing on his skin lightly. His spine arched into her touch, and his voice took on a slightly husky tone, even though she paid no attention to the words he said. Pleasure bloomed in her chest knowing that even after a night of burning-the-sheets-up sex, she could still have him sit up and take notice.

When she reached the base of his spine, she slid a hand over his upper thigh and down into his lap where, to her delight, she found him hard and ready to go.

"Yeah, I hear you," he said into the phone after inhaling sharply at her touch. The warning glance he sent her only served to make her snicker. "Give me ten." He narrowed his eyes at Addison. "Better make that twenty." He ended the call and tossed his phone to the floor, lunging for her.

Laughter bubbled out of her on a whoosh as Del pinned her to the bed, her wrists on either side of her head. "Del, we don't have time for this."

"You started it." He growled and nipped love bites down her neck.

Her breath caught in her throat as he moved lower and flicked a nipple with his tongue. She was beyond wet and ready before he moved to the other nipple.

"But…" She couldn't breathe, much less think when he had his hands, his mouth all over her.

His deep blue eyes met hers, darkened with lust and all sorts of wicked thoughts. He shifted his hips, and his hard length pressed against her thigh.

"Don't worry, I think we have plenty of time." Del reached for a condom on the nightstand.

"I couldn't agree more." She spread her legs, primed and ready for him to shift and slide inside. He lifted one of her legs up to his shoulder and slid his cock into her wet heat. At that angle, he filled her and was so deep it made her pant with need. Words were useless, and her brain couldn't form any that made sense anyhow.

Del moaned when he withdrew and slid home again. "Fuck, you're so hot." His hips moved faster against her, and she fisted the sheets under her hands to keep herself from flying apart too soon. He leaned forward and put his hands on either side of her head, his hips never breaking rhythm. She held onto his forearms, riding out the storm that raged inside them.

It was a heated and sated thirty minutes later before Del made his way out the door.

* * *

Addison didn't want to admit she'd watched the clock from the time Del left to when she would see him next. Today was her day to shoot some of her scenes with him as the owner of the house and the interview portions with Teri. So, while she would get to see him, it was in a professional capacity.

She smoothed down her hair in the mirror and straightened her clothes. This project was more than just her own house. She was sharing it with Del, Jackson, and the whole freaking town of Madison Ridge. There was a reputation and an image to uphold, so being sloppy wouldn't do but neither would being too serious and unapproachable. The sleeveless blouse and skinny jeans paired with ankle boots were casual without being too much.

Addison made it a point to always look put together, was always confident in her choices. But at that moment, her self-confidence had abandoned her.

"When have you ever worried so much about how you looked?" she asked her reflection. The image in the mirror didn't provide any insight. Sighing, she added silver hoops and a matching long necklace to the ensemble and called it done.

She let Murphy out, and as much as she wanted to walk, she decided to drive to the worksite. It wasn't far, but late May in Georgia could be hot, even in the mountains. Showing up a sweaty mess for the camera didn't lend to the put-together look she was striving for. Her nerves were going to provide enough of a challenge—she didn't need weather to make it worse.

She laid a hand on her stomach trying to ward off the butterflies that had set up camp there permanently. When she arrived on the square, she parked in front of The Sweet Spot and headed in for an iced coffee.

"Good morning, sunshine!" Emma Reynolds—soon to be Kavanaugh—called out from behind the counter.

Addison smiled. She always liked Del's cousin and was thrilled she was doing so well on her road to recovery. "Morning, Em. You're cheerful this morning." She tilted her head as she saw the apron Emma wore. "Don't you have a winery to run?"

Emma nodded. "I do, but since most of Amelia's help are college students and most of them have headed home for the summer, she tends to be short-staffed at times. So, I come in to help her out when she needs it." She winked at Addison. "My boss lets me do whatever makes me happy, so it works out well."

Addison laughed. "I always knew Shane was a smart man. Happy wife, happy life."

Emma's face lit up at the mention of her fiancé's name. "Not his wife just yet, but soon. It will be here before I know it!"

"The offer is still open, Em. If you need help, please let me know."

Emma blew out a breath. "You might be sorry you asked because there are things you can help me with."

"Well, just let me know. You've got my number."

Emma nodded. "Now, enough about me. What can I get you?"

Addison looked over the board behind Emma's head. "I'll take a cold brew Americano, two creams, one sugar."

"Sure thing." The bell to the door rang, and the noise level rose as four older women, all dressed in various colored tracksuits and fanny packs, filed through the door talking a mile a minute. The smell of Aqua Net waged war with the coffee aroma.

Addison bit back a sigh. The Poker Posse. The gossip mill was alive and well as long as these ladies were still around. And don't even bother trying to play poker with them. If it weren't for the tourists and the oddball local masochist, these four would never have anyone new to play Texas Hold 'Em with.

She prayed she didn't have *why yes, I did have mind-blowing sex with my ex for the last twenty-four hours thankyouverymuch* written on her forehead. It would be all over town before they left the bakery with their daily coffee and baked goods. Addison swore those women had a hidden beacon that passed out news all over town.

"Good morning, ladies," Emma raised her voice over the noise to get their attention. "What can I get y'all today? Your usual?"

"Well, of course, dear. What else would we have?" Faye Casteel, unspoken ringleader of the quartet, said with a chuckle.

Emma's lips quirked in a smile. "Right. Let me get those for you."

She busied herself with getting coffee and danish, and four sets of eyes turned to Addison.

"Well, hello, Addison." AnnaMae, one-half of the Goodwin twins, drawled with a smile, walking toward her. Her dentures gleamed white, and today, her and her twin sister EllaMae's hair matched their suits. Pink and lavender, respectively. "Aren't you such a pretty thing. I haven't seen you in so long."

The woman had literally seen Addison about a week ago. Still, she smiled. "Why, thank you, Mrs. Goodwin."

AnnaMae rolled her eyes. "Please, child. Call me AnnaMae. Mrs. Goodwin was my mother-in-law and she's long dead. May God rest her soul."

All four crossed their chests like the good little Catholics they weren't.

"I hear you're working with your ex-love. How's that going?" EllaMae said, sidling up beside her sister. She sighed, a hand over her heart. "That Delaney Reynolds sure is a handsome devil."

Clarice Martin raised a brow, a frown on her thin lips. "Those camera crews keep causing a traffic jam on my street."

Addison held back a laugh. If there were more than three cars on the road, Clarice thought there was "too much traffic." She may have been wearing a bright yellow tracksuit, but her disposition was anything but sunny.

"I'm sorry about that, Clarice. I'll see what Del can do about making sure they don't jam up the road, okay?"

Clarice sniffed, then nodded. It was the best she'd get from the woman.

EllaMae leaned closer to Addison. "Those sparks are still there, aren't they?"

"Well, I—"

"I swear, he looks better than he did when he left here." AnnaMae fanned herself. "If only I was fifty years younger."

EllaMae elbowed her twin with a grin. "Then he could have both of us. Now that would have been a fine ménage à trois."

The two of them giggled, and Addison's eyes widened in horror before she looked over at Emma, whose jaw was on the floor.

Had the twins always been so…horny?

Ew.

"For God's sake, EllaMae, AnnaMae. Leave the girl alone and stop being hussies," Clarice Martin grumbled. "Get your stuff and let's go."

Faye paid for the items and then passed out the coffees and small pink boxes to the other women. Clarice shuffled the twins out the door, muttering something about old bats losing their minds.

On her way out, Faye stopped and laid a hand on a still shell-shocked Addison's arm. "Stella told me about the project and how y'all are finishing out both of your fathers' dreams. I think it's a wonderful thing."

Addison didn't mention that they hadn't exactly had a choice or how grateful she was now about the project bringing her and Del back together.

At least for earth-shattering sex anyway.

"Thank you, Faye. I appreciate that."

Faye nodded, a knowing gleam in her eye. "Your daddies would be proud." Her faded blue eyes glanced up and smiled. "Well, speak of that handsome devil."

The bell on the door rang as Addison glanced over her shoulder.

And fire ignited in her instantly when Del smiled at Faye and held the door open for her. She walked out, patting his cheek as she passed, and waved her goodbyes.

Shane Kavanaugh came in behind Del, and if Addison thought Emma's face shone before, the smile she had on her face now could light up the entire Eastern Seaboard and then some.

Damn, these two men side by side were enough to give a girl permanent wet panty syndrome.

Shane leaned against the counter next to Addison and had a smile that matched Emma's on his face. He only had eyes for the dark-haired woman behind the counter. "There's my beautiful woman."

Emma blushed and after starting the coffee machine, crossed to the counter and leaned over it to meet him for a quick kiss. He turned his blue stare to Addison. "Hey, Addison. Good to see you again. How are you?"

"Doing well." She shifted her gaze to Del, who stood beside Shane. "Hey, Del."

"Hey, Addie." The smile on his face said it was good to see her again as well. But preferably naked. Her cheeks burned under his stare.

"What can I get you guys?" Emma asked.

"My usual, babe," Shane answered.

"I'm going with straight up, good old-fashioned coffee, black. I was up all night and need the caffeine." His gaze drifted to Addison's for a moment with a small curve of one side of his mouth before focusing back on Emma.

"Coming up." Emma walked away to complete the orders, and Shane asked Del a question about a mutual friend they had in California. Addison tuned out and picked up a copy of *The Ridge Herald*. The words in front of her were just a bunch of letters because she was too busy watching Del from under her lashes.

His arms were crossed over his chest, the muscles in his forearms on full display. His fingers tapped against his biceps, and she couldn't help but think about what those fingers had been doing just a few hours before. He wore a closefitting black polo shirt today, probably for the filming they would do later. It was tucked into faded jeans that hugged his hips, hips that had spent most of the night between her legs.

Good God almighty, girl. Addison shifted her stance, heat crawling along her skin. Her mouth watered, and she cleared her throat slightly to keep from drooling. When her gaze headed back up to his face, she found him staring back at her, a small smile playing on his lips before he nodded at something Shane said. Damn the man. There was no doubt he knew what she was thinking.

"Here ya go, Addie." Emma's voice snapped Addison's focus back to the present, thankfully. Much more of that kind of thinking and she'd be a puddle of need in the middle of the place.

"Thanks," Addison murmured.

"And here's yours, Del." Emma slid the two cups across the

counter. "Yours will be ready in a minute, babe. Hey, did you find out about that new order of cabernet?"

As the happy couple chatted about their joint venture, Del shifted his stance to be closer to Addison, leaning against the glass cabinet beside her. "Have I told you lately how beautiful you are?" His voice was low and danced along her skin, causing her to shiver.

She kept her eyes on the newspaper and sipped on her straw. "Not since about four o'clock this morning, but I never tire of hearing it," she responded low enough only he could hear. A glance at Emma and Shane told her they weren't paying attention to them anyway.

"Those pants you have on do amazing things to your legs. All those curves. It's going to be tricky to work with you nearby."

She smiled into her straw. "Stop it, Del."

"I can't help it—you're driving me insane just standing there."

Out of the corner of her eye, she watched as he shifted himself covertly, and she bit her lip to keep from giggling. She glanced at the other couple and saw they were still in conversation. "So, um…this thing between us…"

"Is insanely hot."

She pursed her lips to keep them from curving into a smile and tried to slow down her racing heart. "Yes, but what about working with the show? I think we should keep it professional, don't you?" She sipped on her straw and raised her head to look into his eyes.

Which was so not a good idea.

His eyes were nearly navy with desire and watching her lips suck on the straw. The pulse in his throat beat against his tanned skin, and the fact she had that kind of effect on him while standing in a coffee shop was a heady feeling. "If that's what you want, sure." His voice was rough and nonchalant.

"I just don't want any backlash for either one of us. From the town or from the network."

He blinked and looked down, his lips in a half smirk. "Well, you know as well as I do, the town has been talking since I got back into town. We've been seen together, so they'll have a fall wedding all planned out for us."

Seeing that she'd already thought about it, Addison had to concede his point. Still, although they weren't wrong, it was only speculation until she or Del verified it.

"As far as the network goes," Del continued, "some would see it as a ratings grab. On the other hand, we're not that kind of show. Teri already knows we have history. I told her. But she's Ms. Discreet so she'll never say a word about it. It wouldn't help her, anyway." He looked back at her. "But yeah, we can keep it on the down low if that makes you feel better."

Something in the way he said it didn't make her feel better. It made her feel like the bad guy, but she didn't understand why. "Thanks, Del. I appreciate it."

He nodded and glanced over to see Emma and Shane occupied with something on Shane's phone. The shop was empty otherwise. Del turned his head back to her and let his gaze travel back down her body. He moved behind her and lowered his head so his mouth brushed against her ear. "Do you want to secretly meet me in the bathroom? Let me see what color your panties are today?"

Breathing became the hardest thing Addison had ever done. Before she could respond, the bell over the door rang, snagging Emma's attention and breaking their bubble.

"Good morning," Emma greeted a young man as she finished up Shane's coffee. When she handed Shane's coffee to him, she tilted her head and narrowed her eyes at Addison. "Are you feeling okay, Addie? You look flushed."

Son of a bitch, she needed to get out of there and get it together. She would be spending the whole day with Del, and she needed to be the calm, cool Addison Davenport people knew her to be. Not the wanton woman that wanted to do nothing more than spend the day in bed with her ex-fiancé—and work him out of her system once and for all.

"Um, yeah. I'm fine. How much do I owe you?"

"I got it." Del stepped forward and dropped a couple of bills on the counter. "That should cover all three. Keep the change."

Emma nodded. "Thanks, Del." She tossed the change in the tip jar and leaned forward to share a lingering kiss with Shane. "Love you, babe," she murmured.

"Love you too, peaches."

They said their goodbyes and left. Addison started toward her car while Shane and Del did the handshake, half hug thing guys do. She turned on the AC full blast and sighed when the cool air hit her over-heated skin. A tap on the passenger window made her jump, and she turned to find Del bent over looking at her.

"Are you okay?" he asked, his brow furrowed in concern. "I mean," —he dropped his voice low and sensual—"I know what I was thinking as I watched you trying not to watch me, but…"

Uncertainty tinged his voice, and it made Addison's heart hitch. She cleared her throat and looked out the front windshield before she could speak. "I'm fine. I was just thinking about last night." She raised her eyes to his and found he wasn't grinning like he'd taken some sort of prize. She expected that. What she didn't expect was the seriousness mixed with desire in his eyes and his mouth in a set line. He simply stared at her for a few moments, making her grateful the AC blew on her. That stare alone made her hot under the collar despite the cold interior.

"Me too." He finally broke off the stare and looked away, rapping his knuckles against the side of the door. "I'll see you at the site. Filming will be starting soon, and Teri's a real stickler for keeping on time."

She nodded. "Right, I'm headed there now."

He nodded and rose to his full height before walking toward his truck parked a couple of spots behind her.

She signaled and then pulled out into traffic, making her way around the center of town toward the house. As it came into view, she glanced in the rearview mirror, finding Del in his truck a little way behind her, and she blew out a deep breath.

Working next to him after the night they spent together was going to be a challenge, but she could handle it.

It was the rest of her life without him she had no answers for.

CHAPTER SEVENTEEN
ignorant heart

SINCE IT WAS FILMING DAY, Del wouldn't get much done as far as the actual work was concerned. Sure, the crews they hired would continue and things would work out on time and hopefully on budget. But over the years, he'd grown increasingly dissatisfied with being on camera at the expense of not doing what he loved—carpentry.

It also meant he didn't see a whole lot of Addison. She had some of her interview portions to film in addition to her parts with him. It was finally time to get those shots done. Del paced the open area that was still just a skeletal maze of two-by-fours but would end up being the main area for historical pieces. They were waiting on Addison to finish in makeup before they could film. A few minutes later, Addison strode through the opening where the double front doors would eventually be and crossed over to where he stood.

As gorgeous as she was in full makeup for the cameras, Del preferred her everyday look. That's where he found her most stunning.

Scratch that. Her face after coming down from an orgasm he coaxed from her was where she was so beautiful it hurt.

His eyes traveled down her form as she walked toward him. Yeah, those jeans had some hella hot power to them. With the black sleeveless number she had on, the long silver chain that fell between her breasts, and the black boots, she looked sexy, elegant, and a little edgy.

What he wouldn't give to peel her out of those clothes right now. He willed his cock to stand down and behave.

She shot him a sheepish smile and looked at the cameras around them before settling her gaze on him. "Sorry I'm late. Do they always put so much makeup on?" she whispered. "I feel like all I've done is get pancake put on my face all day. I feel like it's melting off."

He chuckled and brushed a lock of hair behind her ear. "On closeups like today, they are more liberal with the makeup." His heart thumped against his ribs as he moved closer to her. "Everything go okay today with your segments?" The need to protect her drummed in his veins and if anyone so much as made her the least bit uncomfortable, heads would roll.

She nodded. "Yeah, it was fine. Teri was great in making me feel comfortable. I mean, we've done some scenes but the ones where I was by myself had me a little nervous."

Del nodded, having no doubt she handled the interviews like a boss in spite of nerves. "Good." He rubbed his hands together. "Ready to get this done?"

She nodded and rubbed her hands down her thighs, drawing his eyes down and making him think back to how those thighs had been wrapped around him earlier today.

Shit. He really needed to get his hormones under control.

"Alright. Teri," he raised his voice over the low din of voices and equipment noise around them, "we're ready to go."

Teri nodded and called out to the crew, who kicked it into motion and set up the equipment to film Del and Addison as they walked through the house. In this segment, Del would be showing Addison the work they'd completed and an area he had to change up due to an issue with a pipe in the powder room off the hallway. She followed him through and asked questions, while he explained things. Del's pulse bumped with excitement at how well they worked together and made jokes with one another. It was easy and after a little while, Del actually forgot a camera followed them around, filming the banter and action between them.

In his mind's eye, he saw the two of them working side by side, renovating homes, working together, but without the cameras, the lights, and the cords running like snakes across the floor.

"Cut!" Teri called out where the segment was paced to end. "Guys, that was awesome! We did that shit all in one take." She shook her head, her eyes wide. "I can't remember the last time that happened on this show or any show I've worked on for that matter." She waved them over to where she stood behind the camera. "Check it out. Gary, play it back."

Through a small screen, Del and Addison huddled behind Teri and Gary, watching themselves go through the last segments they'd filmed. Addison gasped and then a huge smile split her face. "Oh, look at that. I haven't watched myself played back before."

Del shifted and put his lips near her ear. "Everyone always said we looked good together."

She smiled and ducked her head before looking over her shoulder at him, locking eyes with him. Their lips were so close her breath stirred against his skin. "We do, don't we?"

Her husky voice went straight to his cock and he wanted to haul her into his trailer and listen to that voice call out his name while he did naughty things to her.

Instead, he blew out a breath and tilted his head. Del had to admit Addison was made for the camera and they looked damn good on it. If he could ever convince her to work with him on a show…

Nope. There was a reason he was leaving a show he loved and starting over. Sure, the schedule and travel were grueling, but he thrived on adventure and always had. His reason for quitting had everything to do with the illness invading his body. The fucking syndrome was temperamental and showed its hand when he least expected it. He wasn't willing to go so far as to hurt himself or someone else—which was a distinct possibility—just to feed his ego and adventurous side. He'd just have to find it another way.

"Del?"

Addison's voice brought him back to the now and he found her looking at him with a brow raised in a *hello, Earth to Del* gesture. "Sorry, what did you say?"

"I said, I'm headed out." She gestured with a thumb over her shoulder. "Teri said I was done for the day and I need to go by my office."

Teri glanced away from the screen for a minute to where they stood. "Yeah, you guys did great. No need to reshoot this part."

He nodded, arms crossed over his chest. "That's good news. I've got a couple of things to check on here." He turned on his boots to face Addison. "I have something to ask you. Can I walk you to your car?"

"Yeah, I need to go get my purse from the makeup trailer."

"I'll meet you out there then." She nodded and gave him a slow, saucy smile as she walked away.

An elbow to his ribs drew his gaze away from Addison's backside as she walked away. "Ouch, what the hell?"

Teri smirked up at him. "So, you two are an item again?"

Del pursed his lips and glanced down at his producer. "What makes you say that?"

"Oh, I don't know. Maybe the way you're licking your lips and looking at her ass."

He snorted and rolled his eyes. "That doesn't mean we're together. I'm just admiring the scenery."

Teri tapped a finger on her lips. "Or maybe it's the chemistry between you two on camera." She fanned herself. "You guys are going to melt television screens all over the nation."

Del sighed, wishing Teri would for once mind her own fucking business. Though he had to admit this may very well fall under the header of her business. "Always the show," he muttered under his breath. "If you're done with me for the day, I have some other things to take care of around here."

She nodded and turned to walk away. "Yep. Tomorrow morning we have some more we need to do with you in the house."

"I'll be here. Every day until it's done." He walked out the opening of the front door, saying hello to a few of the filming crew as he passed, but his destination was clear. He made a beeline for Addison's car where she leaned against the hood, her fingers flying over the screen of her phone.

As he approached, she lifted her head and met his eyes. Her smile was quick and easy, her eyes lighting up to a bright green. Pleasure filled his chest seeing the happiness in her and knowing he put it there. A smile curved his mouth and without a care to who saw it, he cradled her face in his hands and crushed her lips to his.

Fuck keeping it on the down low.

Her surprised gasp was muffled by his mouth on hers, but half a second later, she leaned into the kiss and wrapped her arms around his neck. Del tilted his head, taking the kiss deeper, their tongues sliding together. Warmth spread through Del's limbs as the kiss continued and Addison pressed her body against him.

When he finally pulled away, he dropped his forehead to hers, their breaths short and mingling between them. Her long, dark eyelashes swept across her cheeks and his thumbs brushed against her skin. The ache in his chest grew. In every way, this woman appealed to him.

"Are you free tonight?" he asked, his voice low and rough. She nodded, her neck rippling as she swallowed. In spite of the work and noise going on around them, Del only heard his own heartbeat and Addison's breathing in his ears.

"Good. Pick you up at seven thirty?"

She nodded again and lifted her gaze to his, a smile kicking up one side of her full, kiss-bruised lips. "Where are you taking me?"

"It's a surprise."

She pulled back slightly and raised a brow. "Now how will I know what to wear?"

He chuckled, contentment warming his heart. "I was thinking we could go out on the lake. So casual works for me." He tilted his head, a wicked thought of short, skimpy sundresses crossing his mind. "Got any more sexy, little sundresses?"

Addison bit her lip, a smile sneaking in behind it. "I think that can be arranged." Her phone dinged and she looked down at the screen, a line forming between her brows. "As much as I'd love to stay and make out with you, I need to go." She rose up on her toes and kissed him quick on the lips.

"Should I bring my swimsuit?"

The thought of her in a skimpy bikini with all of her luscious curves on display had him instantly hard. *Jesus, chill out, horn dog.*

"You won't need your suit tonight, Addison. It will just be another layer of clothing in my way." Satisfaction was his when her eyes dilated with desire. He lowered his head and dropped kisses along her jawline.

"Hmmm...you need to stop, Del." Her phone dinged and she groaned. "As much as I'd love to stay and make out with you, I need to go. Duty calls." She rose up on her toes and kissed him quick on the lips.

With a grimace, he stepped back and walked around to open her door. Once she was settled in, she rolled down the window.

He leaned inside and stole one more kiss, lightly nipping her bottom lip as he pulled back. "See ya tonight."

Smiling, he rose up to his full height and tapped the roof of the car twice before walking away. As he walked back into the house, he questioned whether or not he should have asked her on another date. He couldn't stay when all this was over, they both knew it.

The real question was, did his heart know it?

CHAPTER EIGHTEEN

have you not learned a damn thing?

"I ALWAYS FORGET how beautiful it is out here this time of day." Addison sipped wine from a stemless glass and sighed. With her eyes closed, she leaned against the back of the Adirondack chair and lifted her head to the breeze. The cooling air smelled of Addie's perfume, a light, fresh, delicate scent that never failed to drive him crazy. Del admired the way the wind tangled through her long, golden-red tresses so much like the colors of the sunset in front of them.

He reached over and played with the ends of her hair. "We could take the boat out."

She smiled at him. "Maybe another time. Besides, I didn't bring my suit." She tapped a finger on the rim of the glass and looked up at the sky. "If I recall, you said it would just be another layer of clothing in your way."

Del grinned and glanced over at the red-and-white polka-dot halter top sundress she wore. "I did say that." He reached out and drew a line over the slope of her shoulder and down her arm with his fingertip. Goosebumps dotted her soft skin under his touch. "I appreciate you keeping the clothing to a minimum."

It appeared her tongue was in knots because she simply smiled and kept her stare on the dark expanse of the lake stretched out in front of them.

Del's heart played a rhythm against his sternum. They sat in silence, but the tension in the air between them made breathing in the wide-open space a challenge for him. He wanted nothing more than to peel her out of that little dress that showed off her long legs and bury himself inside her for the night. But he'd promised to cook her dinner and there were things he needed to say to her. Things he wanted to say before they ended up in bed again.

He stood and held out his hand to her. "Dinner should be ready or close to it. Ready to head in?"

Her lips quirked, but she stood. "Can we come back out afterward? It's such a beautiful night."

Del linked their hands together and pulled her close. "We can do whatever you want, beautiful," he murmured against her soft lips before capturing them in a hot kiss that sent a zing all the way down to his toes. She moaned and opened for him even more, her mouth a hot inferno of pleasure he'd happily die in. With her arms wrapped around his neck, she pulled him closer until there was no space between their bodies. His hands slid up into her silky hair, grabbing handfuls in his fists. She moaned against his mouth as he continued his perusal of all the soft curves she was made of and stopped at the flare of her hips.

With a groan, he broke off the kiss and stepped back from the edge of insanity. At least that's where it seemed he had a one-way ticket to if they continued to make out on the dock. He needed to fling himself into the lake just to cool off. He shook his head to clear it of the sexual fog plaguing him. "Hang on, baby."

Addison looked up at him and he almost lost it. Was he fucking crazy? Desire made her green eyes glow in the dusk, the waves of her hair tousled. Those full lips were swollen from the assault of his mouth and her nipples stood erect under the V-shaped neckline of her dress.

Son of a bitch, he was insanely crazy over this woman. And not just in the physical sense. It had always been more than physical with Addison. That very fact was the reason why the cold hand of dread clawed at his throat.

Del cleared his throat. "Let's take this inside. And slow it down a bit. I want to talk with you. Okay?" Before they took it further--again--he needed to get this burden of his illness off his chest. Not telling her weighed on his mind and it finally seemed like a good time to talk.

He entwined their fingers again, and God help him, kissed the back of her hand, where the skin was smooth and warm.

Addison narrowed her eyes at him for a moment, then nodded. "Okay. I'm starving, anyway." Her lips curved into a smile and she leaned into his arm. "What did you cook me?"

His smile matched her own. "Let's go find out."

They retrieved their glasses and walked hand in hand up the grassy slope to the house. When Del opened the back door, Otis Redding sang in the background about sitting on a dock and the aroma of Italian spices, cheese, and meat greeted them. Addison stepped inside and inhaled before her jaw dropped. "Oh my God. You cooked me lasagna?"

Shit. The way she said it had him thinking he'd fucked up again.The last time they'd had dinner together she hadn't asked for anything special. So he didn't even consider she was on one of those diets that didn't allow carbs or counted macros or some shit. He knew all about them after spending so much time in Hollywood. "Um, yeah."

Addison walked farther into the kitchen, sniffing the air. "Is it your mother's recipe?"

"Yeah, I sweet-talked her into giving it to me."

Her wide eyes darted between him and the large kitchen behind him. She held up a hand. "Wait a minute. You mean to tell me you wheedled your mother's prized lasagna recipe from her hands?" She paused and tilted her head. "Is your mother still breathing?"

He chuckled. "Yeah."

She nodded. "Well, that's good. But still...so not only did you get the recipe, you *made it*? As in you bought the ingredients and put it together?"

Del drew his brows down. Where was she going with this? "Yeah." He didn't like the defensive edge to his voice, but damned if it didn't sneak in there anyway.

Her smile could have lit up the dark depths of a black hole as she closed the small distance between them. "Thank you." She looped her arms around his neck, her lashes sweeping against her soft skin before she looked back up at him. "You know, you're the only man who's ever cooked for me."

He wrapped his arms around her waist and pulled her close. "Is that so?" Del wanted to not only be the only man, but the last man that ever cooked for her. But something held him back from voicing that thought out loud.

The oven timer went off, saving him from sliding further down that slippery slope. He dropped a kiss on her forehead and unwrapped himself from her. "Let's see if I can make my mother proud."

He finished the lasagna while Addison set up the table for the two of them and put out the salad she'd brought with her. Minutes later, Addison sat on one side of the large farmhouse breakfast table. Del came out of the kitchen with two plates of lasagna in his hands and set one in front of her. After he put his plate down, he poured her glass half full of red wine and she arched a brow up to him. "Trying to get me drunk and take advantage?"

Del set the bottle on the table and leaned down, bringing his mouth close to her ear. "You like when I take advantage of you." She bit her lip and her breathing hitched. He grinned. Yep, he wasn't the only one in agony over here.

Addison cleared her throat and swallowed a large sip of her wine. "This smells amazing."

He sat down across from her. "Well, I hope it's good. I've never cooked anything like this before."

She rimmed the top of her glass with a finger. "You were always more of the grill master if I recall."

He shrugged and met her eyes. "Yeah, I can make a mean steak. But I thought I'd change it up just a bit for you." Her gaze darted from his but not before he noticed the shadow of vulnerability in her eyes. "Eat up, babe."

At the first bite, Addison's eyes slid closed and she moaned a sound that was almost orgasmic. Stirrings began below the belt for Del and he shifted in his chair. Her eyes popped open and she looked over at him. She pointed to the pile of food on her plate with her fork. "Don't let your mother taste this. She's going to be pissed to know that you can make her lasagna as well as she does."

He couldn't help the expansion in his chest. It was a reminder of how this woman had made him feel ten feet tall and bulletproof when they were together. "You like it?"

"Like it? I could live on this." She rolled her eyes. "And then I'd have to start running again instead of walking just to keep the weight off."

His heart beat faster as he pictured Addison's belly curved in pregnancy. Carrying his baby. God, she'd be fucking gorgeous. *What the hell are you thinking, Ace?*

He shoved that thought from his mind and gave her his best panty-melting smile. "I wouldn't worry. You've grown into your curves quite nicely, Addison Davenport."

A pretty pink blush spread across her cheeks and she took another bite of her dinner. He cleared his throat and opened his mouth.

"You know what being here makes me think of?" Addison asked, a grin on her lips.

Damn it. He forced himself to smile, though when he looked at her face, it wasn't hard for him to fake it. Her grins were infectious. "It could be any number of things. We spent a lot of time here as kids."

"There's one thing in particular though."

She leaned closer to him as though letting him in on a secret. His heart thumped under his chest. Whether it was from her being so close or the fact that he did have a secret, he couldn't be sure. "Well, don't keep me in suspense, Addie."

"Remember that summer I made you do all those dance scenes? We did the Chopsticks number from the movie Big off the dock."

Del chuckled. "I seem to remember recreating the dance break from The Breakfast Club."

Her smile widened. "Yep. But the best was when we did the lift from Dirty Dancing." She sighed and looked down into her plate as though flashing back. A moment later, she looked up at him, her eyes bright and green as grass after a hard rain. "I just remember thinking how strong you were and knew you'd never drop me."

Del's throat closed up and his stomach rolled. *Shit*. He couldn't do it. Not right now, not after she talked about the one thing his illness could rob of him one day.

She shook her head and sipped her wine. "I'm sorry, that's not what you wanted to talk about I'm sure."

He swallowed and found his voice again. "No, but that was a nice jaunt down memory lane. I recall that in great detail. But I wanted to let you know the flooring you picked out looks amazing in the foyer area."

"Oh, I can't wait to see it. The project seems to be on target, too. The wrought iron for the staircase is going to look amazing." She smiled at him and sipped her wine. "Nice touch, Ace."

He grinned. "That's my job." At least it was for now. Just another thought he pushed off the edge of thinking about for the time being.

From there, the conversation continued on about finishes for the museum and drifted into Addie telling him about some of the crazier clients she'd had in her real estate career and how it had been working with her father. A pang hit his chest hard thinking about how he'd never had the opportunity to work with his own father.

They worked next to each other cleaning the dishes and the kitchen. Del topped off her wine and took her outside to sit on the deck. "No wine for you?" she asked, sitting on the lounge chair next to him.

He shook his head and tried to ignore the tightness that set up camp in his chest. How much did he want to tell her about his illness? He and Addie had spent some memorable nights together drinking and sharing all manner of things. But the woman was sharp. Sooner or later, she'd ask him why he never drank.

Del had decisions to make and he needed to give people answers. But now that he and Addie were…something again, he needed to see where her head was before he decided.

"Hmmm…I haven't been this relaxed in a while." She turned her head and reached out for his hand. "Thank you for the wonderful dinner."

"You're welcome. It was my pleasure." He slid his hand around hers. "Addie?"

"Yeah?"

"Dance with me?"

The lazy smile she gave him shouldn't have made a fire light in his belly, but it did. Still, he was trying to spend more time with her where he wasn't just pawing at her or nailing her against the door.

She took his hand when he stood and offered it. With an arm around her waist, he pulled her close and the lavender scent of her shampoo filled his nostrils. Everywhere her body touched his—from the light touch of her hand on his shoulder, to her hand in his, down to her body close against him—set sparks dancing across his skin.

Sam Cooke drifted out the open windows to the deck as they slow danced. He closed his eyes and relished the feel of her in his arms as Sam sang about his woman bringing her sweet lovin' on home to him. *I know how you feel, Sam.*

Halfway through the song, fat drops of rain started to fall. They pulled back and looked up at the sky, while the rain continued to fall faster. Addison covered her head and started for the house.

"Wait." Del grabbed her wrist and pulled her back to him. "You have to finish the dance."

"Del, I'm getting soaked!"

He laughed. "Baby, you're already soaked!"

He continued to laugh and she joined him. She stepped back from him and lifted her face to the sky. With her arms out to her side, she started to spin in a slow circle.

Del's heart raced in his chest. Jesus, he was so in love with this woman he couldn't think straight. How the hell was he ever going to leave her this time?

The realization hit him like a two-by-four to the head. While he'd been a lucky SOB to have the opportunity to help families with their homes for all those years, he didn't want to live that life anymore. After ten years in the business—ten years of working every single day, ten years of living without Addison, the one thing he always wanted— he was ready to hang it up. He'd still renovate and he'd still love doing what he did but he wouldn't do it in front of the camera anymore.

But was Addison ready for him? She'd have to be, that's all there was to it.

Sure, buddy. Because Addie's always been such a pushover. Have you not learned a damn thing?

"This feels wonderful." She lowered her arms and shoved at the golden ropes of hair hung around her face. "Do you know how long it's been since I played in the rain?"

He closed the gap between them and took her face in his hands. "Have I told you lately how beautiful you are?"

Her hands found his hips and rested there. "No, but you can spend the rest of the night reminding me."

With a groan, he captured her mouth with his own and plundered hers. He slid his hands down and gripped the back of her thighs. Her skin heated under his hand as he caressed her inner thigh, drawing circles in her skin with his fingertip. Without hesitation, she jumped up and wrapped her arms around his neck, never breaking the kiss.

The rain fell around them as her lips parted and her tongue darted out to meet his. The skin under his work-worn hands was slick from the cool rain, but smooth as rose petals. Her body was like an inferno in his arms and she tasted faintly of the wine she'd drunk earlier, and it held a hint of spice underneath it. He turned his head slightly and deepened the kiss. Her low, soft moans were swallowed by his ravenous mouth. All combined made her an intoxicating cocktail he would gladly stay drunk on for the rest of his life.

It was the sweetest kiss he'd ever experienced. He wanted to stay just like this.

On second thought, he wanted her underneath him. Her fingers whispering over his skin and crying out his name.

"Inside. Now," he said against her lips.

"Yes, please." Her desperate reply had him kicking his feet into gear and carrying her inside.

Del kicked the door shut behind him before he stopped at the table where they just had dinner and set her on her feet. Her laughter faded when he wrapped an arm around her waist and pulled her to him. With a hand in her hair, he gently tugged until her neck was exposed to his hungry mouth.

He kissed along her collarbone, his tongue darting out to lick the indentation at the base of her neck. The arm around her waist slid down and cupped her ass, bringing her closer to him, before settling his hand on the soft curve of her hip.

He walked her back until she bumped the table, where she slid onto it, and leaned back on her elbows, her dress riding up her thighs. Del stepped back and kneeled down. Holding her stare, he ran a hand up her smooth thighs, pushing the damp fabric up until it bunched around her waist. Addison let her head fall back and opened her legs for him.

Del growled at the sexy as hell picture she made wide open for him, her pussy covered in a sheer white thong. He pushed the fabric aside and ran a finger down her slit, causing her hips to buck and drawing a moan from her lips.

"Hmm…you're so wet," he whispered, half to himself. Leaning forward, he flicked his tongue against her clit, before sucking lightly on that sensitive bundle of nerves.

Addison gasped and arched her hips toward his mouth. He laid a hand over her lower belly to hold her still while he plunged his tongue inside her and feasted on her sweetness. Her moans grew louder and her body writhed on the hard table beneath her. Del inserted two fingers into her tight channel, causing her to pant and her fingernails to rake over his scalp.

"That's right, baby. Come for me." He curled his fingers and she detonated under his ministrations.

She cried out his name as the muscles of her core clenched around his fingers and her clit pulsed on his tongue. When the pulses stopped, he laid light kisses across her pelvic bone before standing and admiring the view in front of him.

"Oh my God." She laid on a hand over her heaving chest. Still breathless, she sat up and with a wicked gleam in her eye, slid of the table. She turned around and gave him her back, which was mostly bare due to the design of her dress. Addison leaned back into him and hooked an arm around his neck. Her breath was hot against his ear. "Take me right here. I can't wait any longer." To emphasize her point, she reached back and rubbed his cock through his shorts. "Oh, and

Del? I'm clean and I'm on the pill."

Fuck, this woman drove him crazy. How he ever lived without her was a mystery to him. He'd been a fucking idiot. And he didn't need to be told twice. "Thank you, Jesus. There's been no one else since my last physical." When she moaned and pushed against him again, his sanity slipped a bit more.

With a growl, he bent her over the side of the table and shoved her dress up, exposing her perfect, smooth ass. He traced a fingertip down the strip of sheer fabric that led down between her cheeks. He bit his lip to keep from exploding. "Sorry, babe. I'll buy a new pair."

Her only response was to lean back into him. When he gave the panties a hard tug, the delicate fabric disintegrated under his hand and she let out a long moan. She continued to rub his length through his jeans. He closed his eyes and moaned at her touch, his hands shifting through the waterfall of her hair. "Please, Del."

Within seconds, he was unzipped and plunging his cock into her tight, wet heat. She was slick and more than ready, making entering her a dream. His fingers dug into her hips and she pushed back into him as they found a rhythm that made this animalistic mating the hottest sex he'd ever had in his life.

Before much longer, their skin was covered in a sheen of sweat and as her pussy contracted around his length, she cried out his name. The tingling at the base of his spine caught him off guard and he exploded inside of her, her name a guttural moan on his lips. He leaned over her to catch his breath. Her chest rose and lowered underneath him as she, too, tried to bring her pulse back to normal.

Fear of crushing her had Del leaning back and pulling out of her. He lowered her dress back over her ass, although it was a shame to cover such beauty. He zipped up and when she turned around, her face was flushed and her hair a riotous mess around her head. But the smile on her face? Well, that made Del stand a little straighter and his pulse pounded in his ears.

"Wow."

He lifted a brow but couldn't hold back a grin. "You liked that, huh?"

"You might say that." She stepped up to him and wrapped her

arms around his neck. "But I don't think I'm quite through with you." Her long lashes swept across her cheek when she looked down for a moment before bringing that green-eyed gaze back to his. "Take me to bed?"

"Absolutely." He carried her off into the bedroom where after another bout of sweaty sex, they finally drifted off to sleep. Sometime in the middle of the night, Addison reached out for him and he was only too happy to oblige. But this time, in the still of the night, it was different.

He settled between her thighs and braced himself on his elbows, framing her face with his hands. His eyes traveled over her face in the moonlight shining through the windows.

"Addison, you're beautiful," he voiced barely above a whisper. He kissed her lips softly. "I've missed you. More than you'll ever know." He buried his face in her hair, nipping a trail down the side of her neck.

"I've missed you, too," she whispered, stroking her hands down his back.

Staring into her eyes, he entered her in one long, slow motion, torturing them both, until he was buried in her silky heat. With every withdrawal, she writhed underneath him, grabbing his ass and pulling him in tighter when he sank back into her.

They kept their gazes on one another with each stroke. It was slow, sweet, and where fucking her on the table was hot and primitive, this was the most sensual thing Del had ever experienced. All breathless moans, whispered kisses, loving caresses. There was a stirring deep in his soul he'd only experienced once before. With her. It overwhelmed him.

"Addison, I..." Del whispered.

She laid her fingertips on his mouth. "Shh...I know."

Did she? He wasn't sure she understood the depth of what he felt for her. Hell, he was just getting used to it again himself.

He hooked an arm behind her knee and lifted it toward her chest, changing the angle and causing him to be deeper in her than he'd ever been. She moaned long and loud each time he slid home. Her hands gripped his forearms, her nails digging into his skin. The pinprick of pain urged him on until the tension built up between them. In spite of wanting to go slow and savor her, his hips picked up the pace.

When she cried out his name softly and fell over the cliff, he was stripped bare of all his defenses. Del couldn't imagine his life without her.

With one last push, he followed her over and into the abyss.

a falling realization

"THE CROWN MOLDING accents are throughout the living room and sitting area." Addison waved a hand toward the ceiling. "I think it gives a nice elegant touch to the rooms."

She smiled at the young couple following behind her through the house. They were on the fourth house of the day—the fourteenth of their search so far—and the young woman smiled as she looked around.

Addison hoped like hell that smile meant they'd hit on a house the woman liked. She continued walking through the two-story living room to the large picture window. "As you can see—"

The phone rang in her hand and she frowned at the number that popped up on the screen. "I'm sorry, can you excuse me a moment?" She walked toward the front of the house, her heels echoing off the hardwoods, and walked out the door.

"Addison Davenport."

"Hey, Addison. It's Teri."

Addison furrowed her brow. Was she supposed to be on set today? "Hey, what's up?"

Teri cleared her throat. "I'm at the Madison Ridge Medical Center with Del."

Addison's stomach dropped and her blood ran cold. "Oh my God, is he okay?"

"He's fine, but he asked me to call you. He won't be able to drive himself home because they had to put him on some painkillers."

"What the hell happened?" She shook her head. "Never mind, I'll be there in fifteen minutes." She ended the call and went back into the house. A whole lot of *what the hell?* ricocheted around her mind along with the resignation she was probably going to have to start over with the young couple inside.

As promised, fifteen minutes later, Addison strode through the doors of the emergency room. Teri met her halfway down the hall. "Hey, he's in room twenty-one."

"What happened?" Addison asked, her mouth as dry as the desert.

Teri shrugged, rubbing her biceps as though trying to warm up, concern clouding her eyes. "I don't know exactly. He was on a scaffold in one of the rooms and then..." she trailed off and blew out a breath. "He fell. It happened so fast. One minute he was talking to the camera, then the next he's falling and lying on the ground. He—"

Her phone rang in her pocket. With a shaky hand, she pulled it out and checked the display. "I need to take this," she said, already bringing the phone to her ear. "Hey. Yeah, I brought him to the hospital." She walked away leaving Addison to her own devices.

Following the signs, Addison found his room with the door slightly ajar. An authoritative male voice reached her just outside the door, causing her to stop and peek through the opening.

"What were you doing before you fell, Mr. Reynolds?"

Del's face was pale as he leaned his head back against the pillow. "We were filming a scene. I was on a scaffold explaining some issues on the house."

The doctor shined a light in each of Del's eyes before stepping back. "Did you trip?"

Del started to shake his head but a grimace crossed his face and he stopped. "I had double vision and I missed a step."

The doctor—Davis, it looked like his coat said—narrowed his eyes. "You had the double vision before you fell? Or you have it now? Have you had this before?"

"I had it before I fell. And I still have some now. And yes, I've had this before. This isn't the first time." Del's voice was resigned and the hair on the back of Addison's neck stood up.

Dr. Davis tilted his head. "Have you seen a doctor for it?"

Del nodded and turned his head toward the doctor. "Yeah, I have a doctor." He sighed heavily and leaned his head back on the pillows propped up behind him. "I was diagnosed with myasthenia gravis about six months ago."

Addison froze and her body went numb. What the hell was myasthenia gravis? Was he sick? Or…she didn't even know what. Did his family know? What did any of this mean? Her mind was simultaneously running through a million questions while also blanking out on any thought whatsoever. She held her breath and leaned forward, trying to hear more.

The doctor slid his hands into his coat pockets and nodded. "I see. Have you had more onset of symptoms recently?"

"Not more so than normal. In fact, it's been a while since I've had any symptoms. My doctor in LA told me right now my symptoms may still come and go."

"Hey, Addison."

At the sound of her name, Addison jumped a mile and put a hand over her heart. She looked over her shoulder to find Lisa, an old friend from high school and an RN in the ER. "Hey, Lisa."

"Aren't you going in?"

"Um, yeah. I just," she gestured with a hand, "I didn't want to disturb the doctor."

Lisa held up a plastic bag of saline with a smile. "Well, I have to disturb him. Come on." She pushed the door open.

"Del, I found someone here for you." Lisa crossed the room, quick and quiet on her sneakered feet, to hang the bag on the pole next to Del's bed. Addison's feet were glued to the floor next to the entryway.

Del smiled at Addison, and she couldn't help it, but the smile—in spite of his fatigue—was sexy and held secret promises just for her. "Hey, Starshine."

Addison mentally stiffened her spine and gave him her best smile. She hadn't missed the *oh shit* expression that crossed his face, leaving as quickly as it came. "Hey, Ace." On the surface, it was light. Easy breezy. The way it was supposed to be. The way it should have stayed until her traitorous heart decided it had a vote.

Sometimes that fucking organ was a huge pain in her ass.

"So doc, am I good to go?" Del asked, his tone as pointed as the stare he gave the doctor, who stared right back.

Dr. Davis cleared his throat before speaking. "The CT came back clear for concussion. But you were dehydrated. How's the vision?"

"Fine." The curt tone from Del sounded foreign to Addison.

Dr. Davis lifted his chin to the bag on the pole. "Let that bag finish and I'll get your discharge paperwork going. Take the weekend, get some rest, follow up with me in my office on Tuesday."

"Will do, doc." Del nodded, his gaze drifting over to Addison.

Dr. Davis walked out, nodding slightly to her as he and Lisa left the room, shutting the door behind them.

They stared at each other from across the room. His eyes were unreadable as he stared quietly at her. Even with his face paler than normal and the bad lighting of the hospital room glinting off his dark blond hair, Del made her heart stutter. He was always bigger than life, more like Hollywood than Madison Ridge.

Now he had this new level of vulnerability to him with his…whatever it was, well, what the hell did it say about her that she found his vulnerability even more appealing? After several moments of silence, she walked over to the chair next to the bed and perched on the edge of it.

His eyes followed her movements. Del finally looked away and leaned his head back on the pillow. "How much did you hear?"

She could play games with him, but she'd quit doing that a long time ago. "Most of it. The part about being diagnosed with myanthe graves or whatever it is may have been in there." Saying it out loud between them started an anger building in her chest and she couldn't help the bitterness in her voice from the nasty pill of disappointment she'd just swallowed.

Del ran a hand down his face and sighed. "It's myasthenia gravis. I'm sorry I didn't tell you sooner. I should have. I tried, but…" he trailed off. "There was never a great time to bring it up."

Her fingers tightened in her lap and narrowed her eyes. "Seriously, Del? You had a million times you could have said something to me. I thought we were past all this bullshit."

He rubbed a hand over his head and groaned. "Okay, sure. When would you have brought it up if you were me, Addie? At the Memorial Day party? When we were reconnecting? Or maybe when we were having sex?" He snapped his fingers. "Oh! I know, maybe I should have announced it in front of all my coworkers—who don't know, by the way—so they could run to the tabloids and spill my private battle."

The word *battle* hit her like a cold burst of water on a hot day. She bit her lip to hold back the gasp and tears that threatened to show up for the party. Delaney Reynolds was usually the epitome of cool. Addison didn't know a thing about his condition—something she was going to change the minute she got home...hello, internet doctors—but if it was throwing Del off his game this bad, it was serious.

A thought hit her hard enough to set her back a step. "Wait a minute. Are you leaving the show because of this condition?"

The door to the room swung open and Lisa sailed through the door with a stack of papers in her hand. "You can get dressed. Dr. Davis says you're ready to go." As Lisa went through the motions of unhooking him and going over discharge instructions with him, Addison tuned them out.

All this time, she thought he was leaving town once the show was over. It was her defense for her heart so she wouldn't fall again this time around. It was just sex and fun. Sex and fun with an expiration date. What did this mean for them now?

Nothing more than it did before. She frowned. Of course, it didn't change anything. It was obvious he didn't want her to know. He went to great lengths to hide it from her if even her best friend—his sister—never said a word to her. Did Grace even know?

The pit in her stomach grew with dread. Absolutely nothing had changed in the ten years since he'd left. They'd been best reminds and he didn't trust her enough to share his dreams years ago. And now, just as they were repairing their relationship, he still didn't trust her enough to tell her about something so serious.

"Addison?" She jerked back to the present when Lisa called her name.

"Yeah?"

"I was just asking if you were taking him home."

She nodded. "Yeah. I'll take care of it."

"I wanted to let you know, word's gotten around he's here. There looks to be a couple of reporters out front. But I have a way to get you out of here without anyone finding out."

"Son of a bitch," Del muttered.

Shock snapped Addison's head back. "Reporters? But he's been here for weeks."

"They're just trying to drum up a story. And that isn't something I need right now." Del flung back the sheet and swung his jean clad legs to the side of the bed. "I need to get out of here."

Lisa patted Del on the shoulder. "I'm going to show Addie where to go and I'll be back for you."

"Thanks." He nodded and reached for his shirt on the nearby chair. His face was like stone with no expression and if she didn't know him so well, she would have missed the small tic in his cheek that told her how pissed off he really was.

Within ten minutes, Addison was pulling away from the hospital with the small group of reporters standing out front none the wiser that Del was safely ensconced in the passenger seat next to her.

Del turned around, looking out the back window, and laughed. "Nice work, Addie. I need you in LA to get me out of places." He turned forward and settled into the seat.

Addison didn't trust herself to say anything. The mix of emotions churning in her gut left her unable to gauge how she would react, so she kept her mouth shut. Del must have understood she was in no mood to talk to him because he kept silent as well.

When she pulled into the driveway of the lake house, it was empty and the house was quiet. "I can come in and help you if you want."

Del had his hand on the door handle but didn't make any moves to get out of the car and kept his gaze trained to the view in front of them. "No, I'm good. Thanks for the ride."

"You're welcome." What the hell was going on here? It was as though they were strangers now.

Maybe they were. And that made her heart ache in a way that was both familiar and new.

He pulled on the handle and the door unlatched but he didn't push it open. Instead, he shifted his long frame as much as the small seats in her Mini Cooper would allow and speared her with his Caribbean-blue eyes.

"To answer your question. Yes, I'm leaving the show primarily because of my condition. It's just perfect timing my contract is up for renewal. As you can see," he lifted his bandaged wrist, "it's starting to affect my work. And it's not going to get better. There's no cure for it."

Addison held his gaze until tears pricked behind her eyes. She turned her head and looked out the driver's side window. "So if it weren't for your condition, you would continue the show. Right?"

Del looked down at the console between them, pausing before responding. "Yeah. I guess I would."

She nodded slowly and rolled her lips inward. Tears continued to threaten to fall, pissing her off. She'd given Delaney Reynolds enough tears. She wasn't giving him any more.

Turning her head, she met his stare head-on. "Why didn't you tell me before? I mean, I know we didn't talk for a long time. But I thought we had gotten back to a semblance of friendship again while working on this project. You could have told me."

"You're right. I should have told you. The truth is only my mother, my siblings, and my doctors know about this. And now you." He shook his head and blew out a breath. "I know I should have told you earlier. I'm truly sorry I didn't. You're family, Addie. You always have been."

"Yeah, I wish you'd have told me earlier, too." She looked down and shifted the car into reverse. "Get some rest, Del. I'll call you later." She was practically pushing him out the door, but she needed to get away from him. There was too much to process and she couldn't do it with him in her space. The heat of his gaze was on her, but she couldn't look at him.

"Yeah, okay. Talk later." He shoved against the door, forgetting his injuries if the grimace that crossed his face was any indication, and got out of the car. The door slammed behind him and she closed her eyes, pushing away the thought that it seemed to punctuate something between them she didn't understand. His tall form walked toward the house, his movements slower than they would normally be. A sob escaped her before she could stop it. Her heart filled with a mix of emotions as she watched the man who had taken her heart years ago.

And she'd never gotten it back.

CHAPTER TWENTY
the grand canyon between us

IN THE LATE AFTERNOON SUN, Del stood, hands on his hips, in the center of the large area that would serve as the entryway to the home, admiring how well the dream was becoming a reality. Although it was quiet except for the workers packing up for the day, the hours had passed with saws whirring, hammers banging, and rock music blaring from the radio upstairs. The electrical work would be done by tomorrow and he received news that the foundation had been lifted less than a decade ago and wouldn't have to be done. This was somewhat offset by learning he would have to redo the entire HVAC system, but all in all it had been a good day.

Things were progressing along nicely.

With the renovations, anyway. When it came to dealing with the owner of said property, that was another matter altogether. He took a deep breath, the smell of the sawdust hanging in the air mingled with the humidity of early summer air. It had been a week since his little accident and his confession to her. Physically, he'd recovered for the most part. Addie was a different story. Their only communication was through text messages that were nothing but professional. Anytime he tried to bring up anything personal, she ignored it and changed the subject. Or didn't respond at all.

She'd been to the job site almost every day over the last week and each time Del hadn't been there for one reason or another. It didn't take a rocket scientist to see she was avoiding him. It pissed him off, and while he wanted to lay the blame at her feet for being unreasonable, Del was mad at himself more than anything.

He'd done his best to get her to trust him and as far as the project was concerned, he'd done it well. And things had been going well personally, too. While the sex had always been the best he'd ever had, it was different this time. He couldn't quite put a finger on it. It had always been more with Addison, but this time it carried a vibe to it that puzzled him. But he hadn't manned up and trusted her enough to tell her about his illness, nor had he made any decisions about what he was going to do after his contract was over.

He'd fucked it all up. Again.

At the sound of an engine and tires crunching on gravel, Del turned. His heart lifted when Addison alighted from her car.

This was his all-business Addison in her sky-high heels that brought them nearly eye to eye, the professional, yet curve-hugging skirt, and the button-down blouse that whispered over her torso. A deep hum of male appreciation rode along his nerves. The dichotomy of her cool, tidy business clothes covering a body that was made for sin drove him crazy.

For fear his knees would give out if he moved, he stayed where he was when she climbed the stairs, looking around at the house.

Damn, she was stunning.

"Hey there."

She shifted her gaze to him, her smile hesitant as she crossed the threshold and approached him. "Hey. Feeling better?"

Her smile didn't reach her eyes, causing his body to tense and a heaviness to weigh in his chest. Damn it, were they back to square one again? "Doing better, thanks. Haven't seen you in a while."

"Yeah," she looked away and a breeze blew her hair, "I've been busy."

Busy avoiding me. "Yeah, we've been busy here, too. I can update you now, if you'd like that instead of a report."

She nodded. "Sure."

He took her through the house and explained some of the larger updates they'd found out that day. Addison didn't say much, only asking a question here or there, but mostly it was just a nod or a hum of approval. It was more of the same when he talked with her about the filming that would be taking place over the next few days as well. Each passing moment they spent together ramped up Del's anxiety.

When they came back downstairs, she thanked him and started for the door. "Hold on a damn minute." His fingers circled her wrist and drew her up short.

She kept her head turned from him for a couple of moments before she squared her shoulders and looked at him. "Yes? What is it, Delaney?"

His gaze roamed her face, looking for the Addison from just a little over a week ago. The Addison before his accident. "I want you. I've missed you."

A faint blush spread across her cheekbones and she ducked her head, setting off a tenderness inside him in spite of the frustration simmering under his skin. Although they'd known each other since childhood and he knew every square inch of her body, she still blushed at his compliments.

"I…I've missed you, too. But…look, I just came by to see how you —things—were going."

"So you have missed me." He brought her hand up to his lips and kissed her palm. Her eyes widened slightly and darkened with desire. His gaze trailed down her neck where her pulse bumped.

She looked away and pulled her hand out of his. "I need to go." Her voice wavered but she didn't attempt to leave.

"Busy tonight?" he asked, shifting closer to her. With a single finger, he traced down her arm. It took everything he had not to touch her further, but he wanted to wrap himself in her essence. And stay there.

She blew out a breath, but still didn't try to move away. "I—"

"Damn, Del. You waste no time, do ya, buddy?"

What in the ever-loving fuck was he doing here?

Del looked down at Addison, who looked away. But he'd caught the closed-off look in her eyes as she avoided his gaze. Mentally cursing the shitty timing, he pushed off the wall and turned to the tall, balding man standing just outside the open door on the front porch.

"Hey, Rick. What the hell are you doing here?"

"Come on, buddy. Is that any way to talk to your agent?" Rick asked.

Addison tensed next to Del. She physically and mentally stepped away from him. The vibe coming off her said whatever progress he'd made just now was gone.

Del could easily throttle the guy and not feel an ounce of remorse.

Rick crossed into the room, looking around at the construction. "Looking good, my man." His gaze landed on Addison and traveled up and down her body. The smile Rick gave her had Del seeing red. "Looking real good." He held out a broad hand to Addison. "Rick Adams."

Her smile was polite but held no warmth when she returned his handshake. "Addison Davenport."

"Ah, the owner. Nice to finally meet you." He smirked at Del and bobbed his eyebrows. The underlying message was clear. *Nice job banging the owner.* Del made a growling sound in his throat and shifted his body between Rick and Addie. Rick—the bastard never missed a trick—dropped her hand but chuckled before walking farther into the house.

Why the hell was this guy his agent? Oh yeah, Del had wanted to make money and his agent made sure he did. He'd overlooked the fact the guy was a douche for too many years.

Rick crossed his arms over his wide chest and walked to the back of the room. Del knew he was sizing up the joint as he was prone to do. A hot ball of anger burned in Del's belly.

He looked out the back windows for a moment before turning and striding back to where Del and Addison stood. "Nice view. Well-sized. Going to be a masterpiece when you finish." He stopped in front of Del. "Which will be when, by the way?"

This was not a conversation he wanted to have right now. Especially not in front of Addison. "I don't—"

Addison suddenly turned to him, catching him off guard. She took advantage of that moment of surprise to shift away. To anyone else, it would have been subtle.

But she didn't fool him. There was a divide the size of the Grand Canyon between them now.

"This sounds like a business conversation. I need to head out, anyway." Her smile was polite but cold and her voice took on a formal, professional tone. She nodded to Rick. "Pleasure to meet you."

He smiled and returned her nod. "The pleasure was mine, Ms. Davenport."

Hands tied, Del pursed his lips. "I'll walk you to your car."

She turned back to Del, false smile and business attitude still in place. "No need. I look forward to your status report." Turning on her heel, she started to walk out of the room.

Del gritted his teeth. "Give me a minute," he muttered to Rick.

He caught up with her at the bottom of the steps. "Addie. Wait." He reached for her arm, his fingers grasping her wrist. "Wait, damn it."

When she turned to him, her face was patient, but the smile was gone and her eyes were bleak. She wouldn't look at him. "Yes, Delaney?"

Her expression brought him up short. He frowned. "I'm sorry about Rick. He can be an ass."

Addison waved her hand. "I've worked with all kinds of men, Del. Guys like him don't bother me."

He opened his mouth, then snapped it shut. Something shifted with Rick's arrival and Addison was shutting him out.

"Okay," he said slowly. With a gentle hand, as though she were a skittish mare, he cupped her chin and turned her head toward him. "Hey." Her lashes swept her cheeks when she looked up at him. "I'll see you later." It was a declaration, not a question.

"It's fine, you don't need to come over."

Del laid his thumb over her lips, sweeping over the petal-soft skin. He wanted to gather her up, dump her in his truck, and speed away from everything and everyone. The town, the house, his agent.

He and Addison holed up in a place all by themselves for the rest of their lives?

It would be heaven on earth.

"I know I don't need to, but we need to talk."

Her eyes bored into his as though looking for answers to...well, he didn't know what she was looking for.

Finally, she moved her head slightly, dislodging his hand, then nodded. "Fine."

When she opened the door to her car, he stepped back and shoved his hands into the front pockets of his jeans. She started the engine and let down her window, her hands on the steering wheel.

Addison looked up at him. "If..." She looked away, licked her lips, and then looked back at him. "If you get caught up with Rick and can't make it by, don't worry about it."

Before he could respond, she dropped the car into gear and pulled away.

What the hell just happened here?

Del curled his hands into fists inside his pockets, as though he were trying to hang on to something that kept slipping away.

"Is there a decent place to get a drink here in Mayberry?"

Pushing that feeling aside for now, he pivoted to face Rick. He really didn't feel like dealing with his ass right now. But the sooner he did, the sooner he could send Rick back to California and leave him in peace. Leave him to repair his life.

"Rick, you're still an asshole."

He spread his arms to his sides. "What did you expect? You know me."

True enough.

Del shook his head with a rueful smile. "Come on, I know a place. First round's on me."

déjà vu all over again

MURPHY'S EARS perked up and he raised his head from the porch when a pickup truck pulled into her driveway. With a deep sigh, Addison closed her eyes. She was in no mood to talk with Del.

He stayed in the truck for several moments, so she stayed where she was to see what he planned to do. Her feet were on the top rail of the porch and she pushed off to keep the chair rocking. She hoped she looked as calm as her surroundings were. The sun was setting so the temperature hovered in the seventies and thankfully the humidity had waned a bit. The cicadas and crickets were singing a rhythmic symphony. Combined with the sight, it was a perfect early summer evening to drink a chilled glass of chardonnay.

Until, that is, the love of your life who has managed to rip your heart out and stomp on it, again, decided to pay a visit. Oh, and never mind the fact she looked a mess with her hair in a messy knot on top of her head, sans bra, old T-shirt, and short shorts. There was nothing perfect about that. As much as the nature song of the surrounding woods usually soothed her, she couldn't shake the burden that had settled between her shoulder blades since she'd dropped him off from the hospital a week ago.

Finally, he stepped out into the night and headed to the front of her house. Murphy stood and greeted him at the top of the stairs, his large chocolate tail wagging. *Traitorous dog.*

Del stopped on the top step, his hands in the pockets of his jeans. "Hello, Addison."

She met Del's gaze over the glass of wine she sipped from. His eyes were confused and what looked to be sad. Addison hardened her heart against the vulnerability that tugged at her heartstrings.

Involuntarily, she stiffened her spine. She had to or she'd get lost in his eyes and his voice and just his presence. "Hello, Delaney."

"Can we talk?"

She sipped the golden liquid courage from her glass again. After she swallowed, she shook her head. "I don't have anything to say." She waved her hand toward the rocking chair next to her. "But if you feel the need, take a seat."

Del lowered himself into the chair next to her and Murphy set up camp in front of her chair. With a small smile, she rubbed the big dog's head. Maybe her pup wasn't so traitorous after all.

Next to her, Del rubbed his palms on the legs of his jeans. She raised a brow. Was the legendary, cool Delaney Reynolds, *Property Ace*, nervous? She had to be in an alternate universe.

She turned her head and stared at him blandly, continuing the slight rocking of the chair. "You wanted to talk, so talk. Otherwise, I'm going to head to bed. Alone."

He frowned and narrowed his eyes at her. "Can you just give me a damn minute?" He blew out a breath. "I want to apologize."

She tilted her head. "Oh? For what? Lying to me about your illness? Or making me fall in love with you again? Or using me and my father's legacy for your personal gain?" Okay, the last one was a stretch and just mean because it was a personal dig.

Del's eyes flashed blue. "That last question is bullshit and you know it, Addison. You signed a contract to have the renovations done on television. Don't act like you don't know that now." His hands clenched and released before he continued. "And don't forget, that museum may be in a trust that has your name on it, but it's only because my father had the misfortune of dying before it could be finished."

Addison looked down into her lap, her cheeks burning. If she was looking to hurt him, it appeared she hit her target, bullseye. She nodded once. "You're right. I'm sorry. That was unkind of me."

Del sighed and looked away. "It's fine. I deserved it. Because I did lie to you about my illness. I had good intentions but… I was trying not to hurt you, to protect you, but I just made it worse." He leaned back in the chair. "I should have been upfront, but I wasn't sure who I could trust."

"Del, you knew you could trust me."

He continued to stare out into the yard, his strong jaw tight. Addison shook her head, disappointment settling heavy on her heart.

"I screwed up. I should have trusted you. We've known each other forever."

She gathered her wine glass and stood. "And yet here we are." She rubbed her forehead to ward off the headache brewing behind her eyes. "I accept your apology, okay? I'm headed to bed now. Good night." Having him near her, admitting fault, reminding her of their history, just made it harder for her to keep her resolve. He needed to get his ass out of there.

"Wait a minute." He stopped her by grabbing her hand as she walked by. "There's another question you had I want to address."

Damn her and her big mouth. He hadn't mentioned it yet, so she had hoped he didn't hear it. She pulled her hand away. "There's nothing more to address, Del. Apology accepted. Go home." She opened the front door and snapped her fingers. "Come on, Murph. Let's go." The dog slipped in ahead of her and when she went to close it, he palmed the door to stop it. There didn't seem to be anything wrong with his muscles at that moment. He pushed it open the rest of the way and walked into the foyer before slamming the heavy door behind him.

"I'm calling bullshit again, Addie."

She threw up her hands. "Do whatever you want, Del." She turned on her heel and walked toward the kitchen. "You always do, anyway."

The clomping of his work boots on her hardwood floors told her he followed her into the kitchen. It took all the willpower she possessed not to throw the wineglass in the sink. She stood at the sink with her back to him in hopes he would get the hint and just go.

"Addison, what did you mean by I made you fall in love with me again?" She hung her head and closed her eyes to ward off the tears. His voice was soft and full of something she didn't want to recognize as hope. Because it would do no good. She lifted her head and opened her eyes. When she turned to face him, the armor she'd used against her feelings for the man who stole her heart when she was just a girl fell into place.

"I love you, Del. I always have and, to my dismay, I always will. But that doesn't change the fact that we just don't work."

His arms were crossed over his broad chest. "We work just fine. Things have been great between us." He frowned. "With the exception of one thing. But I said I was sorry, Addison."

"Of course, you think things are great," she muttered, dropping her chin to her chest.

Del sighed and dropped his hands to shove them in his pockets. "Would you care to explain?"

"Addison?" Del prompted when she stayed silent for a long time.

Stay strong, Addie. Tears pooled in her eyes and she swiped at them. She blew out a breath and lifted her head. It was time to lay out all her cards. She couldn't continue the dance with him any longer.

Addison stared into his eyes. *Now or never.* "Ten years ago when you left, you told me you'd be back in a year. That's all the contract was for. I didn't like it, but I knew I could live with it. For you."

She swallowed hard before continuing. "In the beginning you called me, every day, multiple times a day. As time wore on, those calls turned into once a day, at night when you were done. You have no idea how much I looked forward to those calls."

"Addie, I'm sorry. I—"

She held up a hand in stop sign fashion. "Please let me finish before I can't. Eventually, I ended up talking to your assistant more than you until the phone calls, texts, and emails stopped coming from you completely."

He rubbed a hand over his head and looked at the floor. "I know I really messed up. But before I could fix it, you'd taken matters into your own hands." Del's voice was low and his eyes full of anguish when he looked up and held her gaze. "You ended us, Addison."

She shook her head and her eyes filled with tears. She couldn't look at him. "You'd made your choice long before our last phone call, Delaney. I just made it official. And in your response, you agreed with me."

"You're right. You've always been right." He blew out a breath. "You never took any of my shit, Addie. It's one of the things I love most about you. But back then? I was mad as hell that you ended it. Ended us. At the time, it felt like you decided I wasn't worth waiting for."

Silence filled the space between them for several moments. She couldn't speak. If she did, she'd shatter into a million pieces, never to be whole again.

Silence filled the space between them for several moments.

"Addie," Del's voice sounded as though he'd swallowed sand. "I had to face facts. "I broke a promise. The promise to choose you. I fucked up so badly and the fact was my choice came with consequences. I lost everything when I lost you." His voice cracked a bit on the last word and he looked away from her. "But I also knew I couldn't come back here. The best thing you ever did for me was let me go."

She nodded. "And that's why I'm doing it again" She crossed her arms over her chest and rubbed her hands up and down her biceps to ward off the cold those words brought with them. Her vision blurred with unshed tears.

He shook his head and took a step forward.

When she retreated, he stopped. "No, Addie—"

"Look, I've watched you work over the last several weeks. You're the best at what you do. It's who you are. I can't ask you to change, any more than you would ask me to change who I am."

She laid her fingertips over his lips, not wanting him to say anything that would weaken her resolve. "Delaney, I love you enough to let you go. I wish things were different. I wish our choices coincided. But we both know they don't. If we forced it, we wouldn't be happy for long. We'd end up resenting each other."

"What about all the time we spent together the last few weeks? Were you pretending?"

She stepped back and flinched. If he'd actually hit her, it'd probably hurt less. He closed his eyes and pinched the bridge of his nose.

"No," she said quietly, "I wasn't pretending with you. I fell in love with you again. But I don't trust you not to break me again. And you will."

"It's different this time, Addie."

"How is it different, Del? Because we're older? We have history? Learned from our mistakes? We haven't. Because this," she waved her hand between them, "feels the same as it did all those years ago. You wowed me, wrapped me up until you were all I could think about. But you still withhold the most important parts of your life from me. It isn't the first time and it won't be the last."

"Addison," he started toward her, stopping in his tracks when she backed away from him.

She couldn't let him touch her. That would be it for sure if he did. She shook her head vehemently. "It isn't different and it isn't happening to me again. I won't survive another heartbreak from you, Delaney."

"I won't leave you. I promise."

Her chest ached as tears rolled down her cheeks as she shook her head and moved out of his reach. "I'm sorry for the way things turned out, but this is for the best. We don't know it yet, but this will just make us stronger one day." *Liar, liar.* Maybe so, but she had to believe it to keep one foot in front of the other toward the front door.

"Addie, please."

She opened the front door wide and stood next to it, unable to meet his stare. "Please, Del. If you ever loved me, leave me alone."

He stood there for a moment, his gaze a brand on her skin. Murphy came and stood next to her, bumping his broad body into her legs, effectively putting himself between his mistress and the man across the room. After several angst-filled moments, Del walked through the open doorway. Before he crossed the threshold, he stopped and she looked up at him. The anguish in his eyes shattered what was left of her already fractured heart. He opened his mouth to say something and tears rolled down her face. "Please go," she whispered.

His mouth set in a flat line and he nodded once before walking out the door. She closed it behind him and locked it up. When the deadbolt slid home, the sound was as loud as a gunshot in the quiet of her home. With her back against the door, she slid to the floor, where Murphy came over and sat next to her. His eyes were full of unconditional love, the kind of love she'd wanted from Del but that always seemed to be out of reach.

The floodgates opened. Pulling her dog into her arms, she wept for all she'd lost and all that would never be.

too little, too late?

THE SILVER MOON CAFE was busy as usual for a Saturday night, with people laughing and enjoying themselves. Del wasn't one of those people.

It had been a week since Addison had kicked him out of her life. For the second time. But this time around was more hell on Earth than he thought possible. The first time there'd been an entire country separating them. This time, there wasn't even a *county* to separate them. She made sure to never show up at the house when he was there, but her perfume lingered in the air long after she'd been there. It made him ache so bad, he was sure ripping his own heart out and stomping on it would hurt less. Their communications had been reduced to emails and text messages about the project, curt and to the point. Nothing personal about them. It pissed him off, but he still had a job to finish and he had to remember he hadn't come home with the intention to get back together with Addison Davenport.

He couldn't face being in the lake house alone with nothing but his memories, so he called the guys to let off some steam. Jackson was in town and Del was ready to unwind by playing some pool and shooting the shit.

"You're up, man," Jackson called across the table after breaking.

He took a long sip of his Coke and set it on the bar table next to him. Sliding off the stool, he studied the balls on the table. "Five ball in the side pocket."

Del lined up his shot and sank it and two other solids before banking one too hard and missing the side pocket. "Damn."

"Missed that one, Ace," Noah said. Aidan continued the sibling heckling by making an L with his thumb and forefinger then putting it up against his forehead.

"No shit, Sherlock," Del muttered and flicked off Aidan, who grinned. He walked back over to the table and picked up his drink.

"All this sibling love makes me miss Colin." Shane grinned and shook his head.

"How is the tech tycoon doing?" Aidan asked.

Shane nodded. "He's doing well. In negotiations with some people about an app he and his partner created." He sipped his beer and smiled. "Dad would be happy for him. He quit drinking and partying, so the move to the Valley has been good for him."

"Sounds like he's where he needs to be."

Jackson missed his shot and Del stood to line up his next turn.

"You're quiet, Ace." Shane asked, "You okay, man?"

"Yep. Just fine. Seven, corner pocket." His voice was flat, his words clipped. He hit the cue ball harder than necessary, causing the seven ball to land in the pocket with a sharp thump.

"Right." Shane drew out the word, his tone telling Del that he wasn't buying what Del was selling. "How's the project coming along? I heard there was an accident on set. Everyone okay?"

Del leaned over the table and lined up his shot, trying to regulate his pounding heart against his ribs. Was he ready to tell anyone else about his condition? Now that he'd had an incident here in town, guilt at not telling men who were brothers from other mothers ate at him. How much longer could he dodge the conversation? He'd have to bob and weave for the next few weeks until the show was wrapped up.

"Yeah, everyone's fine." He evaded from commenting further on the accident. "We still have a couple of more weeks of work to be done. We should be finished up about a week before the grand opening." He took his shot and the ball stopped short of the pocket.

"Got any new things lined up after the show wraps?" Jackson asked. His unspoken words were "and is my sister included?"

Del's skin warmed under his T-shirt and he caught the eye of the waitress and signaled for another round of beers for the guys and a Coke for him. The walls seemed to be closing in and he was sick of being in hiding.

When Jackson cleaned up the table and won the game, Del passed his cue to Aidan and plucked his fresh drink off the table. After downing about half of it in one go and slamming the glass to the table, Shane whistled. "Sure, you're okay"

Del cleared his throat. "No. I'm not okay."

Even in the noisy bar, each of the men froze and four pairs of eyes stared him down. Del fought not to laugh like a maniac. The scene in front of him was like a movie where the music stops and everyone looks at you.

Jackson narrowed his green eyes that were so much like Addie's. "What do you mean, you're not okay?" he asked, leaning against the pool table. Del glanced over to his brothers, who both nodded imperceptibly.

Del took a deep breath and let the words spill out. "Six months ago, I was diagnosed with myasthenia gravis."

"What the hell is that?" Shane asked, hooking his feet on the bottom rung of the stool and sitting back.

"It's a neuromuscular disease, similar to multiple sclerosis. There is no cure, but symptoms are manageable. So far my case seems to be mild. My symptoms come and go for now." He took a fortification sip of sugar and caffeine. "But there's a good chance my symptoms will progress and get worse. Or they could go into remission. I just don't know."

"Did this cause your fall last week?" Shane asked. He tilted his head and glanced down at Del's glass. "And is that the reason you aren't drinking?"

Del nodded. "The medication I take doesn't do well with alcohol. And so far, it's affected my vision mostly. That day I had double vision and I stepped where I thought there was a board and fell off the side." He shook his head. "I got lucky that time. My injuries were minor and more importantly, no one else was hurt." He shrugged a shoulder. "With the contract up for renewal, it was the right time to walk away."

"I assume you two knew," Jackson used his cue and motioned toward Noah and Aidan, who nodded. His gaze came back to Del. "Does Addison know?"

Jackson's tone was as hard as stone. He could be intimidating when he used his lawyer tone and stare. Most times, Del wasn't bothered by it. This time, though, Del knew he was skating on paper-thin ice with his friend. Addison was all Jackson had left of his immediate family and Del had fucked over his baby sister before. The likelihood of him getting a reprieve, sick or not sick, was slim to none.

"Yeah, she knows. Now." Del rubbed the back of his neck and fought not to squirm under Jackson's stare. "She found out after my fall."

"Son of a bitch," Jackson muttered and shoved off the pool table. He stalked off toward the bar and was lost in the growing crowd.

Fuck. That did not go how Del wanted it to.

"He'll cool off," Aidan murmured. "Just give him some space."

Del rubbed a hand over his head and blew out a breath. "I don't blame him. If I were in his position and he'd fucked over one of our sisters, not just once, but twice? I'm surprised he didn't throat punch me right now."

Noah crossed his arms over his chest and pinned him with a stare. "Have you made a decision yet?"

"No." Del looked out over the crowd of people milling around, talking, laughing, drinking. Mostly locals and since he knew a good many of them, they didn't bother him for autographs or pictures. It was like any other Saturday night in Madison Ridge. And that monotony is what always gave him itchy feet. Could he stick in one place for very long?

He was in the same place he was years ago, just more money in his bank account and age on his body. But he didn't feel any wiser than he had ten years before when it came to choosing his next move and how that would impact his relationship with Addison.

He was head over heels in love with her. If he were being honest, he'd never stopped being head over heels in love with her, he just learned to control his emotions. Having thousands of miles between them helped, but he'd never truly forgotten about her and he'd certainly never gotten over her.

Del looked over at Noah, who stood with a raised eyebrow. Noah wanted to know if Del would be there or would he run again. It was coming down to the wire and Noah wanted answers. Being his brother only bought Del so much time.

"My agent tracked me down here last week." He took a deep sigh before dropping the bomb. "The network has a new show for me. Some travel, but not a demanding schedule like *Property Ace*. More money."

The other three men were silent for a moment. "And what did you tell him?" Shane finally asked.

Del ran a finger through condensation on his glass. "I told him I'd meet with the production team, see what they have in mind. But I haven't made a decision. And I'm not making any guarantees. To anyone."

"I assume that's what you told Addison, too? No guarantees?" Aidan asked, his brows drawn down.

"Well, no. I didn't tell her about it."

His younger brother's laugh was incredulous. Noah turned and took a sip of beer, looking out over the crowd. Shane just shook his head. Del looked at each of them, unsure as to what he'd said. "What? I didn't want to say anything to her until I decided. I was trying to save her the hurt."

Aidan set his beer bottle down with a snap. "You and Addison have been working on this museum project for weeks, she's filmed scenes for the show, and based on your history with each other and rumors around town, I'd say you guys have picked up where you left off ten years ago." He shifted and moved closer to Del, dropping his voice. "Now I ask you, if you were in her position, wouldn't you want to know you played some part in the man you love's life decision?"

Aidan was right. Addison had figured it out anyway, hadn't she? Before he'd ever said a word. She was sharp and smart as hell. Why did he think she wouldn't put two and two together? And this is why she didn't trust him. He was a fucking dumbass. In that moment, he'd made his decision. Now he just had to hope and pray he hadn't really screwed the pooch again.

Del stood abruptly and looked at Shane. "Is your plane here in town?"

"My plane?"

"Yeah, don't you keep it over in the hangar at the airport?"

Shane nodded and pulled his phone out of his back pocket. "When do you want to leave?"

Del glanced up at the old beer sign clock hanging on the wall, half amazed the thing still told time. He calculated for time differences. "As soon as they can fly me out tonight." Shane nodded and walked away, talking to someone on the phone.

Aidan narrowed his eyes at Del. "What are you going to do?"

"I'm going to take my life back." He held out a fist. "Thanks for looking out, bro."

"It's my job." Aidan returned the fist bump.

When he turned to Noah, his older brother leveled a stare at him. "I don't know what you have planned, but whatever it is, make it right. You won't get another chance."

Del wasn't sure if Noah meant with just Addison or with the whole situation again. Either way, Noah was right, as much as Del hated to admit it.

Shane came back over, phone still in his hand. "Meet me at the airport in an hour. The plane will be ready to go when you get there."

"Thanks, man." He clapped Shane on the shoulder.

Shane's thumbs moved across the screen on his phone. "No worries, man." He finished his typing and put his phone in his back pocket, meeting Del's eyes. "It wasn't so long ago I was in the same position. I understand what it's like."

Del lifted his chin in acknowledgement. "Oh, one more thing. I need the number to your broker." He grinned. "I got a house to put on the market."

Del turned back to Noah. "I'll make it right."

Noah nodded. "I'll handle Jackson. Get on out of here." He lifted a chin toward the side door. "Go out that way. A group of beauties just walked in and I'm thinking they'll only try to stop you on the way out."

"Thanks, big brother." Their identical blue eyes held for a minute before Del ducked down the side hallway and out the door.

He needed to go get his shit together before he ran out of chances with the only thing that mattered.

CHAPTER TWENTY-THREE
shattered hearts

"WHAT DO YOU THINK, ADDISON?"

Addison tuned in when she heard her name. She cleared her throat and tried to think of what the older woman had been jabbering about. "I'm sorry, can you repeat the question?"

The woman harrumphed and rolled her eyes. "I said, if we can negotiate the price, we should be able to use the pumpkin farm from North Georgia."

"Oh. Yes, if we can get the price we want, that would be great." She looked around the small conference area and noticed the odd looks four members were giving her. The fifth member, Stella Reynolds, had a look of concern on her face.

"Ladies," Stella said to the room, "let's take a break, okay? Ten minutes."

Addison wanted to hug Stella but opted to push her chair back and bolt for the door. She double-timed it down the hall to the ladies' room and once inside, locked herself in a stall. Leaning against the flimsy metal wall, she breathed deep, trying to gather her continuously scattered thoughts.

It had been two weeks since she'd told Del it was over. Other than texts and emails, they hadn't spoken at all. Hell yeah, she was avoiding him. She had to in order to get some distance from him, get away from him before he broke her heart again.

That's what her mind said, anyway. But her heart? Oh, that organ was making her life hell and questioning every decision she'd made. What if he was telling the truth? What if it was different this time?

She shook her head. The path she walked on with Del was littered with heartbreak and he was the same, just older, which told her it would continue to be the path of most destruction. Breaking it off before it went too far again was the right choice.

She took one last deep breath and rubbed her hands on her slacks. A tug on her jacket to straighten it and she was ready to face the music. As she reached for the door latch, two women came in talking.

"—what's wrong with her. She's not even listening."

"Well, I know what's wrong with her. The same thing that was wrong with her ten years ago."

She pulled back her hand and held her breath. Two board members, Betty Roberts and Helen Phillips, were solidifying what Addison already believed about the two older women. They stayed on the board to be in on the latest gossip. Otherwise, the pair were about as useless as a one-armed coat hanger.

"You mean?" Betty asked.

"Oh, yes. She and Del were hot and heavy again, rumor has it. And rumor has it, he up and left her again."

Addison rolled her eyes. She left *him*. Apparently, Helen's sources weren't all that reliable.

"Well, she should have known better. Didn't she think about him leaving when he finished that museum her daddy started?" Betty tsked. "Poor Stephen would be rolling over in his grave if he knew they started up again."

"My sources also say her daddy is the reason Del is the one working on it." A pause. "There's something fishy going on with all that, but I haven't heard what."

"Helen, you always think people are fishy. Especially since your husband ran off and left you."

That was the freaking truth.

"Well, all I know is he didn't wait around to finish the project either." Helen's voice was rife with malicious glee.

Wait, what?

Addison swallowed the nausea that threatened to drop her to her knees. *How the hell could he not tell me?* She had wondered why the daily reports started coming from Noah, but now her worst fears were confirmed.

"He left already?" Betty asked, her tone aghast.

"Yep. A few days ago. He went back to California. Noah's been overseeing the project."

"Helen, Betty." Stella's voice came through loud and clear in the time-worn tiled restroom. "That's enough. Helen, you're the last one that needs to be bad-mouthing anyone. Last I heard, that son of yours is following his daddy's path." She paused, and Addison could see in her mind's eye the cold stare she no doubt gave the two old biddies. "Shall I go on with what I know?"

There was a sniff, presumably from Helen. "That won't be necessary."

"Perfect. Break's over." There was shuffling of feet then the door opened and closed. Addison let out a breath and opened the stall door. Stella leaned against the vanity waiting for her in all her casual, calm elegance.

Addison cleared her throat and walked to one of the sinks. "Thanks for that."

The older woman stayed silent while she washed her hands and dried them with a paper towel. "Addison, I'm sorry."

Addison tossed the towel in the trash can and crossed her arms over her chest. "Why are you sorry? What your son does or doesn't do has nothing to do with you."

Stella nodded once but looked down at the floor. "That's true. But I'm also sorry about the gossip girls there."

Addison shrugged. "They don't bother me much. They've been that way as long as I can remember."

Stella smiled, but it didn't reach her eyes when she looked up at Addison. "And I'm sorry about Del. I take it you know about his illness?"

Addison nodded and looked away. "Yeah. I found out by accident when he fell."

Stella's blue eyes sharpened. "What do you mean 'by accident'? Didn't he tell you before?"

"I overheard him and the doctor talking."

Stella sighed and ran a hand through her long dark tresses. "After I saw you two together at the Memorial Day party, I told him then he needed to tell you."

Addison bit her lip. On some level, she may have forgiven him about the illness. It was the fact he was planning to leave again, just like before, and she hadn't factored into his plans. Just like before. It was déjà vu all over again, but worse. "Did he really leave?"

Stella nodded. "Yes. He came by to see me before he left. Said he had some things to take care of in California."

"Did he say if he was coming back?"

Stella frowned. "No, sweetie. I'm sorry, he didn't. He looked like hell. I'm worried he's not taking care of himself like he should be." She pushed off the vanity and turned to Addison, taking her by the shoulders. "Addie, Del is so in love with you, he can't think straight. I can see it in his eyes, just like I see it in yours. Now, I don't know what happened between the two of you, but whatever it is, I think you two can work it out this time around."

Addison shook her head and dropped her chin to her chest. "I don't know, Stella. Del is who he is," she looked up into Stella's eyes, so much like Del's. "I can't stop him from being who he is. I love him for everything he is, but I can't keep getting left behind."

"I know, baby." Stella pushed a lock of Addison's hair behind her ear and cupped her chin. "Everything will work out how it's supposed to. Don't count Delaney out just yet."

Addison's phone vibrated from her pocket. Her heart jumped in her throat, wondering if it was the man in question.

Stella stepped back. "I'll let you take that. See you back in the meeting. I'll cover for you." She smiled and left Addison alone.

Her hands were slippery as she pulled the phone out, but her stomach dropped when she saw the caller was Teri. "Hi, Teri." She tried to infuse some enthusiasm in her voice.

"Hey, I'm glad I got you on the phone," the producer sighed. "I know you were supposed to film some scenes tomorrow, but we're having to shift around a couple of them now that Del left. But I guess you already knew that."

Addison swallowed hard and schooled her voice. "Oh, yeah. Of course. So what do the new times look like?"

She listened as Teri rattled off the last couple of times Addison needed to be on the set before they filmed the live scene on the day of the museum opening. "If Del doesn't come back for the live show, I'm going to kick his ass."

"What makes you think he won't come back?" Addison asked, hoping her tone was nonchalant. But her chest was tight and breathing became a laborious affair.

Teri sighed. "Oh, he'll be back. He has to or he'll be in breach of contract. But I do know he was going to meet with some of the boys at the network on another show. So it may be a quick in and out thing for him. That Rick," she muttered. "He really is a prick. Couldn't wait to wheel and deal another show for Del. You know," her voice changed, hitting a higher pitch, "I'm actually kind of pissed off at Del. I thought he was done with Hollywood. And honestly? I thought you guys were a thing anyway. We had a bet going around here that he was staying here. Damn, I hate losing."

Addison's heart sank and she swallowed the lump in her throat. "We weren't really a thing. Not this time. We're friends and we just… we were hanging out while he was here." *Right. If hanging out meant having sex all the time and making me fall in love with him again.*

"Hanging out. Is that what the kids are calling it these days?" Teri asked, humor coloring her tone.

"Ha ha. Look, I've known Del nearly all my life. He was never planning to stay, Teri. It's just not in him. He's always been the adventurous type. If I'd really seen him for who he was all those years ago, I would have known better than to pin my hopes and dreams on him."

"You're in love with him again." It wasn't a question but rather a statement from Teri.

"More like still. That's why I had to let him go."

Teri was quiet for a few moments. "For what it's worth, Addison, I think the feeling is mutual. The way he looks at you, the chemistry you guys have on film…it's amazing."

They were amazing together. When things were right, they were phenomenal. They knew each other's movements, could read each other's thoughts, and of course, the sex was incredible. But as much as they had proclaimed to love one another, they could never land on the same page when it came to protecting each other's hearts.

"Sometimes love just isn't enough."

Tears threatened. It was truly over. After this, he wasn't coming back. Sure, he had his project, but with Noah handling it, there would be no need for him to come back until right before filming the live show.

She'd sent him away. It had been her decision. It had been the right decision. The best decision to protect herself from being broken by him again.

So why were her heart and soul in a million pieces?

rip property ace

DEL SAT in a fancy leather office chair in a slick, modern conference room. The Los Angeles skyline spread out beyond the glass walls and the mountains rose toward the sky beyond the horizon. It was a beautiful sight and distracted him from the business at hand.

No, that was a lie. The scenery was stunning, but it was a stunning strawberry blonde back on the East Coast that kept his focus anywhere but where he was. He'd left without a word. He knew it would look like he ran, just like he always did. And knowing the way her beautiful, sharp mind worked he could guess she was thinking he left her behind again for another adventure.

He wanted to bang his head on the table to see if he could shake loose the brain he obviously had lost ten years ago. He bit back a sigh and fisted his hand under the table. His plan had to work. It was a gamble. He could lose it all.

But Addison was worth whatever risk he had to take.

"What do you think?" Rick's voice brought him back with a jolt to LA.

Del straightened in the chair. "You explained the concept to me before. And it is a great concept." He released a deep breath, rolling the dice. "But it isn't for me."

Rick and a room full of suits from the network froze. For several beats, no one said a word, silent looks of *what the hell* exchanged between the guys sitting across from him. Rick glanced toward them and cleared his throat. "What do you mean, it isn't for you?"

Del sighed as he looked at his longtime agent. He turned his Hollywood smile to the suits. "Gentlemen, would you give Rick and me a moment?"

Murmurs and shuffling of papers filled the air as the men moved out of the room. Del smiled behind his hand, thinking about how pissed Addison and his sisters would be at the fact that not a single woman was in the room. It did strike Del as odd, since the shows they were doing were geared to a more female demographic.

Rick's leg bounced and his lips were pursed. As soon as the door closed, he was all up in Del's grill. "What the fuck, Del? I thought this was a done deal."

Del tilted his head and rocked gently in the chair. Anger simmered just below the surface of his skin, but he kept his cool. He had no desire to work in Hollywood in the future, but he was not one to burn bridges. Well, at least not anymore. "I never agreed to do the show, Rick. We talked about it. But I never said this was a done deal. The only reason I took this meeting is because I was already in town to meet with a real estate broker."

"You're selling your house? What kind of dumbass move is that?"

Del clenched his fists and glared at him. "Watch it, Rick.""

Rick bunched his jaw and looked to be mentally counting to ten. "It was implied to me you would do this. These guys are expecting you to sign the contract so they can move forward."

"Why would they think that, Rick?" Del leaned forward with his elbows on the table. "What did you tell them?"

Rick opened his mouth and then closed it, looking away, his face turning pink. Del's blood pressure rose and it was hard for him to keep his calm. "Rick." He banged a fist on the table, rattling the glass of water in front of him. "Look at me." When his agent looked back at him, he asked again. "What the hell did you tell them?"

He sighed. "I told them you were in. This was just a formality. I told them you'd already signed the contract."

"Why the hell would you do that?" Del asked, anger and frustration clear in his voice.

Rick tapped a pen against the leather portfolio on the table. "They were going to give me an extra commission if I had the contract signed before the meeting." Del's eyes met his, and the man across from him was a stranger. Rick's brown eyes were cold and flat.

"Are you fucking kidding me?"

"No." Rick shrugged. "Just because you've had a crisis of conscience doesn't mean we all have."

"What the—" Del stared at the man who'd been his agent for over ten years. But it was as though he were seeing the man for the first time. The slicked back hair, the suit and watch worth more than some people make in a year. When had Rick become this slimy asshole?

Del wasn't his only client, but without a doubt Rick had made a shit ton of money off him over the years. Del always made sure he was kept in the loop with deals. Until this time because in his mind this wasn't even a deal. He had to admit since his diagnosis, his only concerns had been getting done with his *Property Ace* contract and figuring out how to salvage his relationship with Addison.

What he liked the most about his job was helping the families whose houses he remodeled and breathed new life into. He didn't need the cameras to get that done. He could do that in his hometown for people who needed it.

Del blew out a slow breath. With that breath went all of his reservations, all the things holding him back from what he'd been looking for since he'd left Madison Ridge. No, that was wrong. It had actually been since his father died.

He wanted to go home.

He shoved the chair back and stood. Rick shot up out of his chair. "Where the hell are you going?"

Del just smiled and held up his hand in a *wait a minute* gesture. He walked over to the door and opened it. "Y'all can come back in."

Rick snorted. "Y'all? You've spent too much time in the south, my friend."

What Del really wanted to do was punch his soon-to-be-former agent in the throat. Instead, he grinned. "Actually, I haven't spent nearly enough time there lately. But that's about to change."

Before Rick could speak, all the suits were seated. "Okay, Del. Are we ready to move forward?" Tim Hanes, the head of show development, looked expectantly between Del and Rick.

Del stood behind his chair, gripping the back of it. "Here's how this is going to go down." He looked each man in the eye, his gaze finally landing on Tim. "There's a plane waiting for me at the airport. I'm headed back to Madison Ridge now to finish filming the end of my last *Property Ace* episode. Once the filming is over, I've fulfilled my contract for *Property Ace*. Then I'm done." He paused as shocked faces stared back at him. Everyone except Tim, who sat with his eyes narrowed and leaned back in the chair. It wasn't the reaction Del expected.

"I appreciate you thinking of me for this project. But it's not for me. I'm ready to move on to a new chapter in my life." He nodded once. "I wish each of you the best."

Del turned on his heel and walked out of the conference room, unable to stop smiling.

"Delaney."

At his name, he turned around and found Tim walking toward him. "Yeah?"

Tim stopped in front of Del. "Are you sure this is what you want to do?"

"Absolutely."

Tim nodded slowly, not taking his eyes off Del's. "Does this change have anything to do with a beautiful blonde who's house your final episode is focused on?" When Del lifted a brow, Tim grinned. "I've seen some of the filming. You guys have some crazy chemistry."

One side of Del's mouth kicked up and he slid his hands into the pockets of his jeans. ""It has everything to do with her. But there are other things going on in my life right now. This lifestyle, while it has been an awesome experience for me, I just can't continue it."

"I understand. Even if some don't." He held out a hand to Del. "Listen, if you're ever interested in doing a special or anything like that, let me know. We always need content like that, and the audience loves you. Maybe you can even include a certain property owner." He winked.

Del laughed and shook Tim's hand. "I'll think about it. Thanks, Tim."

"You're welcome." He slid his hands into the pockets of his slacks. "You better head out, don't want to miss your plane. And I have some anxious yes men to go settle down back there." He paused. "Take care of yourself, Del."

"You too, Tim."

Del turned and walked away from his old life. He had a new life waiting for him on the other side of the country and he was eager to get back to it.

CHAPTER TWENTY-FIVE
remind me

WHEN ADDISON ARRIVED on set for the last day of filming, the area around the house was a chaotic mess. A few of the town commissioners milled around in the shade of a large tent, waiting for filming to begin. The white tissue paper collars they sported told her they'd already been in the makeup trailer and were camera ready.

Crew members ran all over the place hollering out orders, dragging cables, and adjusting lights. In the middle of it all, Teri stood directing everyone as though she were in an air traffic control tower. Del was nowhere in sight. His absence felt like a punch to her gut that she tried to ignore.

One of the production assistants ushered Addison into the makeup trailer. She sat in front of the mirror, wide-eyed at the whirlwind pace things were moving. It was a bit different from the other shoots she'd done so far.

"It's always like this on the final day of shooting." Eve, the makeup artist, must have noticed her deer-in-the-headlights expression. She smiled in the mirror. "It's especially insane today since they are filming this last part live." She lowered her voice and looked around. "Rumor has it there's some surprise happening at the end. I can't wait to see what they've pulled out of their asses this time."

Fifteen minutes later, Teri came through the door of the trailer, a pair of headphones around her neck and a tablet in one hand. "Hey, Addison. Ready for the live show?" Her smile was reassuring in spite of the barely restrained chaotic vibe that came off her.

Addison nodded and blew out a breath. "Ready as I'll ever be."

"Good." Teri went over the things Addison needed to do but since it was a live show there was a little room for improv. "There's a special thing we're doing at the end we haven't put in the beat sheet, so my advice to you is to just go with it."

Addison lifted her chin at Eve's silent direction before the woman brushed on face powder. "I haven't seen Del. Did he make it back?" She hoped her tone was casual but feared her poker face had taken a leave of absence.

"I—" Teri held up a finger. "Hold on." She frowned as she listened to the headset. "Shit. I gotta go. Five minutes, Addie. I'll send a PA to get you." Teri slammed out the door, before Addison could respond. This was a different side to the producer than she'd seen before.

Eve smiled as she swept a large makeup brush across Addison's forehead. "She's always like that on the last day of shooting. And with this one being a live show? She's even more on edge. Don't take it personally. Oh," her smile turned into a gleeful grin. "You should see your team in their makeup."

Addison's eyes widened. With everything going on, she had forgotten about the bet. The bet she'd made with Del that kicked off their reconnecting. Her stomach dropped but she pasted on a smile. "Oh geez. I can tell by the look on your face you had some fun with them."

Eve laughed and turned to pick up a brow pencil. "Hell, yeah. I painted their faces as animals. There's everything from a unicorn to a baboon."

Addison laughed. "I can't wait to see this."

A few minutes later, Teri's PA came in to get Addison and brought her to the side of the trailer, where the house was just out of her vision. "Wait right here, Ms. Davenport. Mr. Reynolds will be here shortly to bring you in for the reveal."

Her heart slammed against her chest at the thought of seeing Del again after over a week of virtually no contact. She nodded and swallowed hard. The PA stood next to her looking around the corner as Addison started to pace back and forth.

"Addison."

His voice never failed to send shivers down her spine. She spun around at the sound of that deep timbre and God, he looked so good. A five o'clock shadow covered his strong jaw, his Caribbean-blue eyes and dark blond hair popping against his tanned skin.

"Hey, Del." She wanted to say more, but all she could do was stare. The only saving grace from making the situation utterly awkward was the fact Del couldn't seem to take his eyes off her either.

"Mr. Reynolds…" The PA's voice broke the stare and he turned to the young girl standing next to him, shuffling her feet. "Teri is signaling."

Del glanced around and an entire camera crew was set up around them. "Okay, let's get started. Ready?" he asked her, holding out his hand with a smile.

Warmth spread through her body at the show of teamwork. She wished with all her heart they could make it work, be together the way she wanted to be, but she knew him too well. He would never settle down, no matter how much she wanted him to. But for today, at this moment, she could share this time with him and work as a team. She loved him and if this was the last time they would be together, she would make the most of it.

She slid her hand into his. "Ready."

After a few minutes of setup, the lights came on and the cameras started rolling. Del spoke to the camera, setting up the narrative and history of why the house had been featured on the show. He walked toward her as he spoke. "Today is the best part of my job," Del said to the camera, "reveal day." He turned to Addison with a huge smile on his handsome face. "Are you ready to see the finished product?"

She nodded with a grin. "I'm more than ready."

"Okay, here we go. Close your eyes." He put his hands on her shoulders. "Three, two…one."

When Addison turned around, her jaw dropped and tears filled her eyes, coursing down her cheeks. Del kept his hands on her shoulders and she lifted hers to twine their fingers together. "Oh my God. Delaney, it's…stunning."

"We did that together, Addie. Our fathers would have been proud." His voice was low and rough in her ear. With the strength of Del's body behind her and the beauty of the estate her father had left behind, the feelings running through her veins were almost too much to bear.

"Come on, let's get a closer look." Del ran his hand down her arm until he linked their hands together and pulled her forward. She swiped the tears off her cheeks and took a deep breath, following him toward the house.

The yard and shrubs against the house were immaculately cut and the window boxes contained all sorts of flowers in a rainbow of colors that popped against the greenery.

The white clapboard, black shutters, and wrought iron had been freshly painted. The red brick steps and porch had been power washed and the half dozen windows that made up the front of the two-story home shone in the late June sunshine. Columns stood tall across the front of the house, giving it a stately historic feel that warmed Addison's heart. Black rocking chairs sat at intervals on the front porch just begging for visitors to stop and take a load off.

As she walked up the stairs with Del, she breathed out a sigh. "Wow, the door came out so beautifully."

Entranced, Addison ran a hand along the etching of the square glass in the center of the front door. She gasped at the tiny detail she almost missed. In the lower right-hand corner of the glass, a "D" and "R" were etched in winding calligraphy. "Oh, Del. I love it."

Del grinned and turned back to the camera. "I think she likes it, guys."

Her enchanted haze wore off when she was reminded cameras were following them around. She turned to him with a smile. "Can we check out the inside?"

"Absolutely." He pushed down the latch on the door handle and opened the door wide. Walking ahead of her, he spread his arms out. "Welcome to the Madison Ridge Historic Museum."

Behind her, murmurs came from some of the chamber members as she walked in. Her jaw dropped as she took in the gleaming hardwood floors. Their dark mahogany color contrasted beautifully with the faintest of grey painted walls and bright white trim throughout the space. The rooms were open concept and spaced out in such a way to keep traffic flowing through the rooms seamlessly. She lifted her head to find the ceiling was covered in ornate tiles that matched the flooring. The pattern on the tiles was trimmed in gold as a nod to the town's history with the metal. It was such an amazing little detail. Everything Del and his crew had done to the house was beyond anything she could have dreamed.

It took another thirty minutes for her to go through the house, oohing and aahing over the details and master craftsmanship in the house. All of the historic items that had been donated by her father to the town were laid out throughout the house to the specifications the late Stephen Davenport and Paul Reynolds put together decades before when they first envisioned it.

With tears in her eyes, Addison walked out the front door, glancing around at the front porch and all the work that had been done. She walked down the stairs side by side with Del and turned back to look at the house again when she was back on the lawn. "Del, I'm just… amazed at the transformation."

Mayor Samson shook Del's hand. "Your crew did the town proud. We couldn't have asked for a better-looking museum."

Stella came up beside him and nodded. "As chairperson of the chamber, I have to say it's more than we could have asked for." She glanced over to Addison, her eyes glistening with tears. "Addison, your father would be beside himself at this."

All she could do was nod, mindful of the cameras still running. Anything more would cause her to break down on national television.

Stella stepped forward and held Del's hands in hers. She dropped her voice low, but Addison was close enough to hear. "Your father is smiling today, Del. I've never been more proud of you than I am today. Thank you." For a moment, mother and son just stared at each other, a million messages passing between them. It was imperceptible, but there was a shift in Del's demeanor. One that made Addison's heart race in anticipation.

"You're welcome," Del said. His mother hugged him before stepping back and the ribbon was brought out for the four of them to cut.

With the flashes popping and the cameras of *Property Ace* rolling, the red ribbon was cut. Hugs were exchanged and then the members walked off to the side. As Addison started to follow them off to the side, Del grabbed her hand and stopped her. "Wait, we're not quite done with you, Addie." His grin was infectious and all Hollywood.

She couldn't help but return the grin and came back to stand beside him, remembering Teri's words about going with the flow. "Okay, what else have we got, Del?"

He sent her a slow smile before dropping her hand. He turned toward the camera trained directly on him and took a step forward. "As you may know, this is the final episode of *Property Ace*. It was with immense pleasure I was able to come full circle and finish my career on the show that changed my life." He held up a finger. "But what you might not know is this particular reveal has a special place in my heart. Madison Ridge is my hometown. And this beautiful estate we renovated was actually a project my late father and," he turned slightly and gestured toward Addison, "Addison's late father had planned for over twenty years. Unfortunately, they both died before they were able to fulfill their dream—and their promise to the town—of bringing the house back to its former glory and making it a museum to celebrate the town's history."

Del took a step back toward Addison until he was standing in front of her. He took both of her hands in his and looked down into her eyes. The fact the cameras were still rolling and aimed at the two of them didn't escape her, but when his bright, ocean-blue eyes stared into hers, everything else faded away. "I could never have done this project without you. Not because we had to," he grinned and she chuckled, "but because it brought me home."

Her eyes widened and her heart virtually stopped when Del lowered to one knee. "Oh my God. Del..." she trailed off and glanced around at the people around them. The cameras were still rolling, and Teri stood next to one giving her the *keep going* gesture. Behind the energetic producer stood the whole Reynolds crew—Noah, Aidan,

Grace, Amelia, and Charley—even Jackson, as well as her face painted softball teammates, with smiles on their face.

"Addison Davenport, I've loved you my entire life. And you make me want to be the best version of myself. Ten years ago, I walked away from you searching for adventure, thinking it was anywhere but here. What I didn't realize at the time is I had all the adventure I'd ever need right here. You're the strongest person I know and you make me want to be a better man. Your man. My life's adventure is you, Addison. I'm not going anywhere without you. Because there's nowhere in this world I'd rather be than here *with* you."

Her jaw dropped, heart racing, when he pulled the ring. "You still have it?" she whispered.

Del smiled. It was the ring he'd given her once before, the one she'd loved so much and it nearly killed her to give it back. An emerald cut, diamond solitaire in a white gold band that twisted like two vines entangled together in an infinite loop.

He looked up at her and those impossible blue eyes were clear and filled with love. No holding back. "Addie, I know I gave you this ring once before. But this time, I give you my whole heart with it. You're my adventure of a lifetime. Will you marry me?"

He was offering her everything she ever wanted from him. And this time she wasn't going to let him walk away. But she also wasn't going to make it easy on him. "Del, stand up." He raised a brow. "Please, stand up."

He stood and looked down into her eyes. "You're killing me, Addie."

She smiled at him and laid her hands on his chest. "Thank you. I wanted to look up into your eyes when I said yes."

That panty-dropping Hollywood smile curved his beautiful mouth as he slid the ring on her finger. Cradling her face in his hands, his eyes roamed her face for a moment. "I love you, Addison."

"I love you, Delaney."

He lowered his mouth over hers and sealed the deal with a searing kiss that burned all the way down to her toes.

When Del pulled away, he glanced around. "She said yes!"

Cheers broke out all around them and Addison laughed, burying her face in his chest. "Oh my God, I can't believe you did that on live television."

With a grin, Del signed off to the audience and Teri yelled, "Cut!" Before Teri could say another word, Del took Addison's hand and led her back inside the now empty house. Once inside, he ran his hands down to her ass and pulled her close, his desire for her pressed against her as he took her mouth and kissed her breathless.

When they broke apart, he laid his forehead on hers. "If you want a different ring, I understand. I'll buy you whatever the hell you want."

She curled her hand into a fist, protecting the ring. "Don't you dare. This ring is perfect. It means everything to me."

He grinned. "This is the first adventure of many, Starshine. Think you can handle it?"

She twined her arms around his neck and pressed her breasts into his hard chest, causing him to moan. "As long as I'm with you, I can handle anything, Ace."

"You know, I'm no longer the Ace."

"Delaney, you'll always be my ace."

"I may need you to remind me of that." His voice was low and sexy, causing tingles along her skin. "You know, like every day for the rest of our lives."

"Every day? I think I can deal with that." A grin curved her lips and she brought his head down to seal their forever with a kiss.

TWO MONTHS LATER

YOU'RE A LUCKY BASTARD.

It was what Delaney thought each and every morning he woke up next to Addison. He was reclined against the dozen or so throw pillows on the bed, his eyes on the woman that was his whole world as she stood in front of the bathroom mirror. She tied a navy blue bandana in her blonde hair and stood back to check out the results. Her fire engine red lips curved when her eyes met his in the mirror. "See anything you like, Ace?"

His eyes took in the legs that looked impossibly tan against her white thigh length shorts and the red tank top that hugged the curves of her breasts and flat belly. Wedge sandals that gave her a couple of inches in height and tied around her slim ankles completed the ensemble. She looked like a patriotic pinup girl. Fireworks indeed.

In one swift motion, Del rolled off the bed and strolled into the bathroom. "I like everything I see."

He walked up behind her, caging her between his body and the vanity. With his stare on hers in the mirror, he swept her ponytail to one side and laid a hot open mouthed kiss on the soft skin of her neck. Her breath hitched when his lips made contact and her eyes slid closed. "You do?" she whispered.

"Fuck yeah." His voice was rough, ragged with need. He'd barely touched her and he was already hard as steel. "Everything. Those eyes that slay me every time you look at me." Another kiss to the neck. "Those lips that are soft as pillows and know how to drive me to the brink every time." Kiss, then a swipe of his tongue. She shuddered. "Those long legs that wrap around my waist just perfectly." A hand slid down her hips and toyed with the edge of her shorts. She pushed back against his hard length and moaned softly.

It took every ounce of willpower he had not to tear off the shorts. "You know what I love the most, though? This." Del moved a hand under her tank top and laid it over her heart. It beat under his hand, strong and quick. "Your heart makes you exquisite, Addison."

Tears pooled in her eyes, making the green stand out like emeralds in sunlight. She raised her arms and hooked an arm around his neck. Her fingertips grazed the short stubble on the back of his head. "Del?" Her whisper was low.

"Hmmm?" He nuzzled his nose along the length of her neck, inhaling her lavender scent.

"I don't mind being late, if you don't."

He grinned at their reflection and slid a hand down to the waistband of her shorts. With a flick of his hand, he had her shorts unbuttoned and unzipped. Finding her wet and ready, they groaned in unison. "We might be really late."

"I don't care." She turned in his arms and crushed her mouth to his. Her arms came up around his neck and without breaking the kiss, Del lifted her onto the vanity, stepping between her thighs. Within seconds, the floor was littered with clothing, the air thick with lust.

Thirty sated minutes later and a retying of Addison's bandana they —along with Murphy on his bright blue leash—were in his truck and headed into downtown Madison Ridge.

"I'm starving. I want one of Amelia's apple turnovers." Addison practically bounced in the seat next to him. "And coffee. Lots of coffee. Someone kept me up late last night."

Del chuckled. God, she was adorable. "Hell yeah, I did. And since I'm such a nice guy, you shall have coffee and pastries, my queen.

Right, Murph?" The big chocolate lab leaned his head forward from the backseat and swiped his tongue on Del's cheek.

Addison's smile rivaled the sun and she looked out the window. "We're still early. That's good. And looks like a nice turn out so far. Oh! Grab that spot!" She pointed to an open parking spot in front of The Sweet Spot. As he stepped out of the truck and opened the backdoor for Murphy to jump out, the late summer heat rose from the pavement and humidity made the air shimmer.

When Del opened the door to the bakery, allowing Addison and Murphy to walk ahead of him, the cold, air conditioned air hit his skin, cooling it instantly. He sighed in relief both for the cool air and that the bakery was empty at the moment.

Amelia stood behind the front counter, a grin on her face. "Hey, chocolate drop. I got a treat for you." Murphy's tail wagged and he trotted forward. When he got to the counter, he jumped and placed his huge paws on the counter. Gingerly, he took the bone from Amelia's hand and plopped down on his feet. Treat securely in between his teeth, he proceeded to walk over to a corner and stretch out, the bone already turning into crumbs as he demolished it. Del looped the leash around a sturdy table leg. Not that the lazy retriever would go anywhere without his mistress.

Amelia turned her gaze to them. "Morning, lovebirds. I didn't expect to see you guys out so early. The parade doesn't start for another couple of hours.

"I have some chamber duties to fulfill with the parade," Addison said. When she swiped at a wisp of hair that escaped her ponytail her ring glinted in her sunlight.

Amelia rolled her eyes. "This town has a parade for everything."

Addison laughed. "Don't I know it. But it is Labor Day and we won't have another one until Halloween."

Amelia leaned against the counter, her arms folded over her chest. "I thought y'all would be holed up in bed all weekend."

Del exchanged a heated look with his girl and a beautiful blush crept up Addie's cheeks. It reminded him of how she looked after they had sex. Flushed and satisfied.

He stepped behind Addison and wrapped his arms around her

waist. "My woman is committed to her position. Otherwise we would still be in bed. Not sleeping mind you."

"Del!" Addison lamented at the same time Amelia said, "Oh God, make it stop." Delighted, he laughed at both of them and planted a loud kiss on Addison's cheek before turning to his sister. "We need two coffees and three of those apple thingees you make that are like heaven in my mouth."

"I thought I was—" Addison started with a grin.

Amelia held a hand in a stop sign motion. "Oh my Lord, please stop. I just threw up in my mouth a bit."

When Addison giggled and popped up on her toes to kiss him on the mouth, Amelia rolled her eyes, but Del caught a small smile on her lips. "I'll be back," Addison said and walked off toward the ladies room. Del's eyes followed her form as she walked away. How long did this fucking parade thing last? It was hot as Hades outside and he wanted nothing more than to strip Addie down and have his way with her. Again.

Amelia snapped her fingers in his face. "Hey, perv."

Del's gaze snapped back to Amelia but even her name calling couldn't wipe the smile off his face. "What the fuck was I thinking for ten years?" In spite of the fact he was here and not going anywhere, the years apart and all they missed still made his chest ache sometimes. "Jesus, I missed her."

Amelia shrugged and chose four apple turnovers before putting them in a white paper bag. "Does it matter at this point? I mean, you guys are engaged and working together professionally. Seems like it's working out well."

The museum opening had gone off without a hitch and exceeded both his and Addison's expectations. After filming finished, Del had gone to work with Noah and the family business, helping on the renovation side so Noah could get back to the business of land development.

He'd had to fly back to California a couple of times to close on his house in Malibu and tie up some loose ends, but Addie had been by his side each time. With the museum project such a success, he and Addie were in talks about a partnership between their respective company's and the Madison Ridge Revitalization Committee to renovate historical houses in the area.

Del nodded. "It is working out well. And the best is yet to come." He laid a hand over hers on the bag as she handed it to him. He leaned close over the counter. "Are you okay? Not working too hard again are you?"

His words were just above a whisper and judging by the shadow that crossed her eyes, they'd packed the punch he intended on.

She tugged at her hand and avoided his stare. "I don't know what you're talking about."

"You know damn well what I'm talking about, Amelia. I understand building a business and career, trust me. But—"

"Stop." She put up a palm and met his stare. "I know you mean well, but let's not go there, okay? I'm fine. I have it all under control this time."

Del's eyes narrowed. "And yet here you stand, with a worried look in your eyes. Oh, you cover it well for most people. But I see it. Tell me if you need help, Amelia."

Amelia's fingers gripped the bag hard enough to cause it to crinkle in protest and tugged hard enough to slip free of his grasp. She closed her eyes a moment before pasting a smile on her face. "Del. I love you. You're my big brother and I respect you. But I need you to stop. Anything I got going on, I can handle. If all goes the way I want it to, you'll be hearing from me. Until then? Leave it be."

Del sighed and hoped she meant what she said. He pulled out his wallet and laid out more than enough cash to cover his order. "I'm sorry. I won't bring it up again. Promise."

"Won't bring what up again?" Addison asked.

"Nothing." Amelia and Del said in unison.

Addison looked back and forth between the siblings. "Okay..." she drew the word out. "So Ame, are you going to have a chance to come out to the parade?"

Amelia shook her head. "Probably not. Especially if my help doesn't show up soon."

"Are you coming to the house tonight for fireworks?" Del asked.

Amelia sighed. "Maybe. I need to be in the shop early tomorrow. I've got a meeting in Atlanta. Which means—"

"Which means you need to make sure everything is just so before you turn your baby over to someone for a day." Del finished Amelia's sentence with a grin.

She pointed a finger at him. "Bingo. You get me, Del."

"Hell, yeah." The two bumped fists and his heart filled with love for his sister.

She tilted her head. "Del, have I told you lately how glad I am you're home?"

He grinned. "Not lately. But I never mind hearing that from my favorite pain in the ass."

Amelia laid a hand over her heart and batted her lashes in mock flattery. "Me? I'm your favorite?"

"Don't you dare tell the other two. I'll deny it to the grave. And then exact cold revenge on you."

She rolled her eyes. "You wish."

Addison chuckled and untied Murphy. "Okay, children. We gotta go." She tugged at his arm as she walked toward the door. "Bye, Ame. I hope we see you tonight."

Throughout the day, Del watched with pride as Addison kicked ass at being a pillar of the community. The town loved her and the devotion she had to it was written all over her face and in the way she interacted with everyone from babies in strollers with sticky fingers to the old timers who wanted to complain about the parking situation and the tourists.

Later, as they sat together on an old quilt, watching the fireworks with family surrounding them, Del thought about where he'd been the year before. He'd been on the beach, alone, and missing Addison just like he had every day since he'd left.

He hugged her tighter and she turned her head to look up at him. "I love you, Starshine."

She brought a hand up to caress his face. "I love you too, Ace."

Their lips met in a kiss that started soft, but grew more passionate until calls of "Get a room!" rang out.

Del pulled back and smiled down into her eyes that held his future. "Let's go home."

Thank you for reading **REMIND ME**! Want a peek into the happily ever after for Del & Addison? Get access to their bonus scene by signing up to my newsletter.

Flip the page for a preview of book 3 in the Madison Ridge: Homecoming series, Wreck Me. This is Aidan and Megan's steamy, grumpy sunshine story.

wreck me:
chapter one

CRASH INTO ME

AFTER PULLING AN ALL-NIGHTER, Aidan Reynolds was exhausted.

Thankfully, the good citizens of Madison Ridge had managed to behave most of the day, a relief after he and a couple of other deputies had broken up a bonfire get-together gone sideways. Of course, the Brewster brothers had never done anything quietly—even when they were all back in grade school together—especially when they'd tied one on…maybe even two. Aidan's bad shoulder throbbed from where one of them had taken a cheap shot at it.

It wasn't the first time he'd had to haul in the two knuckleheads for fighting, and he figured it wouldn't be his last.

But damn, at thirty-two, they were all getting too old for that kind of stupid shit.

He circled through the square, headed for the station, where a mountain of paperwork waited for him. With Sheriff Thompkins only working part-time due to his cancer treatments, Aidan had been picking up a lot of slack as Deputy Sheriff. Part of that slack included hiring some new staff, especially with the fall festival in a couple of weeks and the holiday season coming up.

Their small town would swell in population for the next few

months. As would the number of calls for crime and accidents from the influx of tourists who seemed to forget the laws of the road when visiting. It would tax their already woefully understaffed department.

At least he had the next day off. He could get some much needed sleep and work on the paperwork from the comfort of his cabin.

If he ever got there. There was some sort of traffic jam in the usually free flowing square. It's why they'd put in the roundabout thing, to keep traffic moving. Aidan peered out the windshield to see the bottleneck was coming from the circle. Turning on the lights and siren, he maneuvered the SUV along the edge of the one way street through the town square, cars moving off to the side however they could.

The cause of the traffic jam sat in the middle of the curve where a red late-model sedan looked like it had failed to yield to an old turquoise-colored sportster. Unfortunately, the coupe looked like it got the worse end of the deal.

That was a shame. It'd been years since he'd seen a Karmann Ghia on the road. And because it had been a while, he didn't have to look at the plates to know that they weren't local.

He made a U-turn in the middle of the road, blocking it off to traffic until he could ascertain what went down. A woman with dark hair was talking to the other driver through the driver's window, but started to walk his way when he parked.

Aidan slid on his glasses and got out, meeting her halfway in the middle of the road. "Ma'am, I'm Deputy Aidan Reynolds. Are you okay?"

She blinked, full pink lips parted. "Um, yes?"

"You're not sure?" He ran his gaze over her, the professional in him looking for injuries, the man in him taking in the curves that her hip-length sweater tried but failed to cover.

He gestured to her forehead where a bright red gash marred the pale skin. "You're bleeding."

"Oh..." A hand went to her hairline and when she pulled it away, she frowned. "I didn't notice."

"Shock. Why don't you walk over here with me to the sidewalk, and I'll get you something to stop the bleeding. Then you can tell me what happened."

She nodded and winced, sending concern skittering around his chest, especially when her eyes seemed to glass over.

"Ma'am?" He waved a hand in front of her face, but she didn't react. "Can you hear me?"

"Yes...I..."

Her eyes fluttered closed and her knees buckled.

"Shit," he muttered, but moved fast, catching her as she fell. He picked her up and carried her to the bench, laying her flat and elevating her feet on the back of it.

"Hey, Aid. Need some help?"

He glanced up to see his sister Charley jogging toward him. "Where'd you come from?"

She lifted the cup and bag that was looped over her wrist. "I was picking up my lunch over at the deli. Saw her go down. Nice catch, by the way."

"Can you sit with her while I go check the rest of the scene?"

Charley waved him off. "Yep, go ahead. I got this."

"There's a first aid kit in my cruiser. Get some gauze for her head."

"Aidan, I got this. Go."

For some inexplicable reason, he didn't want to leave the woman, even though he trusted his sister. Something in her hazel-colored eyes made his gut tighten, and he itched to protect her.

But he had a job to do and he didn't need any distractions.

He jogged over to where a smattering of onlookers talked to a young girl. "How's everything..." he trailed off when the girl turned to him. "Damn it. Again, Ashley?"

When the girl broke into tears, Aidan blew out a breath, wanting to kick his own ass for making her cry. Maggie, an older lady who owned the local diner, wrapped an arm around her and shot him a look. He held up his hands in a silent apology. "Ashley, are you okay? Any bumps, bruises?"

She shook her head against Maggie's shoulder. "No," she squeaked out through tears.

"Okay, good. Can you tell me what happened?"

Ashley hiccupped through a short explanation of how she was making a right turn but never saw the car she hit.

Aidan nodded. "Did you call your dad yet?"

She shook her head and Aidan frowned. "I hate to do this, but you know we have to call him, right?"

Tears coursed down her face, but she nodded and swiped them away. "Yeah, I know. But I don't know where my phone ended up. It was in my hand when…" She stopped and her mouth formed an O.

Busted. Aidan dropped his head and shook it. He pulled his phone out of his back pocket and handed it to her. "Call your dad, Ashley."

While Ashley made a phone call Aidan didn't envy, he took pictures of the scene from several angles for his report. Maggie brought his phone back to him and could only shake her head with a grim smile.

"Not good, huh?" he asked.

"Nope. We may not see Ashley much this year. Or next. Sounds like she might be grounded for the rest of her teenage years."

"Thanks for staying with her, Maggie."

"No problem, son. Come by for breakfast soon and tell your mama I said hi." Her eyes crinkled at the corners when she smiled and patted her beehive hair, a style she'd had since he was a kid and probably before that.

"Will do."

He called a tow truck, since it looked like the sporty little coupe wasn't going anywhere on its own, and walked over to the bench, where the woman was awake and sitting up. Charley ran a hand over her back in a way that reminded him of their mother. The woman's head bent forward, holding the bandage to her head with one hand and a bottle of water in the other. The gauze had a bright red spot that was stark against her increasingly pale skin. He squatted down to catch her gaze.

"Hey, feeling any better? Did I need to call 911 for you?"

"There's no need for all of that. I'll be fine." Her voice was low and barely a rasp over the sounds of the birds chirping and the cars and activity in the square behind them.

"What's your name?"

She lifted her head and closed her eyes as she leaned back against the bench. The movement made her wince before she answered. "Megan."

"Okay, Megan." He stood and shoved his hands into the back pockets of his tactical pants. "Can you tell me what happened?"

She opened her eyes and looked up at him. Fuck. Those eyes. Grayish green with gold flecks and a brown ring circled her slightly dilated pupils. He supposed they would be called hazel. He called them incredible.

Click here to order Wreck Me

———

Thank you so much for reading REMIND ME. It means the world to me that you took a chance on my book! A review on **your favorite retailer** or Goodreads would mean the world to me and makes a HUGE difference for new indie authors like me!

also by eliza peake

The Madison Ridge Series

(Standalone Steamy, Emotional, Small Town Romances)

Trouble Me

Remind Me

Wreck Me

———

Tormented Bastard

A Cocky Hero Club Production

(A second chance, sports romance written in

Vi Keeland & Penelope Ward's Cocky Hero World)

———

Love's Kaleidoscope

A unique collection of love themed short stories.

———

NON FICTION

30 Days Until "The End": An Inspirational Guide to Finishing Your Novel in 30 Days

If you're looking for humor, positivity, and a swift kick to your flagging motivation, Eliza Peake's inspirational guide to completing a draft in thirty days is a must have.

get a sneak peek in all things eliza!

If you'd like to be a part of my street team where you receive access to ARC's first, join my Elite Street Team!

If you like to talk about books, hot guys, and general fun stuff in a drama free zone, join my reader group, Eliza Peake's Reader Group. We have a fun group going and growing all the time!

author's note

Dear Reader,

Welcome back to Madison Ridge! I hope you enjoyed Delaney & Addison's story. These two have been with me off and on for about ten years now. Their story has changed a bit, but I always knew that they would be a second chance romance. High school sweethearts, growing up in a small town with so much history tied to it, and their families are so intertwined.

Delaney isn't perfect, but he holds a special place in my heart. Delaney was one of the first characters I wrote when I started writing again. And I knew that he would not only be handsome and sexy, but kind and strong yet vulnerable. I enjoyed spending time with him to see how he would handle dealing with the love of his life he'd left behind. I knew Addison would need to be smart and strong. Delaney is an alpha man, but Addison doesn't take shit from him no matter how much she loves him. She's beautiful but full of doubt, especially when it comes to the men in her life that she loves. In the end though, they have their HEA. Whew!!

If you liked *Remind Me,* would you consider leaving me a review? I can be found on Goodreads, Bookbub, and **all major retailers.** I also have a super fun newsletter, The Sneak Peake, where you can get exclusive news, find out about all the trouble I'm getting into, join my Elite Street Team, author events, and upcoming books. If you want to talk more about books and hot guys and general fun stuff, join my reader group, Eliza's Peak Reader Group. Hot guys and book recs? What more could you want??

Happy Reading!

Love fearlessly and live intentionally,

Eliza

acknowledgments

Where do I start?

To my hubs and daughter for being my biggest cheerleaders.

To my sister who isn't a romance reader but pimps my books out any chance she gets. I love you guys!!

To Julianne Burke for being a cover design wizard!

To my Magster girls who are always just a group text away from talking me off the writing ledge or just to hear me bitch about something going on in my life. Your friendship means the world to me.

To my accountability partner Deana, who keeps me motivated to keep typing those words every day and being a friend in all faucets of life.

To Happily Editing Ann's, who make my words make sense to someone besides me.

To Kelly Fletcher, fellow romance writer, who is always ready and willing to read any word that I write and give insight.

To Keurig for making a machine that spits out coffee in record time.

To my Elite street team and my Eliza Peake Reader Facebook group. I seriously love you guys for reading my books, for chatting with me daily about other books, hot guys, wine, tacos, and funny memes. I'm a lucky girl!

Eliza Peake is an international bestselling author of sexy, swoon-worthy, contemporary romance. She writes stories with smart, sassy heroines, charming yet broody heroes who love their women in all the right ways, and happily ever afters with all the feels. She also co-hosts The Misfits Guide to Writing Indie Romance podcast.

In her downtime, she reads all the panty-melting romances she can get her hands on, drinks gallons of coffee, and tries to wrangle her addiction to Mexican food.

She currently resides in North Georgia with her family and dreams of retiring to the beach someday where she will continue writing steamy romance stories to her heart's content.

Sign up for her newsletter, The Sneak Peake for exclusive content and to first look at her latest news.

Find her at www.elizapeake.com.